Leopard Directive

Russell C. Arslan

First Edition – March 2012

Edited by Mary Ann Peck
Cover by Mary Ann Peck

ISBN
978-0-9857695-2-9 (Paperback)
978-0-9857695-5-0 (eBook)

russellcarslan.com

Books previously published

By Russell C. Arslan

"Those People"

"Highest Stakes, All In"

Leopard Directive

PART I

SAN JOSE, COSTA RICA

Matt Papaz, in his new identity, Matt Shaw, Chief-of-Staff to Costa Rican President Roberto Coto sat staring at the email. Any contact from Frederic Valance was shocking. This one shook his entire world.

For more than thirty-six months the only relationship between the two good friends, Valance and Papaz, had been clandestine asset movements from United States to Costa Rica. Purposely legitimizing hundreds of millions of dollars of investments on behalf of Costa Rican President, Roberto Coto, had gone smoothly. Purchases of raw land, farms, undervalued industrial assets, and private Costa Rican infrastructure projects on the country's Caribbean side, made with illicit funds laundered by Valance, were filtered into Costa Rica, developing a political machine and base for Coto.

Capitalized by the Tijuana cartel's boss, Ricardo Vargas, the arrangement had been born four years earlier when the narco world of illegal drugs and violence suddenly became quasi-legalized or decriminalized depending on which region of the world one was referencing. The underbelly of the world's largest economic activity, drug dealing, had reinvented itself to such an extent governments could now collect taxes on the new commodity.

Prisons were no longer flooded with drug dealers and addicts. Violent acts monopolizing production and drug distribution were curtailed, and the legal status of taking drugs was all but acceptable except for a few isolated countries. No longer were day to day drug cartel's business practices perceived as threats to governments. Authorities turned a blind eye towards the drug world's non-violent illegal activities. They could now use their new found financial resources to tackle other social evils. The forward thinking nations had freed-up billions of dollars from policing narcotics. Their monies and personnel could now be used for the betterment of society.

Roberto Coto, the new democratically elected President of Costa Rica with his assistants help had no outward ties to drugs or violence. Matt Papaz and his old friend, Frederic Valance, had carefully circumvented the usual money laundering techniques and the millions of dollars infused into the Latin American country from the notorious Tijuana cartel were being used by the new president for his personal gain. His political and personal persona manufactured after the Porter affair was clean and impervious to public scrutiny. His identity for the entirety of the past four years had been safe.

Breaking his three year's silence, Frederic Valance's email was an unexpected shock to Matt Papaz. The communication was a horrifying prospect to the Chief-of-Staff. Years earlier arrangements had been set for Valance's communication. If a disturbance large enough to affect the lives of his past associates and partners, a distress signal had been established.

Matt Papaz would have to unlock and review electronic protocols to receive communication from his once best friend and cohort. Passwords, electronic inscriptions, and a trial communiqué would be generated before the correspondence between Valance and Papaz would take place. The serious nature of a personal communication with Valance would wake up the past and jeopardize the future of the Costa Rican President and his Chief-of-Staff. A new chapter in the lives of the two men awaited them.

Once the door opened it could never be closed. Papaz had to prepare before answering Valance's email and subsequent phone con-versation. The technical part of the correspond-dence was easy mechanics but Papaz had to clearly lay out a scenario describing the past three years for himself and Coto before he talked to Valance.

What could be so important that the past relationship of dirty monies, drug dealings, and violence could be awakened from their slumber and jeopardize the Costa Rican President's populist movement?

Chief-of-Staff, Matt Shaw called his secretary, Carmen Oliveira and asked, "Please hold all my incoming calls, except those from the President. I'm going to review our trip to Nicaragua and Panama. I need some uninter-rupted time to myself. I'll skip lunch, don't bother to have it sent up, I'll need about two to three hours, so I can immerse myself in total seclusion."

Carman said, "Are you all right? You never shut off your staff. Can I be some assistance to you? This is highly unusual, are you okay?"

"Carman," Shaw responds, "I'm a little behind on our agenda and travel arrangements. I know it's unusual but I really need to catch up. Don't personalize it. It has nothing to do with you. I really don't need any help. I just need my computer and some time alone. I appreciate your concern. I really do, but I'm okay. I just don't want to let the President down by not being prepared. Some things came to my attention and I want to think about them before I present anything to the President."

"The problems of illegal Nicaraguan workers and trade agreements with Panama seemed so disparate. I'm having troubles putting them together. Presenting this agenda is incongruent to the needs of President Jearta and President Morales in the tri-lateral meeting with our neighbors. I don't think we should be going on a Trip-of-State when we can have subordinates do all the work for us. It just doesn't make sense right now that President Coto must hold hands with the Nicaraguan and Panamanian Presidents. I do have to make the trip more substantial or figure out a diplomatic way to cancel it. I must make sense of it, so I need a little time to myself. Then I can be more comfortable with my decision."

She walked out of the room and Matt Shaw stood there asking himself how credible his performance was. He was unsure. Carman Oliveira knew her boss's every impulse and action and he felt to his core that she would be suspicious of his not wanting to collaborate with her on duties of state. Shaw walked back to the door of his opulent office and poked his head out with his hands in the air and waved to Carmen to come back in for a second.

He said, "Carmen I know it's out of place for me not to ask for your help or counsel. I guess I just need to think some things out. I'm a little tired; I know this is out of character. Please don't personalize it. It's me not you," he said again.

He shut the door with a smile on his face hoping he had placated her. He had to get to his work and access the John Porter

Chronicle, a file hidden deep in the bowels of his computer and prepare for the past. He had a few hours at most to sort out things before calling Valance and talking to Coto.

Almost four years previous, Matt Papaz, a.k.a. Matt Shaw, and Jose Guzman, *a.k.a.* Roberto Coto, were forced to create a convenience partnership for survival.

John Porter, Deputy Director of US Homeland Security fabricated an identity for Papaz and Guzman as international terrorists with resources both physical and financial. Supposedly, they were inherently dangerous and presented a creditable threat to US security. The overriding resources of the United States and European intelligence agencies were utilized to apprehend both men. Porter created an elaborate scheme hiding his theft and fraud activities using US assets to feed his gambling addiction. Papaz and Guzman were presented as straw men to take the fall. Before the far-fetched plot of this brilliant sociopath, John Porter, came to fruition, Papaz and Guzman forged an intricate relationship leading them to Costa Rica.

Matt Papaz, a law-abiding US citizen of Armenian ancestry and Jose Guzman, Tijuana drug cartel narco kingpin, formed an alliance which had existed for almost four years. Their pasts included false identities, purchasing mercenary armies, consolidations of Central America drug trade, expanding African and Middle Eastern drug trafficking, created a complete re-identification for the two men and the eventuality of the politicization of the Tijuana cartel's dirty drug money leading to the Costa Rican Presidency.

The two men's initial adversarial relationship ultimately consolidated to trust and brotherhood. The unimaginable and almost unbelievable events leading both men to their present lives in Costa Rica could be destroyed by one simple communication from Frederic Valance. A literal avalanche of events could make both men hide again in the dark corners, residing in the evil that men do to one another.

Matt Papaz needed time to deliberate and assess how to deal with the inevitable repercussions of the call from his old friend. His blank stare's backdrop was the view of San Jose's government district central plaza.

Seated directly in front of his desk, Matt Shaw was deeply slumped into a grand baroque chair. The deep red Philippine mahogany floors, the Persian carpets, gifts to President Arias for his Nobel Prize recognition in the 1990s and the Indian artifacts decorating his office comforted him.

This was his new world. As Chief-of-Staff he had immersed himself into the political affairs of Central America's most respected democracy. His analytical mind had developed and engi-neered an economic renaissance for Costa Rica. Prior training in electrical engineering and his business expertise learned in another life far removed from this tropical paradise was a skill-set perfectly suited for Matt Shaw.

The Costa Rican government needs for pursuing a populist agenda developing higher education, poverty eradication, greater oppor-tunity access and increasingly higher living standards for the poor and middle class seemed simple, even easily attainable compared to the events of his recent past and relationship with Guzman and his narco associates. Matt Shaw now in his early forties had three distinct lives; his life and family in Los Angeles, the Porter affair and consequent drug world association and now the Costa Rican Chief-of-Staff.

For a few brief moments Shaw, sat in his chair with deep regrets and reflections of what he left behind in California. Then his anger rose as he reflected on his recent past. A cerebral list of players in the Porter Chronicle flashed before his eyes: Alvarez, Handle, and Gardner head of the mercenary force that he helped form; Rodriguez and Vargas the Tijuana cartel leaders; Arnouk the Turkish financier; Kasogi the most powerful man in the Middle East; Davis and Rapoport Los Angeles legal counsel; Frederic Valance computer and data analyst; and many more were prominent in his mind.

Accomplishments of Matt Shaw and Roberto Coto's pushing for greater equity, access, and conditions for Costa Rica's middle and poor classes had felt like a calling. The past had no right to rear its head and jeopardize all they had done and represented. The past had no right to threaten the work of Roberto Coto and his triumphs as the most progressive Central American President.

Everything the two men exemplified could disintegrate in an instant. For the first time in Matt Shaw/Matt Papaz's life he felt lugubrious. The metamorphosis from being framed by Porter and hunted down as one of the ten most wanted terrorists in the world with the five million dollars bounty on his head transformed into the Chief-of-Staff to the Costa Rican President was mind boggling. Creating the blueprint for Costa Rica's future and redirecting its landscape was an overwhelming accom-plishment but it paled in comparison to what he had done in the narco world and what might lay ahead for him.

The thoughts of Costa Rica being a major player and regional leader in Central America without having a standing army was income-prehensible to Matt Papaz taking into consideration what he and Jose Guzman's past experiences were. The violence, the drugs and the alliances with some of the world's worst psychopaths could all resurface and Shaw/Papaz, Coto/Guzman would be unable to restructure their lives and create new identities without the real threat of death or incarceration. They could not go back, just as importantly, they should not have contact with the villainous characters of their past. It could be life changing and not in a positive way.

The Valance communiqué was awaiting response. Matt Shaw had to be mentally flexible and dexterous enough for both himself and Coto. He made the decision to limit the involvement of Roberto Coto.

The proverbial Pied Piper was waiting; he had to call Valance post haste. All the exaggerated thoughts brought about by stress and chaotic sensationalism was pressuring Matt Shaw's actions. A psychological state of paralysis was not an option no matter how he resented having to face his past. His stomach ached. Water didn't quench the deep thirst caused by stress. The lost control feeling had to be overcome before he could review the simple mechanical protocols enabling the call-back to Frederic Valance.

The virtual eternity, two to three hours of seclusion he'd requested had no upside. As in the colloquial sense, he had to just do it. In reality he only needed a few seconds to facilitate the email and call. He opened his laptop Mac Book Pro typed in the acronym J.P.C. which stood for John Porter Chronicle and in an agonizingly long few seconds the screen gave untraceable communication protocol directions. Scripted code enabling him to use his landline clear of any electronic surveillance was before his eyes. Years earlier Valance had developed a clear channel of communication that could slip by any satellite detection or bugging device. Shaw's stomach was churning, his lips were parched, and he typed in a few simple words, and then pressed send. His life changed forever with that simple email sent to a Gmail account.

A new Matt Shaw episode was beginning. The call would tell him if he was being asked to become a simple comic-like action hero to combat evil once again and do unimaginable things. Or the other choice, he was on the run again without any options or hope.

Would his Matt Shaw work of the last three and one-half years in Costa Rica be relegated to the inevitability of going back into the world of terrorism and drugs? Was it all for naught?

His major concern would be self presser-vation and keeping Coto at arms length. If he engaged the underworld, would it be the Middle Eastern power brokers, American drug dealers or the security mongers in Europe and the United States. Every horrifying thought he had of being sucked back into the past was flashing before his eyes.

His and Roberto Coto's new lives and identities were in jeopardy. He would know soon enough. His e-mail and expected phone call were just seconds away.

-----o-----

"Frederic, I don't know what to say except I am scared shitless. I have rehearsed this call over and over in my head, it seems like forever and it's worse than I thought. I figured hearing your voice would be a calming influence but I'm terrified. The past is rearing its ugly head."

Frederic interrupted, "Matt, you know I would not have called unless there was an eminent threat to us. There is a new dynamic; all kinds of stuff can unravel everywhere. I'll be more specific in a few minutes but events in the Middle East are moving at such a rapid rate I had to contact you. For the last three and one-half years I have been investing the cartel's money for you and Guzman in the accounts of President Coto."

He continued, "Coto's investment information is part of the Costa Rican public domain and is open to the sunshine, they are public knowledge, and I don't know how you and Guzman have a relationship with him, since I'm not privy to the interactions. There is a high risk that knowledge of the cartel's relationship into his investment funds may come to light. If everything in the Middle East falls apart whatever you guys are doing with Coto is sure to surface."

"Up to this point, no financial transactions have come up in the public domain. The Coto funds sourced from the cartel have been co-mingled with his parent's estate. They can't be traced. I just don't know about the future. That's why we have to talk. I know you said you're scared shitless, so am I. This whole thing can unravel. Let me slow down for a second. I guess I'm so nervous about this stuff I just jumped in with both feet. Hell, I didn't even ask how you're doing. How are you? It's been a long time, old friend."

Matt Shaw interrupted, "It has been a longtime. How are you? In fact, where are you? I've seen your electronic communiqués, it sounds like you're doing well; the last three years I've wondered a lot about you. Kind of felt in my heart that when I finally did talk to you it would be under better circumstances, but shit, it never seems like things are easy for us. All I can tell you is that I am in Costa Rica and life's been good to me. I'm in contact with Guzman and he's also doing well. I have wanted to break our covenant and contact you but I knew I couldn't. It just seemed too dangerous. I really miss you, but I knew someday we would talk but not like this. Before I start feeling sorry for myself and looking back at the past I need a second."

He started discussing Costa Rica and his involvement in general pedestrian terms not to reveal his new identity even to his best friend. Matt Shaw was obfuscating on any particulars of the past three and one-half years. He knew if he became too specific, his role with Guzman, literally creating and hijacking the identity of the new Costa Rican President could jeopardize not only themselves but their populist movement.

Matt took a long breath and continued, "What the hell happened and what's going on?"

Valance said after listening to his friend articulating about his past, "Let me first describe what's happening on my side of the world. The cartel's actions and all the events in Spain not only defined you but defined all of us. After we cleaned up the mess in Porto Banus, Spain and you and Guzman went undercover, our partners, Vargas (Pedro Vargas the ahead of the Tijuana drug cartel) and Kosagi (Agnon Kosagi the influential Middle Eastern financier and arms dealer) implemented our plan for legalizing drugs and making alliances with governments, terrorists and insurgent groups."

Shaw responded, "Yeah, you guys did a great mop-up, while we were getting our new identity"

"Our relationships with al Qaeda, Hamas, the Shining Path, Hezbollah, the Revolutionary Front in Sierra Leone, and a lot more I don't have time to mention became solidified.

-----o-----

A quasi-peace and turning a blind eye by most governments to the narco world became acceptable as long as terrorist activities were held in check. You remember we set-up groups who were allowed to flourish, if they didn't export terrorism to the US or Europe. We gave them arms, financial support, and in some cases military support so they could entrench themselves in their own countries with the proviso they would leave Western Europe and the United States alone. This gave us room for the cartel to monopolize the drug trade without the threat of government interference."

Matt interrupted, "I've followed your activities closely."

"Everybody was happy with the agreement, we basically legalized drugs and created a new tobacco type industry and governments now tax narcotics and have more resources to deal with other social problems. Legalizing drugs took everything out of the criminal mindset and opened up resources for us and Western Europe."

"All everyone did was turn their heads to the happenings of democracy in Africa and the Middle East. It was supposed to be a win-win situation for all of us. We figured the insurgents or religious fanatics would be happy enough to control their own countries and not spread threats outside their own environments. Everything went smoothly for three and one-half years. Now it's all in jeopardy."

Frederic took a deep breath and continued, "We had an agreement of no threat to the west and we would let them do whatever they wanted in their own backyards and would all be better off for it. The reason I am calling you is everything has come crashing down. Not only are some of the agreements unraveling, but we are being held hostage by the threat of some players divulging our past activities. We're all in jeopardy. Simply put, we've got to talk."

"You might have to come out from whatever rock you are under. How's that for the first time talking in over three years?"

Shaw said, "Slow down for a second. Start at the beginning. How did all this unravel, what the hell happened?"

Valance deliberately ratcheted lower his pace of speech and became more articulate and succinct. "Matt, we first noticed splintering of Taliban's regular players and al Qaeda's sub-groups seeking autonomy and more political sway in their indigenous regions. Some of our phone intercepts showed they were tiring of the old guard and their perceived collaborations with us and Kasogi. There are probably no more than twenty or thirty of them, but they are threatening our alliance. We know there are only a handful of lower level terrorists, but they have their own followers of maybe a hundred or hundred and fifty people in Afghanistan they are breaking with Mullah Omar. He hasn't changed much since the old days against the Russians. He is still tyrannical, corrupt and way too sanctimonious for these young Turks. They have the backing of Mustafa Al Bin a secondary player in the Pakistan Swat Valley. He's unceremoniously declaring to be next after Osama bin Laden. He is ambitious, ruthless and appears to be the leader, or at least the titular head of his dissident group."

Frederic continued, "Kasogi became aware of the split. We monitored it as we do all events that can lead to political destabilization in the undeveloped regions of the Middle East or South Asia. You know quite well we don't care what their internal politics are; they can kill themselves we don't care. They can wreak havoc on their own people, we could care less. All we care about is that we control the drugs and the arms sales and they abide by the agreement of not exporting terrorism to Western Europe or the United States."

"Here's where things are going wrong. Kasogi has evidence they are planning an attack on the United States with a dirty bomb."

"Any threat to the 'Evil West,' as Al Bin called us is an extremely unifying force which he will use to his advantage to create blind loyalty. He is solidifying his position as an old guard alternative. The more saber rattling the greater his influence, but this is more. We think he's trying to move as a replacement of bin Laden. We have Intel that his splinter group is preparing a jihad against United States; it's that simple."

"He consolidates his power base, breaks our agreements and becomes the most powerful person in the Middle East. Pretty ambitious for an unknown, it could cause the unraveling of everything, if we don't stop him now."

"He's using the old rhetoric, to show that al Qaeda and Omar look like lackeys, you know, just Western puppets, patronizing and protecting American and European interests to subjugate Islamic people. He's even gone as far as to express deep hatred for bin Laden and called him a blasphemer. A man unworthy to have carried the banner of Islam."

"Do we know where he is? He's probably in western Pakistan."

"Matt, here's where it all gets really screwed up. We have information his people are in contact with a South African fascist reactionary group. Through back channels we've heard reports he's entertaining the idea of purchasing weapons grade nuclear materials and trying to buy the technology to create a dirty bomb."

"Frederic, is this guy for real?"

"He's real enough that the South Africans are in negotiations with him, and we hear numbers as large as ten million dollars being floated around. There's another big problem, though."

"Alright, let's hear the big problem."

"The matter of security in South Africa is iffy at best. With the ANC fully entrenched and Zuma as president there are no clear guarantees these guys can't either obtain or steal nuclear materials. They can pull it off and it seems likely the South Africans will sell materials to Al Bin. If we don't intervene everything on our end could fall apart. Our partnerships of the last three years especially in Afghanistan and Pakistan have not proven helpful to their disenfranchised people. Our goals of narcotics legalization for social betterment have not panned out. No benefits to the poor. No measurable progress at all. These places are again becoming a hotbed of radicalism. Be assured if we don't act quickly, the Al Bin terrorist groups will get a bomb. We have no control over them. The crazies will use it. When they attack the U.S., everything will be like 9/11 and our narcotic dealings will lead directly back to us. You know all our inter-governmental and intra-governmental arrangements meant to camouflage our illegal activities will have to cease. Blame America, threaten them, and consolidate your power base, it's by the book for Al Bin. It's death for us. The problem is we will come to light when the west is targeted. That's why I called. We need your help."

"Frederic, you know I'm available when you need me."

"Matt, Kasogi wants to see you and me. He knows it's dangerous, but imperative. I know this is a shitty way to say hello after three years, but as some people say, it's why we make the big bucks. We both knew someday this whole decriminalizing thing could come down like a house of cards. Shit, legalize drugs, rein in the terrorist groups, use the money for social good, let the druggies kill themselves, save the Western world, and every other good deed, you name it we thought good would come of it. Were we stupid? For three years it's been a great run. Were we dumb to think this would last forever? All we know is that it's coming apart. We need your help; we hope we can stop him. Kasogi wants to see us as soon as possible. The South Africans are serious and are really motivated sellers."

"There's something else, we cannot pinpoint where Al Bin and his organization are getting their money. We figure there has to be more to it, deeper involvement by somebody. There must be other players with deep pockets for numbers like ten million dollars to be thrown around."

"Listen old buddy; get back to me as soon as possible. When you put your arms around this and have some ideas we have to meet Kasogi. I will leave it up to you if you want Guzman to be brought into it. You know the channels to get back to me."

"Frederic, in many ways I'm scared shitless but I really like talking to you again. We have to do something about our set-up so we can communicate."

"Matt, I really miss hearing your voice. I've thought long and hard about the eventuality of all this. It looks like we're in the thick of it again. We've had a good run so far. Screw this guy Al Bin. We must stop him. Do whatever you need to free yourself up. Hell, it's actually been pretty boring around here for three years. There's no place I would rather be than at your back. I guess I can't really get used to prosperity and the easy life, I'll probably feel better reliving hell with you than living the good life. I must sound like a sentimental idiot. Look forward to seeing you. You know something; it's going to be hard to see a new face on the same old Matt. Can't believe it's been three years. When I see you I won't even know what you look like. Unbelievable, just unbelievable, that it's been three years since you and Guzman had plastic surgery. I guess I'll see the results of the hundred and thirty thousand bucks you guys spent to get new faces and identities," Valance said jokingly. "I'll see if you look better than the old tired Matt Papaz."

-----o-----

Following Frederic's protocols, Matt Shaw secured a safe line and called Agnon Kasogi.

Picking up his landline receiver Kasogi said, "Matt, it is of great pleasure to hear your voice, my old friend. I wish the circumstances were different, but I had no alternatives but to get the attention of you and Guzman. I'm sorry to bring the two of you so close to the fire, but after I explain you'll know I have no other alternatives."

"Frederic has told me of your conversation and I am aghast knowing the scope of our dilemma." Matt replied.

Kosagi continued, "You must know he's acting as a third man and cannot always relate we must talk, I am truly sorry for the formalities but a simple hello is all I can say until I bring this matter to your full view. It has come to pass that there is treachery and problems within the ranks of our partners in Afghanistan and Pakistan. We must act quickly and harshly before things are totally out of our control. I'm seeking your input and I'm asking you to be on the ground and give us your leadership."

"Kosagi, you know I'll be there for this."

"Our intelligence gathered by our old friend Alvarez shows Al Bin is real and is an impending threat. He came out of some hole and was not in our sights at all. As we say quite a shock. I will send you all materials so you can judge for yourself before we meet. You will see why we all agreed there is no time to lose."

Kasogi explained in detail all of the intercepts of Taliban and the Al Qaeda subgroup and their simplistic plot having such great international and personal ramifications. He expressed how tirelessly Al Bin was engaged with South Africans for the nuclear materials procurement.

"Matt, I'm sending you a complete file from the Johannesburg's antiterrorist units and their assessment of the threat and the subsequent apprehension of six people who were trying to steal nuclear waste from the Soweto General Hospital."

"The nuclear medicinal radiation depart-ment had contracted the Johannesburg Waste Management Corp for disposal of barium isotopes, dirty syringes, gauze, medical wraps, and hematological waste from HIV patients. South Africa has the highest HIV rates in the world, almost thirty-five percent."

Kasogi continued, "The idea was create a dirty bomb with radioactive barium and HIV patients' waste contaminants. Even though the technical aspects of the bomb were unsophisticated, they could create an explosion with things as simple as a phosphorous bomb using radio activated detonating devices. They could dispatch it anyplace in the world without being caught. It would have a thirty square blocks destructive radius. One radio intercept sent to a small subgroup had them throwing around numbers like potentially one hundred thousand affected people. Even if the estimated number is double or triple, the actual damage would be the biggest attack since the World War II A-bomb in Japan."

"Because of money movement intercepts from Afghanistan to South Africa, we detected the plot. We covertly contacted Johannesburg authorities. The antiterrorist squad uncovered arrangements with Johannesburg freight forwarders sending materials to the United States, first Atlantic City then to New York. It was to be shipped by small carrier van to New Jersey and then by a larger truck to an industrial building in New York City. We don't know the significance of off loading it twice, maybe they were going to leave back up materials in New Jersey, we just don't know. The movement from small to large truck doesn't make any sense either. Altogether five Arab and seven South Africans were apprehended and questioned, all we learned was the plan was hatched by Mustafa Al Bin but we couldn't trace it any further. I'm sorry to say we've been unsuccessful apprehending any top level people associated with the potential attack."

The explanation continued, "With all our money and powers of persuasion Al

Bin is not in our hands. And what makes it worse he has not been intimidated by our pursuit. We have a $1 million reward on his head and it has just made him more brazen and aggressive in pursuing dirty bomb materials. He is now seeking nuclear weapons grade uranium. How far is he willing to go? We don't know."

"We've been in contact with Osama bin Laden's successor and Mullah Omar, and they have concurred with us that killing Al Bin was a necessity. They're concerned with the split in their ranks and they know the importance of stopping disloyalty. Bin Laden's successor has issued a fatwa on Al Bin decrying him as religiously impure and a traitor. I know politics within the Afghanistan and Pakistan groups are complex and very sophisticated but if we don't do something now Al Bin can potentially unravel everything we've done. Our business activities are in jeopardy. Our heroine trade, hashish trade and of course, the arms sales will come under the eyes of our once friendly international organizations. They can't stand by idly if one of *our's*, as they view him, blows up New York.

Artificial ties between him and us have been fabricated and laid out for all to see. It leads to us. We are being set up. All the men captured in Johannesburg were tortured and their religious fanaticism and loyalty to Al Bin was quite evident. Every one of them died and nothing of the plot passed their lips. We got his name but none of them would give up his whereabouts. Matt, this is very serious indeed."

Kosagi continued, "The Mullah Omar sees it as a religious breach and an affront to Islam.

Matt asked, "What about bin Laden's successor?"

Kosagi answered, "He sees it more as a political radicalization. I see it as a death blow to our organization."

Matt suggested, "There are perceived inequities existing in Afghanistan because of US military presence, it could be a reason for our losing control."

Kosagi continued, "That could be part of this. I'm also troubled by the financial backing from sources we can't identify. Frederic says Al Bin had access to ten million dollars for the nuclear materials procurement, but my information indicates the money at his disposal might be double that amount. Our informants tell us he is pushing so hard for these materials he is in effect negotiating against himself and is now willing to pay almost twenty million dollars.

Matt asked, "We don't know who his benefactors are?"

"We don't know their names or motives. However, if there's a terrorist attack on the United States, we do know we will be blamed. They will think it is us. It's that simple."

"Yes, I see," Matt responded, "everything can come to the surface. All you, me, Guzman, Frederic have so carefully put together."

The whole time Matt Shaw's stomach was in knots. The thought of having to change his life one more time was enormously disturbing. The threat of running from authorities, the actual threat of life in a federal prison or death or even worse imprisonment in some Middle East or African hell hole, was overwhelming. There were two things of clarity and dispatch:

- One, he had to protect the President of Costa Rica, Roberto

- Two, he would have to surface.

He said to Kasogi, "I need about a week at most my old friend. Tell me when and where you want to meet. My first intuition is that we should meet in Johannesburg and start from there. Like I said I can be there in a few short days. I need time to straighten up things here and talk to Guzman. I just wish my first conversations with you would have been under better conditions. Let me know when and where."

-----o-----

Matt Shaw, Chief-of-Staff, to Costa Rican President Roberto Coto slowly walked from his office, made a quick right turn following the corridor and arrived at the President's office.

"Estella," he said to the beautiful thirty-five year old dark-haired, brown eyed, appointment secretary. Coto's personal staff was extra-ordinarily professional and young. The President's staff prerequisite of youth, attractiveness, and loyalty were outward characteristics. Coto's political appointees were between the ages of thirty and forty a notable distinction from the aged group of long-standing bureaucrats who had controlled political events in an inefficient and corrupt manner for decades before Coto's arrival on the scene.

"Tell President Coto I'm here without appointment and I need his immediate undivided attention."

Roberto Coto dressed in his usual casual attire, slacks and a button-down golf shirt, opened his office door, extended his hand and pulled Matt close for a hug.

"Come on in," he said. "This is unusual. What's so important? Why so formal?" He shut the door.

Matt sat down and looked across the great room and stared directly into Coto's eyes.

"Well, it's happened. The whole thing has come un-glued; the shit has hit the fan."

Before he could say another word Coto interrupted. "Slow down," he said, "what's come unglued? You are very upset; I see it all over your face. Like I said slowdown, what has happen?"

Matt Shaw took off his coat and began. "José, I have not uttered that name in three years. It's our past. I got a communication from Frederic, not the usual financial stuff. Its nature was so important he used the back channels we set up three years ago. He asked for direct contact and arranged for a clear line and the ability to transfer electronic data. Well, José the long and short of it is that Kasogi received information of the breakdown of our agree-ments with our partners in Afghanistan. There is now a new player who is hell-bent on attacking New York City. He is willing to cross us, Mullah Omar and even al Qaeda to strike a terrorist attack on the US for his own personal gain. If our quasi peace with Europe and the Americans is broken because of an attack all our work in the last three years will be for nothing and Western security authorities will come after us. All our work securing safety for the Western world for the right to sell legal drugs will fall apart in an instant."

Matt stopped to breathe and continued, "If there is an attack on New York with the new security levels needed to apprehend the son of a bitch it will certainly bring us into the light."

Roberto asked, "What does Frederic say?"

"Frederic says there's no way our covers will not be blown. This guy is willing to do anything to advance his own position. He is a *wanabe* bin Laden named Mustafa Al Bin. He has already tried to purchase nuclear materials for a dirty bomb he plans to set off in New York City. If he does, global security will be heightened like post 9/11 and all our tacit arrangements with Western governments to protect them from terrorist acts in exchange for a blind eye to our operations will be dismissed in an instance. Everything we've done to bring about world stability will be as they say, null and void. I don't want to sound sanctimonious but we have done an incredible job creating a safer world even though we dealt in arms, drugs, extortion, and everything else under the sun. We know how it has benefited you and me directly, but our business has changed the world. If this Al Bin moves on the Western world they will move on us. It will be just like when Porter put a price on our heads. We will have to run, but this time they won't stop until we are dead."

Matt went into detail and showed all the information Frederic had electronically sent him. He told Guzman of his conversation with Kasogi and the fact he needed at least a week before the two would meet.

"It's clear you have to be out of this," he said. "Hell, you're the President of Costa Rica for God's sake; you can't be part of this. I suggested I meet him in Johannesburg. I'll have to change my identity. I need some cover. Maybe a medical leave of absence, whatever you think will work. I can't have another plastic surgery. Shit, I would look like a ghoul. My face can't take any more surgeries; we both had so much work done it just won't work on me any more. Even though, I'm thirty pounds heavier I'll need some work not to be detected by face recognition technology at some of the international airports. I think the only way to circumvent the electronics will be the use of theatrical prosthetics and makeup. I know the technology they're using at the airports is much more sophisticated than three years ago but hopefully I can beat the face recognition algorithms with my weight and makeup. Kasogi has not seen me in the three years since the surgeries so he won't know how I look."

"If I have a new face for Kasogi then when this is over I can resume being the Chief-of-Staff to the Costa Rican President. Jose you're out of it as far as anything tactical is concerned but we really need your help. We will bounce ideas off you. You run logistics from here. Be our contact person with the cartel and act as a conduit with Pedro. Look, I know this is your life and you feel you have to do something but you have to trust me enough to leave it in my hands. There's nothing you can do, you're the President of Costa Rica. Shit, you're stuck here. I know all this is out of your control but we'll get the son of a bitch."

José Guzman looked out into the rose garden below. This was not the real Matt Shaw. He had not seen his friend like this in more than three years. Guzman said in the cold calculating manner, "I accept your reading on the events for my staying here, but I must have access to everything you do. I can be useful. When you get to South Africa is when you will need me the most."

"Matt, finding and killing the son of a bitch is what I do and I do it well. You more than anyone knows this Roberto Coto person that I am is only a disguise. I am and will always be of another world. The one that can help you catch this Al Bin. You, my friend, are once again venturing into my realm. When you get hold of Kasogi the three of us will talk. I will tell him it's better if only you and he handle this affair. I will take my position in the background. We must not have too many heads and no proper leadership, just you and him. I will take, as you call it, a logistic position and therefore not be directly involved. I can see its better this way. I'll say I need my fullest attention in oversight or all of us could be jeopardized. He will understand. Matt, at no time should you think I'm abandoning the two of you but it's better for all of us if it's just you two."

-----o-----

"Jose, there is no question; you must remain in obscurity on this."

"Matt, I have no other options; realistically I can't leave here for even one minute and not be discovered. While here I can still handle our holdings and keep a tight rein on everything we have worked for these years. Kasogi does not know what we are or what we have done since we last saw him. He is comfortable with that. Let's leave things in their present state. He won't push for me to be there if we tell him it's just the two of you. We both know I sure as hell can't come out from the cold. He'll accept that."

"Yes, Jose, I believe it's the best way," replied Matt Shaw.

"Matt, I do have some ideas you should pass on to Kasogi as yours. Tell him there must be cleaner lines of authority for all operations, only you and he make the final decisions. You only need the rest of us for support. There will be what I call the killing party to get al Bin. I say killing party because that's what it will be, make no mistake about it. Many people will die. You should start in Johannesburg.

All those leads aren't dead. I mean that literally. The antiterrorist squads interrogated and tortured the men trying to obtain the bomb making materials aren't going to say much. Don't be fooled, there is always more. The police don't always know what men can endure, and how much pressure can be applied. They are cowardly, week scum just like the men who tried to steal the hospital waste. These interrogators will give up information we need to save their own lives. They know something."

"I agree, Jose."

"Even though all the men who tried to commit the robbery are dead there is still information out there that will help us get al Bin. You and Kasogi must talk to the antiterrorist's squad with either money or a threat on their lives, trust me, you will get the information you need. Remember, Johan-nesburg is just the start of your journey. From there I would go to Afghanistan and I would bring Vargas. Have him represent the cartel in purchasing large quantities of heroin but only if you can deal with al Bin in person. Make sure Vargas throws around lots of money. His name and money will bring this pig al Bin out into the open. Men like him are vain and arrogant. The thought of money and power will bring him to us. He will look to Vargas as a source of needed capital when his money dries up. After we apply the right pressure it will dry up, believe me, it will dry up in a hurry."

In an instant Jose Guzman returned to his President Roberto Coto persona and said, "Matt you know my schedule. I have what you call, duties of state. I am expected in parliament at 11:30am. Come with me and we will discuss your trip to Johannesburg."

Matt rose knowing his friend always responded to crises said, "Jose, thank you for understanding."

"We have lots to talk about. We have to be downstairs in five minutes. Let me get my jacket. We'll talk on the way."

-----o-----

After the discussion with Jose, Matt called Valance. "Frederic, everything is a go from our side. I talked to Jose and Kasogi and am leaving here in six to seven days. I need your help with some logistics: ID, credit cards, checking accounts, a safe phone so I can contact Jose, and anything else you think necessary. You know, the whole nine yards. I'm assuming you have resources available and can get me everything I need within the time frame. I'll send you an e-mail with my picture attached. I'm a little desperate. There are things I can only ask you to do for me so when this is over I can come back here to Costa Rica. I will fill you in later. I'll send a list of my needs in the e-mail. But for now shit, I know you, the first thing you will do is look at my picture. You better brace yourself, I ain't no beauty."

"You know me and my planning. I'm still as compulsive as ever. I guess nothing changes. Let me summarize my wish list verbally so you can give me some input. An e-mail is so God damn impersonal, but it will give you a record of our conversation. Hey man it's good to hear your voice," Matt said. "It's been a long time."

Frederic laughed, "I haven't said a word yet. Finally hearing from the real Matt is good. I guess, we both feel we're hearing voices from the dead," he laughed again. "So go on, tell me what you need."

Matt laughed for the first time in days and said, "You always could get to the point."

"Before we get started, what the hell do you look like," Frederic said with a deep evil sounding belly laugh. "I guess I'll find out when I get the email." The whole time he had a chuckle in his voice.

Matt replied, "Let me be serious for a few minutes, my man. I plan leaving from here and flying through Dallas and going to Las Vegas for a couple of days to create a cover. I need a line of credit with some casinos, maybe four to five hundred thousand dollars. I want to stay at the Encore and present myself as a high stakes player. With that kind of money it won't be difficult. They have an Omaha tournament and I need some time to hone my skills and be competitive again. When I meet Kasogi in South Africa we will ultimately go to Sun City and play in a big time, hotel sponsored, no limit game. Kasogi is arranging it; it's all part of my cover. You know me and cards. Omaha is so much different than Texas hold them,

I'll need a lot of practice. The Encore by reputation is a really good card room. Playing cards will be a diversion from all the work I have to do for my trip to Johannesburg. This is where you come in. I need specific Intel on the antiterrorist police squads in the Soweto Township in Johan-nesburg. I'll need all the information on the interrogators of Al Bin's men who broke into the hospital and tried stealing the nuclear materials. Get me their service records, their financials, family history and pictures, the whereabouts of their wives and children. Jose says we will have to interview them. They probably have information knowingly or un-knowningly. That's his polite way of saying torturing them to get information. We also need some kind of safe house if we have to kidnap any of their team. They won't part with any information for nothing so Jose thinks we should make the stakes their lives. We'll have to use whatever tactics it takes to pry it out of them. He said if money doesn't work we will have to kill one of them and the others will be more open to our demands. Shit, I can't believe how we, including me, have such a dark side and for the most part hide it until it's needed. Jose has a history of how effective pure violence can be. Its success speaks for itself. There's a reason why he was the most feared man in all Mexico when he was with the cartel."

Valence interrupted, "You're getting a little off track here."

Matt took a breath and went on, "I also need you to contact Pedro and tell them to set up a trip to Afghanistan. We'll be purchasing some heroine and will need lots of money to throw around. Tell them to use whatever channels he has but we will only deal with Al Bin none of his underlings. He will know how to set it up. Tell Pedro to bring Alverez."

Frederic listened and felt a sense of growing tension and emotion which he always said was a good thing. He felt stress made him better and certainly more careful.

"Matt, man it sounds like yesterday. I wish I could've been there for the last three years and been involved with you guys but I knew that's out of the question, I won't even ask what you did. You sound like you're old self again. You have not skipped a beat. When the heat is up you've always been formidable. I can easily get you all of the stuff you need. Your idea of talking to the terrorists' squad makes a lot of sense and I think it will get us to Al Bin. You know me the old pessimist, an analytical sense tells me there has to be more to all of this than a new bin Laden type guy vying for power. So far I can't find out much about Al Bin so I would suggest he is a front for somebody. He has too much access to money and support for him to just appear out of nowhere. Somebody's pulling his strings, but I can't figure out who."

"I agree with that also."

"We've found out about almost everything he is not capable of doing. It shows he ain't no mastermind. He is just a second rate, new generation Afghan mullah. Shit, he's just another religious fanatic. None of our sources think he's smart and they're not under estimating the guy. I've read a summary of his religious writings. He is not that bright. From what our Intel tells me he's not overly charismatic either. It just doesn't add up unless there's somebody behind him. I always look to who will gain from our loss and he's not smart enough to be around for the long haul. He's not big time enough for our whole world to fall apart because of him. I took the analytical tack of looking at our organization as a house of cards, but it is evident we were built to sustain any kind of major friction. In general we are impermeable to almost all political currents. The analysis shows we're much stronger than I thought, so it's got to be someone who's directly targeting us. Too much of the Al Bin plan points back to us, there is no coincidence that the police are who, when, and where have our name all over them. I don't know why, I don't know who, but there's got to be someone gaining from our loss. As far as I'm concerned Al Bin's arrival on the scene is a direct shot at us. It's not by chance; this terrorist threat against us came out in the open. The results are too specific. It's meant to dismantle our organization. Many players have benefited from our narco arrangements during the last three years. I can't figure any losers being big enough to come after us. On first blush I thought a terrorist attack on New York

City would only do incidental damage to our organization. We will be collateral damage in whatever global security must do to bring about world peace. The effect of the proposed attack would destroy our organization as surely as reality, but, for the life of me I can't figure out who would shoulder such a cost to put this together and what benefits they will get. Not only is it costly to pull this off but the people involved, the secrecy and the shear amounts of time and effort to make it work clearly says it's not our guy Al Bin. If an attack takes place in New York then Europe and the U.S. would be on a global security lockdown. Without knowing the consequence of an all out security alert or the big risk for anybody trying to pull this off, these guys some how projected it would target us and I think they are right. Whoever these guys are they know we will be the losers. I just can't figure out how they think they will be the winners."

Matt responded, "You're right. I've racked my brain over this and so has José. We're pretty much in concurrence with you. It has to be someone big that sees us as some sort of competitor and wants to eliminate us. This end game of terrorism is a public statement meaning they are not strong enough to directly attack us. Every time someone portrays themselves as being weak and not directly coming after me it just means they're big and have me in their sights. I can't figure out who they are, but we sure as hell are in their cross hairs. If we go down in flames there will be a vacuum. Who will fill it, that's the question? The bastards, whoever they are, are coming after us. Whatever they have to do to get us out of the game they will do it. If killing a hundred thousand people is an acceptable risk to them they are either crazy bastards or cold sons of bitches. Man, if they can get the materials and attack New York City that's big-time. Only religious fanatics would kill with impunity, but it doesn't make sense, religious nuts don't have the money and power that's behind this plot. I want to throw something stupid at you. Do you think it could be someone like Ricardo, the military head of the Tijuana cartel, power wrestling with Pedro? Things have been so quiet for the last three years and his position in the cartel has made him a person of no consequence, I think he might be crazy enough and capable enough to do something like this. I don't know I'm just all over the place. Ricardo thrives on chaos and is capable of killing thousands of people without any guilt. I'm just throwing stuff against the wall. Don't listen to me, its just conspiracy shit."

"All I know," Matt continued, "is José thinks killing everyone involved will solve this. You and I think we can intellectually outsmart everyone to solve it. I guess we'll find out what Kasogi thinks in the next couple days."

"He'll come up with something. You know Arab intrigue and people behind every corner syndrome. I gotta admit he's a pretty smart guy, though, I guess I shouldn't discount his herit-age."

"Actually, Frederic, I like him a lot. He probably has a greater clarity on this than any of us. As I said before, I don't know if I'm just grabbing at straws. Before I start indicting more people, like I just did with Ricardo, I should slow down. If I keep this up I will think it's you. After you see my picture and you mercilessly give me all kinds of shit I'll be so pissed at you I'll tell everyone it's your plan to get the hell out of New York. Listen just send me all the stuff I need and hopefully after a couple days in Vegas maybe I will have sorted this out enough so I can make some sense. When I meet Kasogi in Johannesburg I hope I can be of some help to him when we interrogate the police. I wish I could bring José with me but it just doesn't work that way. He has to stay in the background. He would really be brutal and we might need that. He has mentioned to me on numerous occasions we are now venturing into his world. I'm sure he's right. Frederic, I can't say it strongly enough but it's great to have heard your voice. I can hardly wait to be with you again. It's been too long but circumstances sometimes limit what a man can do. Not communicating with you for three years was not what I wanted to do. Hell, you know that. I know I shouldn't say it, it will go to your IT head, but I've missed you. There couldn't be any one in the whole world I'd rather have at my back than you. Well buddy, wait till you see what I look like. You'll laugh your ass off, but I'm still tough as nails."

Matt Shaw received a FedEx package at the prearranged address outside San Jose's central business district. The Post Office Box was innocuous in this adjunct of the ever expanding airport complex. Matt felt he could not be too careful if he wanted to keep the prospects of returning to Costa Rica alive after his venture to South Africa and beyond. Keeping Frederic in the dark to his actual whereabouts and real identity had been amenable to both men. This would probably have to change. Wearing theatrical prosthetics and makeup he picked up the package to see if he could still move around in the covert world with the same ease and confidence as he did in his past life. The stealth of his movements were encouraging but at the same time frightening. The adage of getting back on the horse felt appropriate he thought to himself.

Upon returning to San Jose proper, in a clandestine apartment, he opened the white FedEx box and scrutinized its contents. Not much had changed in the world of cloak and dagger in three years. The array of passports, two US and one

British, and their accompanying printed materials summarizing each fictitious character's history were all-too-familiar. He was amazed that each passport with the same picture had such striking differences in the supposed lives of the men whose names were in bold print, Matt Clayton Shaw, Brooke Antone, and Robert Tashjian. The passport with the name Matt Clayton Shaw had an attached note from Frederic. The notes were short but insightful: *I thought this might be the safest identity for you. It's counterintuitive using your name. National security will never connect all the dots together even if you were on their radar. Sometimes it's better not to be too complicated and have too many aliases, cluttering up things. If your name ever surfaces and security agencies cross reference data you are already captured or dead* the handwritten note said.

"I have arranged some things for you in Las Vegas. Even though it will be a working vacation I think you'll love it. You will have a line of credit of two million dollars, not the five hundred thousand you asked for. Be sure to read and learn all the materials about your new identity." In bold letters that almost jumped off the page, Frederic wrote, "that was some kind of picture. I can't believe how fat your face looks. I hope it's a mask or something. When Kasogi sees you in Johannesburg he better be in a hotel lobby. If not he will think he ran into some hippo on the loose. Just kidding old buddy, but the new faces is really good, there's no way you'll ever be recognized. I almost want to say, 'is Matt Shaw in there somewhere.' Whatever you need, get back to me I'm at your disposal. You know what our capabilities are. There is nothing that's too much to ask. Good luck, I know its work but have fun in Vegas."

Sitting in the modest apartment in San Jose that he would use as a safe house to expedite his departure from Costa Rica he looked at the note again and just chuckled. It was good to have contact with Frederic. His sense of humor was sharp. His loyalty was unparalleled. He knew he was lucky to have Frederic Valance at his side. He called José and asked if everything was set up for his medical leave of absence and the pending trip to Argentina for a diagnosis and treatment if necessary for what was called symptomatic arrhythmia. That could keep him out of country for months. After a brief conversation he told Jose that he would keep him in the loop on what went on in Las Vegas. He would send him a working draft on operation Johannesburg as a living document. Each reiteration and every possibility would be forwarded to Jose.

He said, "You know me and how I have to put ideas on paper to have some clarity. As soon as I get a handle on this you'll have a final draft, but until then I'll send you everything piece meal."

PART II

LAS VEGAS, NEVADA

The new Matt Shaw felt comfortable boarding the American Airlines Boeing 737 for the one hour and fifty minutes flight to Dallas without political portfolio, wearing a new face, an old pair of jeans, a short sleeve shirt and shouldering a small carry-on bag. He passed through Costa Rican electronic security and was just another American vacationer returning home.

Blending in with the hundreds of forlorn revelers who felt their vacations were too short, his plump tanned face and less than fit body were part of an amalgam, passengers walking down the skyway to their seats. The other two hundred thirty-five passengers were more certain of their futures than Matt Shaw. They were returning home after a brief respite from their everyday lives. He was once again beginning a jeopardizing scenario of life and death for himself and the people he held dear.

After landing in Dallas he cleared customs by simply walking through the green declaration lane of the massive American Airlines complex he had one hour and thirty five minutes to transfer terminals and board his plane to Las Vegas. He had flown first class from San Jose to Dallas and would again sit in the expensive seats as they were colloquially known. It was better for his high roller cover.

It was always amazing, first-class seats in smaller older Boeing 737s were no more than ceremonial. They were functionally too small for his 6 foot 2 inch frame. He thought to himself, this is going to be a miserable trip. I'm too tall and too heavy even for first-class. He now had the frame and girth of an out of shape American tourist and the extra room was only marginally better than coach. It still didn't seem acceptable for him to be in this much discomfort so he boarded the plane and used meditation to fall into a light sleep.

He slept from wheel to wheel, from takeoff to landing as he called it. Being able to sleep was a sign his mindset for survival was beginning to permeate his psyche. He was amazed at how low his level of anxiety was. His pulse rate was low, and with deep breathing meditation he could focus on the task at hand. He had control of all his faculties for taking on whatever lay between him and Mustafa Al Bin.

-----o-----

At McCarran Airport in Las Vegas he was taken back by one of Frederic's surprises. A sign with his name held high above the most beautiful woman he had ever seen was awaiting him. His image of her was that of an Amazon woman, six feet, one inch tall with translucent white skin overshadowed by her body and the face of an angel. Las Vegas had a reputation for the city with the most beautiful women in the world and Matt Shaw could not argue with that proposition. He ventured towards her and she immediately acknowledged him by making reference to a picture that she had in her left hand and put forth your right hand asking for his carryon bag.

Mr. Shaw she said, "I'm BiBa Lamanas your personal assistant while you're at the Encore Hotel. Please come with me, a car is waiting. I have an itinerary for your stay with us at the hotel. Of course it's only a suggestion, but I hope you will be pleased by it. You are an honored guest and anything you request will be our pleasure."

She discussed the personal shopper who would outfit him at the extensive retail center situated between the Encore and

Wynn Hotels. He would discard his garb of jeans, T-shirt, and carry-on bag as scripted by Frederic and put on a display of ostentatious capricious spending to lend credence to his most important card playing asset, money. She had plans for him to have dinner across the street at the Capital Grille, Las Vegas' preeminent steakhouse and a seat at a no-limit Omaha game at the Bellagio Hotel.

Matt questioned why the Encore would send a high roller to another hotel, eatery, or card room. "It's unusual," he said.

Ms. Lamanas replied, "Tonight is like an exhibition game for a professional basketball team. Like the Lakers in pre-season. Tomorrow is the season's opener. Everything will take place here. We are flying in four players for the Omaha game and of course we have some locals with incredible skills and reputation for what we call our little home game. The buy-in is three hundred thousand dollars but with your line of credit we feel you will be comfortable. I hope I've not overstepped my bounds and presumptuously locked you into such a game, but we were given instructions stating you wanted to play the highest level of no limit poker."

Matt smiled, "May I call you BiBa? Of course your arrangements are okay, that's why I'm here. I'm sure you are appreciated not only by the guests, but viewed as a valuable asset to the hotel. You are really good at what you do. Your itinerary is just fine; you surely were not presumptuous in putting things in play for me."

She countered, "Tomorrow we made a golf time at the Bears Best course. It's only about twenty minutes from here. We have you playing with a threesome at eleven o'clock. The starters said that the course will be relatively empty. It's a Jack Nicholson course and features eighteen of the most beautiful holes he has ever designed."

The other players in the foursome were going to be Alverez, Malique, and Bill, cohorts from the past who Frederic engaged for the operation. They were already in Las Vegas and had been dispatched from Mexico virtually the same time that Matt Shaw left Costa Rica. The three men were staying at the new Aria Hotel as not to intertwine their activities with his. He thought to himself, Frederic said there would be surprises and he sure as hell didn't overstate it. There was no safer place for meeting them than in the open spaces of the fairway or greens on a golf course in the middle of the desert. The seclusion of the desert course in the midst of the beautiful Ridge Rim housing development made it secure.

Ms. Lamanas' script for the four days was exacting but as she said, "Mr. Shaw it's all open to change from the smallest to the biggest. Let's face it, if you are happy we'll be happy. You're gambling is our business and when you play at our tables it is a win-win situation for all of us. There's nothing you can ask for that is legal that we will not comply with. You are a very valued guest. I hope everything meets your standards."

The car pulled up in front of the Encore and Matt could not help but notice there was a Penske Ferrari dealership on the hotel grounds. He looked at her and said, "Isn't a dealership a bit much even for Las Vegas?"

She smiled, "Mr. Shaw, it's amazing how many men of your station in life come here on a gambling vacation after a successful run at the tables bring home a trifle for their wives."

"Maybe if you are a big winner," she smiled and said, "Maybe you get one for me. Oh, I'm just kidding we can't take gifts from our guests. The hotel is very serious about that. You know this is Las Vegas and the extraordinary is commonplace here."

They walked past the registration desk and took the elevator to the 59th floor. She walked him to his suite and said, "Just call me if you need anything. I'm at your disposal twenty-four/seven. She handed him a cell phone. Speed dial me by pressing #-one. I'm going to leave you here."

She gave him his room key card and walked back to the elevator.

He placed the card in the key slot and waited for the green light. When door opened, the Las Vegas panoramic view stretched more than twenty-five miles, all the way to Red Rock. Walking across the suite to a full-length glass window that acted as a wall to his room's living area he passed another of Frederic's surprises. He heard a murmur from the bedroom. He looked where the voice emanated and saw a pure vision of sex. Totally nude except for a handwritten note she walked over. He was stunned and could not take his eyes off her brown statuesque body with swollen breasts and a waste that created an hourglass shape. He did not even look at her face which was angular punctuated with high cheekbones and olive colored eyes.

She finally got eye contact by saying; "I am supposed to tell you I am one of Frederic's surprises."

She handed him the note. Las Vegas indeed had the most beautiful women in the world he said to himself. He took the note.

All it said was, *Old buddy, even Fatso's get lucky sometimes. Tonight is yours. Tomorrow we have a lot of work to do. Frederic*

-----o-----

One hour of pure unadulterated sex comprised of every pleasure offered a male by a female lead to total physical and emotional exhaustion. Matt Shaw literally passed out on the king sized bed flanked by wall to ceiling mirrors as the soft sounds of jazz on an acoustical system befitting a luxury room in a luxury hotel played soft seductive music.

His companion, Kerry Shannon, of Spanish Irish descent was draped on top of him as he slept on his back. Her soft naked body rested with her arms and legs draped over his slightly rotated body.

The phone rang. He picked it up out of a sense of obligation to technology. A man and his phone in this new age of electronics was no more than the extension of a man and his dog. In this case the phone wagged the person.

BiBa Lamanas was on the other end. "Mr. Shaw, please forgive my rudeness but your benefactor, Mr. Frederic, instructed me to call no matter what the consequences. He said he would accept the blame. Before you hang up he has a message for you. Dial 9611 after placing down the receiver. I'm embarrassed and I'm sorry about disturbing you but Mr. Frederic said it was important. I will fully understand if you would like another assistant so again please accept my apology."

He said, "I am the one that's embarrassed about the situation Mr. Frederic put you in. Now I understand why you left me at the door so abruptly earlier today. Forgive my friend for putting you in a position of knowing someone was in my room and feeling awkward about disturbing me. Of course I want you to still help me while I am here in Las Vegas. It's embarrassing, I guess I've used that word a couple times now, I apologize for my friend, and he put you in a position of being treated like a purser and not as a professional. I again apologize for his rudeness. He is an old friend and his aggressive nature is a burden I should only be burdened with. Of course I would like you to stay as my assistant but if it in any way is offensive to you I will understand. There is one thing I would like to do. I would like to break the hotel's convention of no gratuities. I'll take care of that myself before I call 9611. You are going to have to transfer me to the hotel president's office. Don't say no, don't say anything, this is out of your hands. I will get special dispensation, and it will not fall back on you. It's the least I can do. By the way, I'm not giving you a car, think of something you might like. One more thing, that's enough of these apologies on both sides. Please make an additional reservation for my guest, Kerry Shannon, for dinner and her company at the Bellagio later tonight. She will also need a personal shopper downstairs; of course it will be at my expense. Can you have someone take care of her? I should attend to my business with Mr. Frederic but before I do, I want you to know that you can call me, interrupt me, saying anything to me about my stay here in Las Vegas and it will not be offensive. I have a good enough sense of self except for my fat body and that should be taken care of soon enough to stop you if I feel you are being too assertive. I now know that will never be the case. I know it is your job to be a good host and advocate for me here in Las Vegas. I will let you do your job."

She was stunned. She took a deep breath, "Mr. Shaw I am shocked. I did not expect a man of your resources to be so understanding of my interruption of you at such a sensitive time. I personally would have called it a violation of my space. Excuse me but I'm overwhelmed by how you've handled this. Thank you and before I say goodbye is there anything else I can do?"

"Yes there is," he said, "I just remembered, can you have the desk wake me up at 8:00am tomorrow morning and have a car waiting for me so I can get to the golf course. I probably want to leave around 9:15am. Thanks," he hung up.

He looked at Kerry Shannon lying next to him and said, "I'm sure you've heard everything, I guess I should have asked you if you wanted to have dinner, come with me, and be my escort while I play cards for a few hours."

She nodded her head in affirmation.

"Well," he said, "we should clean up; you have some shopping to do. We have at least three hours before dinner. That should give you plenty of time."

She looked at him and said, "I'm sure we can fill some of that time before we go downstairs. She pulled him softly on top of her."

-----o-----

Matt Shaw frozen in thought for a moment began to question himself, "Why am I being so nice to everybody. Why am I treating her, Kerry, like she's a date and BiBa like she's a treasured friend? Maybe it's the calm before the storm." he said to himself.

He did not need to be a tough guy now; he did not need to practice. He kept saying to himself when the time comes I will be ready. It wasn't like golf or cards when you practice to be on your game. He knew he would be up to the task of going after Mustafa Al Bin. For now being a nice guy just seemed appropriate. He didn't know why he just felt it in the deep recesses of his emotions. Soon enough

Johannesburg and Kasogi would be waiting.

Tonight and intermittently for the next few days for some reason he felt he needed the company of a woman. He could be good to someone and have some pleasures. It was kind of like Mayberry Street. The task of survival loomed over his head but for now he just wanted to feel safe and cared for. He knew it wasn't true, he knew he was paying for all of this.

Isn't that what money is for, he said to himself.

As Matt left the room in Kerry's company and took the elevator to the large retail complex downstairs, he noticed he was not getting the same attention usually afforded a Chief-of-Staff from politicos but now he was getting the attention of a man accompanied by a lovely companion. For the last three years not having sustained any meaningful relationships it felt good to be seen by others as a couple engaged in normal activities rather than a man with a woman on his arm. Even though Kerry was beautiful and as he said to himself, I ain't much to look at; it felt good being viewed as a couple. Their dinner at the

Capital Grille, the card playing, and the lovemaking all went by in an instant.

As Frederic had said, "This day was for his pleasure."

In the next couple of days there would be some important work, so don't get too comfortable old buddy, Frederic had warned him. As he closed his eyes with Kerry next to him he felt the anticipation of seeing Alverez, Malique and Bill. It had truly been a good day.

The phone rang at 8am. Matt woke up by himself with a note affixed to his pillow.

"Thank you, yesterday and last night were special for me. I thought you could start fresh this morning. Kerry, 571-324-0383."

He showered and called the front desk, "In twenty minutes please have my driver wait for me in front."

Upon walking through the hotel's double front doors he saw a Cadillac Escalade. Standing next to it the driver held a sign with the name Matt Shaw in deep black letters.

"Mr. Shaw," the driver said, "My name is Tony may I open the car for you," as he opened the back door.

"Tony," said Matt, "the front seat is fine. How long do you think it will take to get to the golf course? Is there a chance to stop for some coffee or something on the way?"

Tony responded, "Once we get behind the hotels away from Las Vegas Blvd. it should be clear sailing. We should be there in about twenty minutes. We can find a Starbucks on the way if that's okay with you."

"A cup of coffee would be great and maybe I'll get a scone or something." Matt thought when Alvarez saw him with a coffee in his hand he would think nothing much had changed in more than three years since he had seen his friend. Then it hit him. How would he react to the new fat Matt Papaz, and for that matter how would Malique and Bill?

When he got to the course, Tony gave him his card and said, "Call me from the seventeenth hole. I'll be there by the time you get done. I'll pick you up in front of the clubhouse. Have a good time. Take as long as you want, in fact if you would like I'll wait for you. To be honest with you I'm supposed to be with you all day so I guess I should just wait."

Matt looked at Tony and said, "Don't be foolish I'll call from the seventeenth hole and thanks for being honest. Just so you know I'm not a fast player. I'll probably be done in five and one-half to six hours."

He walked into the golf shop and purchased a pair of shoes then asked the starter for a set of rental clubs. He would wait for his three friends at the driving range. In what seem like an instant he heard familiar voices and turned to see the threesome. As they approached the practice area they did not recognize him. With consternation and deep insecurity he walked over to Alvarez first, and then Malique and Bill.

"Well, it's me."

They rushed up to him and before he could crack a joke or say something to deflect how he looked he noticed how they had all taken care of themselves as if time had never passed. They greeted him warmly. One by one they pulled him in for long hard hugs. Time stood still. They would have plenty of work. It would start shortly, but at this moment his emotional, not the warrior heart had surfaced. Three long years had come to pass.

Once more men of action had been called together. The golf was tertiary, the mission became suddenly secondary, and seeing his friends for the first time in three years became primary in his heart. They conversed for a few minutes knowing this was not the main reason for their gathering.

Bill said, "Come on guys lets get to the first tee. Who wants to hit first?"

The long par four was a dog leg right with water on the left side and desert sand on the right of the fairway. Funny Matt thought how images bring back memories. The hole was reminiscent of an oasis in Tamanossete, Algeria on the northern boundary of the Sahara Desert. It was one of the images etched in Matt's mind from one of his many travels as a young man. The symbolism did not escape him and also caught the attention of Alverez.

Alverez said, "Isn't it interesting Frederic picked a place in the middle of a desert for us to discuss Al Bin who's in Afghanistan. We are in one of the most expensive and opulent deserts in the world planning to kill this Al Bin guy who is living in one of the poorest and most rugged regions of the world. The only commonality between us and the son of a bitch is sand. I can't believe that flea bitten little Arab ass hole is planning on bringing us down. Man this whole thing is out of control."

As they played they talked in generalities and passed simplified theories around. There was a collective anguish that time was precious and the golf that was their cover was a wasteful use of it. Their anxieties precipitated calls from their cells as they drove from one shot to another. They knew they needed a safe house and equipment to formulate a plan.

Alverez decided to call Frederic, "Hey it's me, and can you set up a house rental here at Bears Best. You brought us here for some reason, I'm thinking the seclusion. Am I right? There are many unoccupied houses on the course and they're big enough for all of us to stay. You think you can get it done old buddy?"

Frederic said, "I am way ahead of you. That is why I picked this course. The Ridge Rim project is one of Las Vegas' most upscale but as you can see it's in Chapter 13. I have already rented a house on the 16th tee. Have you guys been there yet?"

Alverez said they were on the 14th tee as they spoke.

Frederic replied, "When you get there the door has an electronic code, 1220. I have equipped it with everything you will need. It's amazing how great minds think alike. Call me at 16. Don't do anything more than look at it from the course. When you're finished playing golf, drive to 12743 Lava Rock Drive. Like I said the code is 1220. Come through the front door, you won't be as conspicuous. I want the three of you to go to the house and have Matt go back to the hotel and then come back to the house after dark. I don't want the four of you to be seen together other than playing golf."

After finishing the course they went to the 19th hole, the bar, and had a drink. The talk was of their round of golf. Matt called Tony to be picked up in twenty-five to thirty minutes. He would go back to the hotel wait around for a couple hours, clean up and take a taxi cab back to the foursome's command center. Matt would stay there until about 10:00pm and head back to the Encore preparing himself for the arranged Omaha game at 11:30pm. He placed a call to BiBa to inform her he would be back at the hotel by 10:00pm. He said he had been shopping and had something lite to eat. He assured her that he was looking forward to being at the table. His salutation to her as he ended the short conversation was, "I was looking forward to hearing your voice I was not disappointed. Thanks, wish me luck."

The four men sat in the entertainment room of the ten thousand square feet house designed by Cliff May. The view from their makeshift headquarters on the course with its backdrop of Red Rock Canyon lent a kind of Afghanistan imagery. They were here in Las Vegas but soon enough they would be near the Khyber Pass region of Afghanistan. The Las Vegas streets were paved with gold and people were looking for a get-rich opportunity of a lifetime. Shortly they would be in Kabul and then in the eastern frontier where there were no streets only dusty impassable roads where people had no hope, only desperation.

Malique stressed that Sun Tzu's Art of War described preparation for battle as preparation for victory. The four men would work on stratagem, tactical dispositions, tactics variation and as the fourth century warrior said the use of spies. For them to be successful and reach the plot's underpinnings and originators they needed people on the ground. They called Frederic and Kasogi and discussed the need for tactical Intel support and local assets. They only had a few hours before Matt would have to leave so they set work parameters for the coming days.

-----o-----

At 8:30pm Matt requested a ride from Alvarez taking him from the Ridge Rim house and dropping him off at Caesars Palace. He did not want it to appear the two were together so he started walking back to the Encore Hotel. He ventured into the Forum, the most exclusive shopping center in Las Vegas. He walked into a

Vantanos, purchased two shirts and a pair of pants from the rack. Walking across Las Vegas Boulevard towards Encore, he picked up some magazines at a liquor store, entered the Encore and went directly to the bell captain's desk. There he asked one of the attendants to have his clothes ironed and sent up to his room as quickly as possible and gave him a fifty dollar tip. He knew that BiBa would be monitoring his expenses at the hotel. She was his personal assistant but more importantly the hotel's P.I. when it came to its guests. She was like having personnel on the ground used for Intel and surveillance. BiBa just happened to be prettier than most. She would make notes of his expenses with notations of his comings and goings and it would all fit into his cover of shopping and sightseeing after golf.

Once inside the room he called the number Kerry had given him. "Hello," he said. "Are you free tonight?"

She paused for a second and said, "I don't know if the correct word is free, but I'll sure entertain offers." then she laughed.

He continued, "I know it's late and it is really inconsiderate of me, and of course I don't know the business arrangement you have with the hotel, but all the same, I would really like it if you could make it work no matter how much trouble or whatever the cost."

He could barely breathe after uttering such a lengthy and rapid sentence. While catching his breath, Kerry replied, "Sure, what do you have in mind? I thought you were playing cards, isn't that a solitary activity? I told you I enjoyed myself yesterday, so sure I'll make it work."

He said, "I want you with me at the table. I'll just say I need you as my good luck charm. The hotel has a private game at 11:30pm. Can you be at my room at 11:15pm? We will go down from there."

She said, "Are you sure you don't want me to come there earlier, I can be there in 25 minutes. I'm sure I can calm you down and get you into a rhythm for cards."

She had a way of displaying her intelligence by using double entendres. He said, "I don't think I could take it if you came by early. I would have nothing left for the game." He paused for a second then added, "Except great memories. No, come up at 11:15pm I take cards seriously. There's lots of money at stake. You know there must be something about Las Vegas. I really don't know how lucky I feel tonight. Usually when I played cards it had nothing to do with luck, just percentages and timing. But tonight I hope I'm lucky."

She shot back, "You don't have to be lucky. It's a sure thing. Okay, I'll see you at 11:15pm"

The two went down to the casino. BiBa was waiting for him and felt a little awkward seeing Matt with Kerry Shannon. Her script had not taken into account that he might want to be in Kerry's company again. Trying not to show any disappointment she said, "Mr. Shaw, Ms. Shannon may I escort you to the game. The other players are already assembled. I have a buy-in of three hundred thousand dollars in front of your seat. Excuse me for asking the question but where would you like Ms. Shannon to sit. Should I get her a permanent seat for guests or assume she will be coming in and out and standing by your side intermittently?"

She felt strange asking the question of Matt rather than addressing Ms. Shannon. "Mr. Frederic has increased your line of credit to three million dollars; of course the table is aware of it," she continued, "Good luck."

Matt wondered if Frederic was saying lose big time. It will all be part of your cover for South Africa. There are no secrets in the world of professional gambling. Word would travel fast if he lost and he would be welcomed with open arms when he and Kasogi were in Sun City. His own intentions were to play it slow, if that were possible in Omaha, and breaking even would be a victory considering his ambivalent state of mind for cards tonight. His attention to the work at Ridge Rim and the two women from Las Vegas who stood next to him weighed heavily on his mind. Free money and lack of focus were not good partners for success. If you just brake even it would be a good night he thought. He had looked forward to playing cards in high stake games for almost three years. The circumstances and artificial nature of this game didn't seem terribly enticing. He reflected, this is going to be more work than pleasure. His mind was flashing back and forth from one thought to another. He didn't want to be at the table, the game, or with two women. He had paid for one, he yearned for the other. He was unable to focus and it bothered him.

He stayed at the table for almost 3 hours. A little before 2:00am he called it quits with winnings of almost eighty thousand dollars. For such a big game and its emotional demands for focus and total concentration it was a little like mental masturbation. He got up and thanked his adversaries. He and Kerry slowly walked through the casino back to the elevators and arrived at his suite just a little after 2:00am. They made long passionate sex for almost two hours. By 5:00am she was gone again as he slept for another two hours until an all familiar Las Vegas pattern began anew.

BiBa called and apologized for Frederic's presumptuous intrusion. "Mr. Frederic wanted you to be up by 7:30am so you can call him and give him full account of last night. He said something about a percentage of your winnings. Since I've awakened you is there anything I can do for you. It's none of my business but does he always do this? Do you want me to screen his calls and let you sleep in the rest of your time here at the hotel?"

"BiBa, no no no. I'm used to it. You will have to be just a little more patient with him. He's like you. You're both just looking out for me in your own ways. It's tough being taken care of. Being kept ain't all it's cracked up to be." He laughed, "It's good to hear your voice in the morning, even if it's a directive from my man Frederic. Thanks for calling," he said in a sarcastic manner, but she knew he was just trying to sound funny.

He showered and went down to get some breakfast before he left the hotel. Once he got outside he asked a valet to call a cab for him. He asked the driver, "Can you take me to 12743 Lava Rock Dr. it's in Ridge Rim just off Bear's Best golf course. On the way there find me a Starbucks."

-----o-----

The door opened, Alvarez said, "Come in. Everyone's in the living room."

"Frederic had made the house a command center. Whoever his people were that put this together, they did a spectacular job," he said.

"The electronics are the most sophisticated any of us have ever seen. I think we're about a hundred years behind in Mexico. We have a conference call on a secure line with one of Frederic's people in New York. Her name is Gisele Lapiner. She is an ex-national security agency deputy assistant who you might say is a hired gun. Her field of expertise is Afghanistan and the Taliban. She should be calling in a few minutes. I can't imagine what she costs Frederic but he said she's the best. Between her and his ability to break into Homeland's mainframe we have resources galore at our disposal."

Matt said, "I thought we were off-line a couple years ago with Homeland. I didn't think we had the ability to tap into their database anymore."

I know it's been a long time and I've been out of the loop but I guess Frederic still does his Magic. How the heck did he ever maintain a window into their operations? Who in the hell is this woman Gisele? We're just a few of the thoughts running through his head. They walked into the house's huge entertainment area now the command center. The room's back wall had four sixty inch touch screen monitors with computer systems flanking the rest of the room. As Matt scanned the huge thirty by thirty foot room he saw Bill and Malique. There were three people he did not recognize sitting at monitors next to what appeared to be a mainframe computer. He surmised they were technical support, obviously part of the team. He counted eleven large forty-two inch monitors complementary to the large touchtone screens.

He looked at his three cohorts and said, "We sure have all the bells and whistles. I've never seen this much electronic stuff in my life. For some reason I thought we would just brainstorm, you know, walk around in circles, with one of us writing down notes or using a white board. This is overwhelming."

Malique said, "I know you've been out in the cold, so to speak, but a lot has changed in three years."

Matt thought to himself, "You have no idea."

In Costa Rica where he oversaw the seat of government they must be fifteen years behind the technical ability of this room and Costa Rica was a reasonably developed nation. He was amazed at what Frederic had put together in such a short time.

Before the three men could start a dialogue and interchange ideas, a very polished looking woman appeared on the large touch screen monitor. She looked in her mid-forties, classically stoic, with an air of self-assurance.

Alvarez said, "You must be Gisele. Around here we use first names. I'm Jose, let me introduce: Matt, Bill and Malique. We are all ears, the floor's yours."

The attractive woman on the screen surprised all four men. She had a beautiful thick French accent. She was concise and direct. Her delivery was fluid and her enunciation was perfect. The clear intellect Gisele brought to the table was evident in a few short moments. Matt would later comment to the other three men that she changed his opinion of the French. Up until this working relationship with her he had never met a French person he liked or respected.

After an impressive but brief overview Gisele continued, "I've put together a framework we can proceed from. Our goal is to stop the execution of the bombing plots in New York. Al Bin is probably incidental but he is our starting point. Our vector of thought has to be connecting him to whoever gains the most from this episode. We still have no clarity as to whom and why somebody would hire him. Answers always come to the foreground after the fact but we can't afford to deal in hindsight. The devastation of such an attack is not only unthinkable but it's irreparable. Our goals must be defined as,

- Stop the attack
- Find the responsible party or parties
- Eliminate them at the source

I have been in contact with Frederic for the past thirty-six hours. We have exhausted all our intelligence both on the ground and electronically. We have no substantive evaluations of who's behind this. We do have some working assumptions that might be helpful to you in your analysis. We feel the black-market is sophisticated enough to provide nuclear waste materials, i.e. medical refuse and spent uranium reactor rods from the old Soviet Union for a dirty bomb. A dirty bomb is feasible. Allegedly Al Bin has been throwing money around to buy enriched plutonium, weapons grade. We think it's a diversion. Our estimates are, there's a little less than three hundred fifty pounds of highly enriched weapon grade plutonium garnered and protected by governments both allies and adversaries of the United States. Eighty-seven percent of these materials are accounted for by Homeland's actual visual inspection. We're not exactly sure what that means. If they are okay with that definition for verification I guess we have to be as well. Therefore it's safe to say that approximately ninety percent of these materials are locked up and are out of the reach for any nefarious group. Our estimates of the other thirteen percent show a little less than nine percent is accounted for by the government's materials housing. We think they are being honest with the international inspectors. That means three to four percent of the world's highly enriched plutonium is unaccounted. Most of it is from the old Soviet Union. We don't know how much is in the hands of the black-market. A percentage of the four percent is probably lost somewhere. Our best guess is these dispersed black marketeers do not have working relationships. For Al Bin or anyone else to obtain the nine or ten pounds of materials needed for a bomb would take numerous purchases and red flags would be activated throughout the world's security organizations. There's something else that makes the purchase of these materials difficult. Because of their high radioactivity once in transit they would be easily recognized. Plutonium's DNA or radioactive blueprint would set off alarms at almost all major transit points in the world."

"Al Bin or whoever is behind this is trying to purchase nuclear waste. That's what he's trying to do. We feel one hundred percent assured this is the case.

Putting out feelers to purchase plutonium in the black-market is just a diversion. We do however think the money he's throwing around is real. To that end, we are trying to trace it and may I say, with little luck. There are no electronic paper trails, so whoever has that kind of money must be substantial. It must be in house money that's not traceable. His backers are sophisticated, well-financed, and appear to be targeting us. We don't have a timeline for the attack but gentleman, it's eminent. Our estimates are, if we don't act Al Bin will have the materials and be able to deliver the bomb to his operatives in New York in less than ninety days."

"We feel Al Bin is unwittingly complicit pursuing his own goals of ousting bin Laden's regime as the major figure in the Middle East. Whoever the deep pockets are, they are using him. We feel he doesn't have the ability nor the intellect to pull this off by himself. At this time, we have no, may I express that again, no leads to whoever is using him. Money is not only being used for the purchase of materials but we have evidence some funds are being used to destabilize many of your arrangements and agreements that legalize drugs and promote internal stability, particularly in the Middle East."

"Inquiries are being followed through a couple of lines. Throughout the world, we're investigating all nuclear waste sources, hospitals, industrial sites, and government storage facilities, and their disposal. We're setting up a matrix of where they are and the accountability of all materials. We're also trying to determine where Al Bin is and the easiest way to apprehend him. We find it most interesting that he is under the radar with US, Russian, and Israeli security apparatus. Only Kasogi's people have him on their screens as a threat. This is very troubling. He should be very transparent because he's so unsophisticated, but that's not the case. As I said before, we are trying to track down his source of capital and that has been a dead end. We are trying to work backwards and find out who will gain most by a terrorist attack but we are at a loss. Nothing has come to the light."

Alvarez said, "Gisele, we are late into this so can you please send us everything you have so we can get up to speed. You have at least 36 hours on us and maybe if we glean your materials we will come up with something different. Don't send us anything that's annotated. We don't want to be influenced by you or Frederic. Send over the materials then we'll talk. It shouldn't take more than 24 hours for us to digest it all."

Matt interrupted, "I want you to include Kasogi and send him everything. He looked around the room and everyone agreed. We'll all have a better take on this tomorrow. We'll talk to you then."

Gisele was predictably exacting and prompt in her response to Alverez's requests for materials. In a few short hours the big screen was filled with a topographical map of Afghanistan and the western tribal regions of Pakistan. All the suspected hideaways for Al Bin were highlighted with summaries of his possible whereabouts. The province of Helmed was the last sighting of Al Bin. He was seen in the Marja district in its urban environs less than three weeks earlier. He gave an impromptu sermon at the al Ashan mosque. His trademark of fiery rhetoric and the impassioned need for strict Sharia law was closely followed and scrutinized by NSA. Their analyst's summaries and profiling of Al Bin had been combed over by Gisele with no profound result. She concluded that he was ambitious for his own personal gain. He was not particularly intelligent; in fact her abstract suggested he could not digest more than one complex idea at a time. His rise to power was meteoric and not consistent with any of his actions. His body of work as a mullah had no history that could be traced back more than one year. His reputation was manufactured but his ability as a word merchant propelled him to a position of prominence in the eyes of the young and the poor. He did not say much but he said it well, was a fitting summation of his persona. She felt he had to be sponsored by someone and shepherded to attract the attention he was receiving. His first public recognition came in the Kandahar province at a shura, a tribal gathering, where he openly questioned the wisdom of following al Qaeda and the mullah Omar. He passionately criticized the two for being rooted in compliance with the American infidels. The old leader's insistence on foregoing the campaign of terrorism existed from 2001 to the present was no more than acquiescence to the power of the devils in the West he said. Two weeks later his rhetoric precipitated an impassive fatwa against him by the Taliban leader mullah Omar. It was seen as perfunctorily only. A gesture without teeth and enacted as a measure to save face. Al Bin oratory was so scripted at the shura and its response was so anticipated that after the meeting he sought safe haven in the northern Afghanistan Baghlan province where treacherous terrain made it impossible for even the Taliban leader's minions to follow him. Al Bin had support of the poorer, less educated Pashtuns of the desolate region. Gisele's analysis included transcriptions of his website chatter and phone conversations during his limited stay in what was thought to be a cave complex. When he finally came into public view near Kandahar he was with a mercenary guard of at least ten Arabs. It was clear they were not Afghan, they were a splinter group or offshoot of bin Laden's loyalists. Al Bin's clandestine nature and his infrequent sightings coupled with his fiery rhetoric when he did surface for impromptu appearances made him a mystical religious figure. The orchestration of his accent was coupled with large sums of money being spent on the poor. The vast majority of Gisele's Intel had Al Bin in Afghanistan and in the neighboring Pakistan tribal provinces.

At the prescribed twenty-four hours Gisele appeared on the big monitor. "Gentlemen, good morning. You've had time to digest the materials. What are your conclusions?"

Matt spoke up. "Gisele your assessment is pretty much the same as ours. We have information from Kasogi that as we speak is being sent to you. It suggests Al Bin will be going to Johannesburg to procure the materials. It's a second try, but only a measured risk on his part. Let me fill you in. He obviously knows the plot was foiled and his operatives were tortured and killed. Kasogi's intelligence placed him in Pakistan on his way to South Africa. He's more than tenacious in his pursuit of the nuclear waste. We suspect the only reason he feels comfortable going there himself is the original transaction was botched and he has assurances for his safety this time around. Our intelligence suspects the Johannesburg's police depart-ment's antiterrorist division was not part of the arrangement between the waste management company and Al Bin. We have definitive proof that President Zuma's minister-of-defense and the disposal company were working together. The minister's name is Martin Magumba. There are ties between him and funds from Al Bin. He was supposed to broker the deal for the nuclear waste and provide protection so the materials transfer and shipment to the United States would go undetected. We feel the Johannesburg authorities either intervened because there was money in it for them or they were not informed and unexpectedly fell upon the transaction. Kasogi calls it a jurisdictional dispute. He says the depth of corruption in South Africa is impossible to measure but it goes all the way to the top. It's clear to him that all the perpetrators were killed after interrogation so the anti-terrorist squad would have leverage against whoever was behind this endeavor."

"After going over the files you have given us," Matt continued, "it is pretty clear our attention should be in Johannesburg and my meeting with Kasogi is imperative."

Gisele countered, "Yes I think you're correct. We have information that Al Bin is out of country. We place him in the western Pakistan tribal territories. The money move-ments and personnel suggest he is planning to move in a few days. There is a high probability he will be in Johannesburg shortly. We are in the midst of placing people in his camp in the Swat Valley to monitor his activities. The only way we can obtain a disposition of his intended actions is to place spies into his operation. We have some people in the local area willing to gather information and take pictures of any Al Bin sightings. Just as in the use of any spies we have to manage them with straightforwardness and we need to make sure their needs are consistent with ours. Money doesn't buy loyal partners. Shared ideas and values do. There is perceived anger at Al Bin's strident oppressive read on Sharia law and its repression of women. We feel we have an opening there. Some of Al Bin's inner circle seemed jealous of his newfound power and they openly purport he is hypocritical when it comes to the virtue of austerity. We think he has a need or at least a fetish for little boys. This will be a problem for him. Not only is he a pedophile but he drinks and has a porn collection, unthinkable for the Muslim world. We think we can turn one of his lieutenants; his name is Kasar, on moral or idealistic grounds. But if that doesn't work we will turn Kasar by taking his children. We have one of his sons in our sites and we can commandeer him at any time. We're also working on a scenario of sacrificing one of his inner circles for our own purposes. We will frame el Mohammed Abdul, his most trusted underling. We're putting money into one of his accounts to show he sold out Al Bin's associates in South Africa for mere pittance. We'll sacrifice him to make Al Bin look over his shoulder. He will have to think a little harder about who his benefactors are and he might even loosen his allegiance with them knowing his own people may sell him out. No matter what our spies will soon have names of his click that he relies on for protection. We feel we can pressure him enough to be reckless and lead us to people behind this. He will feel pressure he has never felt before."

Alvarez added himself into the conference call. "Gisele, we have been in close contact with Kasogi as you can imagine. He has his ways of course. Let me fill you in on what he proposes to do. When we are down in Johannesburg, oh yeah, Bill, Malique, and I will be going there in a support role. As I was saying Kasogi thinks it will be hard to get our hands on Al Bin. But there's a possible opening at the disposal company. He says he has a way of persuading one of the principles to give up Al Bin, and I believe him. One of the company's vice presidents was being paid very handsomely for the waste materials from the hospital. He needs the money. He is in financial trouble and his whole world is coming down on him. As the plan goes he will create an opening to steal the waste again, this time with full protection of the Defense

Minister. We feel he will cave in with Kasogi's threat of being kidnapped and sent to prison in Zambia. Kasogi has ties to President Olingo. All desperate men cave in especially when they are shown the prospects of their future. The disposal company VP's name is Stephan Van Deer He is also a ten percent owner. He agreed to act as conduit setting the deal in motion for minister Mugumba. His cut will be $1 million American. With the threat of incarceration Kasogi thinks Van Deer will turn. We can have him placed in Zambia's Mukobeko maximum prison at any time. He is ready to shit himself just with the thought of it. The prison is the worst in Africa. It was built in 1950 to house four hundred men. Today it's overrun by more than 1700. Only thirty percent of the prisoners have ever been before a magistrate. The death rate after two years is more than fifty percent. When Van Deer gets there they will strip him naked and place them in solitary confinement for at least two weeks. His cell will have ankle deep waste water in it. He will have to live in his own excrement. He will get dysentery because the only water he will have at his disposal is the filth he lives in. The rate of tuberculosis at the prison is close to eighty percent. He will be given a loaf of bread a day, they usually just through it into the cell and it lands in the water. Lastly and probably the worst of all he will have a cell captain who will rape his white ass."

Alverez got embarrassed, "I'm sorry Gisele I got a little carried away."

She laughed, "I certainly have heard worse. Don't worry about it."

Alverez continued, "I could go on and on but you see the picture. Zambia's prison system is the world's most brutal. It's called the deathtrap. The thought of this place can change any man. Van Deer will turn on anybody. That's how we'll get Al Bin. With these two leads, Al Bin and Van Deer, Kasogi figures we have a good chance to get to the money people."

Gisele countered, "We also have resources on our end, and may I say a very persuasive resource we can use to obtain information if our operations in Johannesburg fail. It is what we call the last option. It is costly but we can get access to Scorpion drones. They are

Lockheed Martin small drones weighing 35 pounds, usually fired from predators. They also have the ability to fly land to land. We can reconfigure them and they are easy to launch. They're about the diameter of a coffee cup and about two and a half feet long. They traveled about two hundred miles an hour and have an accuracy of one square foot per thirty miles. They are so precise and their electronics are so accurate they can detect a person walking in a crowd and take them out without any collateral damage. We also have access to the thermobalic pressure wave bombs that can be dropped by our own drones. There will be no structural damage to buildings or their contents. The pressure waves can turn corners or penetrate deep bunkers or caves. As a last resort we can go after Al Bin's people or his family, wherever we turn up. This last option as we call it should signal something in him. Maybe he can be persuaded. Keep this stuff in mind if you think you need it. It's at your disposal."

Five intensive days of brainstorming lead to the conclusion that Mustafa Al Bin was definitely not behind such a sophisticated plot and he did not even have minimal input. Every instinct of the four men and their support staff in Las Vegas coupled with Gisele's, Frederic's, and Kasogi's input all pointed to the same conclusion.

Al bin was ambitious but he was too myopic and not smart enough to be behind such a far reaching complex operation. His primary attention was directed at dethroning al Qaeda as the de facto power in the Middle East. Doing the bidding for the person or persons behind the plot would give him the resources to wage a power struggle with the head of al Qaeda and nothing more. He was for hire. He was incapable of heading an operation of this magnitude. The information scraps about his financial benefactors painted an empty mosaic. Someone was filling his coffers with money through a hawala, a money-laundering system, but left no trail identifying themselves or their financial resources.

The four men's final disposition was sending Matt to Johannesburg for a meeting with the ANC (African National

Congress) and Kasogi. Contact with old AMC loyalists would facilitate the kidnapping and interrogation of the police antiterrorist squad for the right price. Johannesburg was one of the most corrupt and a lawless city's in the world and taking its police for ransom was commonplace. The botched operation to steal waste materials from Soweto hospital would not stop Al Bin from a second attempt or some kind of reprisal against the people responsible for the first plot's failure. Redundancy was an operative word in the criminal world of South Africa's largest city. To pull off a successful second heist the police would have to be involved. A reckoning with the anti-terror squad by ANC's and Kasogi's men would hopefully provide the information needed to capture whoever was behind the New York City bomb plot.

As with all plans the risk factor was high for such a task as kidnapping the police for information.

Plans were formulated following the quasi-military procedures of the Russian mafia when it established a power base in the old Soviet Union as it was disintegrating in the early 1990s. Kasogi's men, an all Arab, Cairo contingent, would blend in with their ANC multicultural mega-city counterparts. The fourteen mercenaries, nine from the ANC and the five Arabs flown in from Egypt, would simply march into the prefecture and assume command and control. They would only need thirty minutes to extract information and do what ever they had to with the hostages. Some police would be killed and others would be threatened with the lives of their loved ones if they failed to comply and supply the needed information. The ANC had its ways of getting information. The old guard was notorious for their brutality. A plausible deniability of their acts would be constructed in such a way that their barbaric and brazen interrogation of the police would point to Al Bin as a religious fanatic trying to punish the people who intervened in God's earthly matters.

They felt the plan would accomplish two things:

Bring Al Bin into the light where the international authorities could pursue him and

Generate information leading to whoever was behind the intended New York bombing.

The five days' fact-finding and analyzing materials had gone by slowly. Matt's routine, getting to Ridge Rim at midmorning and staying until late, left him exhausted and in an emotional state of uneasiness. His paid rela-tionship with Kerry Shannon had lasted for only two nights. He was drained and lonely. He longed to hear BiBa's voice. She had called nearly every day with a message in the morning, a prompting from Frederic that on face was always about some inane matter. Her voice was consoling and had a magic about it. His five days' work had led to his isolation and the need for her female companionship.

The warrior in him knew what he had to do in the future but it was tempered by his immediate need for BiBa. He called her and asked if she would meet with him. Her promise of 24 hour accessibility rang true and she said she would see him whenever and wherever was most convenient.

"BiBa," he said, "how about if we meet tomorrow morning at ten o'clock in the lobby. Wear a shopping outfit. I do believe I owe you a gift of gratitude. Before you say anything, I want you to know I've talked to your employer and he has conceded to my demands. You can't say no. Just so you sleep better, I want you to know there is no Ferrari or Maserati or anything like that. I'm not trying to buy you I just want to show you my thanks. I would like to get you something thoughtful."

"Mr. Shaw," she said.

He quickly interrupted, "Matt, its okay to call me Matt."

She finished, "You don't need to buy me anything. Just your company will be enough. I mean that. I will dress casually but not for shopping. You don't need to buy me a thing. I don't really want to talk about it anymore, I'm looking forward to seeing you tomorrow morning and the operative word is seeing not getting anything from you. I mean it. Don't ruin the day by being overly generous. Sharing the day is reward enough."

He went to sleep in an instant with a boyish grin on his face. He had not felt smitten by a woman in many years. His marriage of fifteen years and his subsequent three years of whoring around and buying women with money and political power were all empty exercises of a lonely man. He knew BiBa would be different. He woke up at 7am and called Frederic. He started the conversation by saying, "We've tied down everything and I'll be leaving for Johannesburg in about a week. Knowing you will want to script a travel itinerary for me. First though, I have to get out of Las Vegas for a couple of days to collect my thoughts. I'll be going to La Jolla so you can send everything I need; passports, papers, and Intel to the Hotel Valencia."

Frederic broke in, "Don't go back to L.A. Leave yesterday exactly where it belongs, yesterday. Don't be foolish and try to contact your old friends and of course, I shouldn't have to say this, don't even think about trying to get in touch with Janis and the kids."

Matt shot back, "You don't have to say a word. I know. That's not why I'm going to Southern California."

"Listen old buddy," Matt said, "make sure I carry my line of credit as Matt Shaw. I'm also going to make some purchases here before we leave. That's right, we. So don't be surprised when you see some big-ticket items. If things work out I'm going to ask Ms. Lamanas to come with me to La Jolla. She ain't yesterday."

Frederic replied, "I've only talked to her a couple times and she does seem extraordinary. Have a good time partner. Call me when you get the packet of materials, I will have them delivered to the hotel tomorrow by 12:00pm. Sounds like you are a lucky guy. Don't get carried away, you'll be in Johannesburg in a week."

-----o-----

Matt had to make more calls before his ten o'clock rendezvous with BiBa. His mind was racing. He felt like he was in high school trying to figure out how to impress the most beautiful girl on the campus. He was not good at dating he thought, but buying women was easy. Money does make you more charming and handsome he said to himself. This was different; BiBa was not for sale. He got to the lobby at 9:45am to be there before she arrived. He wanted the advantage of being early so he could collect himself and settle his nerves. He kept telling himself she must mean a lot for him to be so lacking in confidence and tripping over his own feet. He laughed inside thinking how absurd it was for him to be so child like about her and that within a week he would be in harms way with the prospect of killing to protect himself and his compatriots. His reflections changed and once again they were focused totally towards BiBa. He had doubts about her response towards him. He did not exactly know what he wanted to do but he knew he wanted to be with her. He continued talking to himself; I'll just play this out. I'll just play it by ear. Oh shit, I hope I don't come off as a nerd falling all over myself. BiBa first appeared in the mirror adjacent to the elevators. It was 9:55am. She was wearing tight jeans, a simple pink low strapped T-shirt, and tennis shoes. She had no bag, just a wallet in her back pocket and she was wearing a Cartier Roadster watch on her left wrist. She walked up to him at the registration desk contiguous to the large patio in the hotel's main lobby.

She smiled for a brief second and said, "It's good we're both early. That must mean something. In all honesty I shouldn't say this, but I couldn't wait to see you."

He placed a kiss on her cheek and responded, "I've been looking forward to seeing you in the morning. It's certainly better than the messages you relay to me from Frederic. It's kind of silly of me but I really do like to hear your voice when I get up. I think maybe that means a lot as well."

"Let's get out of here," he said.

She grabbed his arm as they walked to the front of the hotel and ventured towards the valet parking. An attendant was standing next to a white four-door XJ Jaguar with a sign that said the Shaw party. They walked over to the car.

He said, "I hope you don't mind driving I don't know my way around here."

She setup her automatic seat as he entered the car's passenger side and said, "I have a feeling you have this day planned out for us." She gave him a big kiss on his cheek, "I am at your disposal. Whatever you want sounds great to me."

He smiled and retorted, "Where ever you want to go is fine but I'm really embarrassed about what I want to do. I want to bring something up first. I don't know where to start, so I will just say it. I want you to come to La Jolla with me for a couple of days. I know it's presumptuous and I probably shouldn't have done it, but I cleared a couple days for you with the hotel. I have two rooms at this old style hotel in the heart of La Jolla. Boy, I'm really uncomfortable asking you this, but I would understand if you want to have a room by yourself, and I would sadly understand if you didn't want to come. This is all very new to me and everything seems so fast, but I know I would regret it the rest of my life if I didn't ask. Before you say a word," he said in a suddenly deep voice, "I have to leave the United States in six days. I'm really at a loss, I can't explain where I'm going or why.

There are a whole bunch of things I would like to tell you but I can't. I feel like a fool. Being cloaked in mystery must sound stupid and immature but there's nothing else I can say. I would truly understand if you don't want to come with me. I'm asking a lot. I just want you to take me on faith. I promise I will explain everything as soon as I possibly can, how stupid does this sound, I can't even tell you where I'm going. I just want to be with you. I know it's a lot to ask," as he sighed and dropped his head, "how about it?"

"Let me just say one last thing. When I first met you I apologized for the actions of my friend Frederic. Now I'm apologizing for my own actions. I must sound like an idiot. If you want out of the car I wouldn't blame you."

She did not hesitate. She looked deep into his eyes and said, "It's crazy but its okay. You promised me you would tell me some day and I'll sure as hell hold you to it. Matt, don't make a fool of me. Usually my first impressions are correct and my intuitions about you are all good. Don't poison my well. That would really be hard to take. Enough said, since I'm driving what do we do with the car?"

He looked at her and said, "It's mine as of this morning. Why don't we just take it to La Jolla? It's only a 5 hour drive and we'll ship it back here to Vegas when we're done. Oh yeah, one more thing, I am going to ask you to take care of it for me while I'm gone. What a team, I guess it's pretty easy for both of us to make impetuous decisions, especially when they are the right ones."

As they left the hotel BiBa was behind the wheel of the one hundred twenty thousand dollar car. She made a left turn on Las Vegas Boulevard and followed it to Frank Sinatra Boulevard and got onto the Interstate15 West. They would follow the desert freeway for thirty miles until they reached the California/ Nevada border.

She said, in a very facetious tone, "There is a factory outlet at the border. I want to get a few things. I just need some night garments, underwear, bathing suit, and some casual clothes. He looked at her in amazement."

He said, "I was thinking along the lines of a more upscale kind of place to take you. They have some real nice places in San Diego."

She smiled and said, "I can't help myself. I just have to say it, I'm not Ms. Shannon. I don't need Beverly Hills boutiques to feel good. The outlets are just fine. Sorry, I guess I'm just a little jealous of her, but really I don't need much. She was so," she stopped herself and continued, "it's your company not your money that I want."

He was taken back. "Shannon meant very little to me," he said. "I did treat her well; she deserved at least that much. I must've made a bad impression on you, but I must've done something right as well." grabbing her hand.

They both agreed not to discuss what had gone on in Las Vegas. Their brief discussion of clothing and Kerry Shannon made for an uncomfortable moment and they both didn't want to start their trip that way.

-----O-----

About forty-five minutes from the border, BiBa pointed out a sign that spelled the word ZZYZX. She told him that it was the last word in the dictionary. It was the name of an old health spa taken over by the California Department of Parks. The oasis style facility was a mineral spring for the rich and famous in the pre-Depression era. A promoter named Dr. Springer, who she described as a snake oil salesman, had developed the hotel and sold vacation shares to Hollywood types, as she called them, for its curative properties. The history of Zzyzx was of interest to her, she had the soul of a tour guide who loved trivial out-of-the-way spots. It was evident that BiBa was a complex woman with many interests and travel was one of them. For about 15 minutes, they walked around the old oasis and dilapidated hotel grounds.

Getting back into the car she activated the GPS system and typed in the words La Valencia Hotel, La Jolla Ca. They would take the Interstate 15 to the interstate 210 and from there heads south on the 605 and continue on the 405 to Interstate 5 and get off at Carmel Valley Road then follow it into La Jolla proper. Estimated time of arrival five hours and ten minutes, the drive through the desert was almost nondescript except for her travel advisories, as Matt called her tidbits of knowledge. The conversation was engaging even though it was only one sided.

Matt was to learn about her past which gave him a greater appreciation of her as a person. She knew little of Matt's history and anything sensitive and was met with, I can't discuss it now, I promise when this is over.

He found BiBa was a product of first-generation Latvian family who found new roots in New Jersey. She considered herself a tomboy only acknowledging her beauty in terms of her mother's adage, beauty is what beauty does not how one looks. Her mother drummed into her that people's actions not their looks were the most important thing in life. Her accomplishments were taken very seriously.

She must have expressed to Matt on four or five occasions that she was an over achiever and sometimes bothered people by her compulsivity. She was an all-state soccer player in high school which garnered her athletic scholarships. She was the valedictorian at Wilson High School in Hoboken but more importantly she was a member of Habitat for Humanity and had traveled to Alabama to help build houses for the rural poor. Upon graduation she accepted an academic scholarship to Columbia University in the Hotel and Restaurant Management School.

"You know," she said, "sometimes I look back and I was very accomplished but I was a social blunder. I don't have many social skills. I'm more like the person you want to hire because they get things done. I'm really good at what I do. I think I work so hard because being attractive is a curse and I really feel what mother said about beauty is correct."

Matt said, "We all have hurdles. None are higher than anybody else's but boy can they get in our way and make life tough. I guess it's the people who get over them that are the happiest and live the most normal lives. On face I think lots of people would like to have your problems, but I do know they are real as long as you think they are. I don't complain much but it is pretty obvious I'm being overly secretive. I have some really big hurdles and I want them over with as soon as possible. I want things to work out for you and me."

She looked at him and said, "I know you're not going to believe this but I'm usually not very spontaneous. This is really crazy for me. I'm a planner, I think too much, I don't like risks, and I can't believe it but I find myself with you in some kind of secretive relationship. This is really exciting and I don't know what I'm doing. But it's alright, as you said, we have six days."

She looked at him taking her eyes off the road for a second and said, "We both must be crazy but what the hell, you only live once."

He thought to himself that was an ominous cliché.

She said, "As tightlipped as you are about your past you could be a spy or something," and then she laughed."

Matt got serious for a moment and said, have to say something. I am living what I call a seminal sense. Two different lives, one I am not proud of and the other I would like to get back. To be honest, sometimes it's almost too much for me. Its cloak and dagger, that kind of stuff."

He knew he couldn't go much further he thought to himself. He probably had gone too far but he said, "I must sound like the biggest piece of crap in the world. You know, like a guy making some stuff up to get a beautiful woman's attention. I really am one of the good guys and when this is over all I want is the ability to prove it to you. Heck, just pretend that I have retrograde amnesia and I will be fully functional and get my memory back in a short period of time. Then you can find out everything about me, really, I'm one of the good guys."

"Look, we have both apologized for things we can't help. You apologized for your beauty and don't want to be treated only for your looks and I apologized for my secrets and all I want is your respect and," he sighed, "ah maybe a little bit of your heart. Hell of a way to start a relationship isn't it? Let's just enjoy each other and see where it goes from here. I've been right about a many things in my life and I know this is right. This will be the greatest six days two people could ever share. I want you to know no one will respect you more than I or treat you better than me. I think we sound a little too serious. How about a little more running commentary from my tour guide? You are an unbelievable wealth of knowledge. Really, you should have been a tour guide. You probably could have worked for the California Department of Parks."

Then he laughed, "The pay would not have been fitting for a big spender like you. I can't believe we went to a factory outlet. I have to admit, that was a first for me. You can get away with it. Hell, you can ware crap and look great. I better keep my mouth shut. I'll say it again; I really want to get you some stuff in La Jolla. Not so I can parade you around as a trophy, but more because of my need to do something for you."

-----o-----

"You were right," BiBa said. "The hotel is just up the street. When the guy at the desk said it was pink and we couldn't miss it, he wasn't kidding."

The Hotel La Valencia was on Prospect Avenue, the main street of La Jolla. It was early 19th Spanish-style architecture with the courtyard behind a 6 foot stucco wall which encircled the main building front. The entryway was dark and decorated with early Spanish colonial furniture. A long hallway off the fountain courtyard led to a beautiful open high ceiling room with a one hundred eighty degree view of La Jolla Beach. They proceeded to the registration desk where they were greeted with moist towelettes and mimosas. After registering Matt said they would wait in the lobby overlooking the scenic coastline while the bellboy took BiBa's bags of clothing purchased at the factory outlet to the room. They walked through a room paneled with Spanish-style windows overlooking Black's Beach, San Diego's most beautiful coastline.

BiBa noticed that Matt gave every employee he came in contact with at least a five dollar tip. She said, "We've only been ten minutes and anybody that even looks at you gets a tip. That's pretty extravagant isn't it? That's kind of obnoxious if you ask me," she mumbled.

Matt just laughed, with his acknowledgment of her constructive criticism.

She continued, "You didn't do that in Las Vegas, except once at the desk. Why here? He continued smiling and said, I didn't have to, I had you in Vegas. I think for five dollars it's not obnoxious as you call it. They will treat us well. I want this to be a special occasion and it can't be bad if everybody acts like we are royalty even if I have to pay for it. It's just tipping money to me but it means a lot to them. I'm the one who sounds like I'm in the hotel business. I thought this was just a general convention in your line of work, you know treat the help well. If we act like jerks it won't bring anything but contempt, but being the nice people we are," he smiled, "people around here will treat us like home. It works every time if you're nice about it. I told you I was one of the good guys."

While they were having a drink Matt could not but notice how the decor of the hotel was almost like his office in San Jose. The lobby's deep dark colonial style red chairs and antique end table situated between them and nestled near a window duplicated the layout of Matt's office in the presidential complex. The view of the water below was reminiscent of the presidential gardens' sightline outside his office windows with its unfettered beauty. Of course, he thought this feast for the eyes was the Pacific, not the view of the gardens he walked through every morning. The openness of both views, the Pacific and the botanical gardens, were calming and therapeutic. He knew he had picked the right hotel and the right woman. To be here with BiBa, he thought was what made life worthwhile.

In the midst of his daydreaming a bellboy came over to the couple and said, "Mr. Shaw, I have a package for you. The instructions were to deliver this to you as soon as you entered the hotel."

To BiBa's surprise receiving the package dimmed Matt's demeanor for a brief second as if he were thrown off balance. He looked into space and said, "BiBa I'm sorry, this is business as he held the package, and I will not let it interrupt our day. Let's finish our drinks and drop this stuff off in our room. Then we will walk around town for a few minutes so I can recover from the drive. My legs get all cramped up after a long car ride."

They walked over to the iron gated elevator and took it to the fifth floor where an attendant was waiting for them with a room key.

Entering the room, Matt opened the curtains and started to say, "Is this one room okay with you?"

Before he could utter another word BiBa closed curtain and pull back the blackout drapes and walked him over to the king size bed.

"Two rooms," she said. "Two beds, haw? I think I like this better."

As she kissed him and pulled him onto her, "We'll walk later if you still want to and are able to. The sex was the most anticipated of Matt Shaw's life and it bettered anything he had ever wished. It seems different for him. He didn't feel self-conscious about his body or his ability to perform. All he cared about was pleasing her and sharing his need for companionship. BiBa was surprised by his tenderness and non-aggressive nature. After deep hard romantic sex for almost 45 minutes they lay in each other's arms and took a brief nap. When they awoke they took separate showers, dressed, and walked out of the hotel hand in hand.

She said, "Well Mr. Tough guy. What was that seminal sense stuff all about, you know good guy bad guy? I think the tough guy was blown out of proportion and it was just all hype. I can't imagine you having a rough side. No one that makes love like you can be a bad guy."

She looked into his eyes and said, "Let's get you some clothes, a few shirts, a pair of Bermuda shorts, and some tennis shoes. It's on me. Hell, I'm on vacation and don't have any expenses. Don't say no. I want a good looking man on my arm. You know eye candy."

Matt knew the good looking part was not true. He also knew deep in his gut that he would not be her trophy if she knew what he had to do. He soon would be a tough guy doing unimaginable things that only the most evil men could do. He chose to close down his mind of tomorrow. He would leave Frederic's materials in the room safe and any thoughts of Johannesburg in abeyance.

He was in La Jolla with BiBa that was his reality.

Five days of unfettered sex, in the cliché, fed and fucked before breakfast, fed and fucked before sunset, and fed and fucked before sleep were part of their daily routine. They exhausted themselves in pleasures of the soul as well as carnally. Just before sleep on their last night Matt felt compelled to say something about who he was and what he had to do. He found himself saying, "BiBa, I can't leave without saying anything about me and you. It's killing me. It could endanger you if you find out what I have to do, I'm not trying to be melodramatic but it's that serious. I should rephrase that, I shouldn't say could endanger you but it would endanger you."

"Look," he started to stammer, "in the next couple days or weeks I have to do some really bad things. Its better you never know any particulars but I will let you know enough. You will feel more comfortable about all this when it's over. There are some really bad guys out there and they're threatening me and some people very close to me. I have no choice but to act. That's what's taking me away from you. When I get back, shit, I can't even tell you how long I will be gone. Please wait for me I will make it up to you. I know I'm talking in circles and obfuscating everything but I don't know what else to do. I've had the most wonderful five days of my life and I don't want the future to ruin it."

He became reflective and businesslike, "One more thing, please don't be mad, tomorrow I'll need some time to go over the materials I got the other day. I just need a couple of hours. I hope you understand. I might even have to make some phone calls. You really can't be any part of this, so I'm going to set up a time for you at the spa."

She looked at him with a strong sense of conviction and said, "I kind of understand. I really want you to know that for some damn reason I trust you. But, there is always *a but* isn't there? Don't lie to me or ever hurt me. I don't deserve it. So if you want to walk away now I'll understand. We have an agreement, when this is over; you come clean and tell me everything. I don't need to know every chapter and verse but I do need to know enough that I can trust you."

He kissed her gently on the lips and said, "I'm getting tired of promising you everything and not delivering. When this is over you will understand."

The next morning after breakfast and the most uninhibited sex either one had ever had BiBa went down to the spa.

Matt opened the safe seconds after she left and grabbed the materials sent by Frederic. Inside a large Manila envelope was a smaller packet containing two passports, two sets of credit cards, attendant materials and story lines with IDs for each passport. There were three words written on the face of the envelope: The Leopard Directive. The file was the last article to come out of the packet of materials. Matt felt it was strange that it was entitled but Frederic was always a little unconventional and never predictable.

He read the first passage: Gisele's forecast for success in Johannesburg is problematic at best, a ten percent chance of obtaining any meaningful information on the whereabouts of Al Bin and less than a two percent chance of obtaining any leads as to his benefactors.

The designated name Leopard Directive was her title and her way of showing the lethality of the operation. Leopards have the highest kill ratio versus attempts of any big cats in Africa. One attempt to two kills, whereas the lowest ratio was the cheetah at nearly twelve attempts to one kill.

Fredric and Gisele were telling Matt he had to be lethal and stealth like in his South Africa activities, the trademark of the Leopard. The cats mostly killed for survival and dragged carcasses of their vanquished prey up a tree for safety from scavengers and other predators. Leopards are one of the few cats to kill for sport. Their practices have an extraordinarily chilling effect on animals found in their killing sites. Just the intuitive thoughts or the DNA recognition of a predator like a leopard made all their victims self-destructive and counterintuitive in their self protective subconscious. All tactical advantages were in the predator's hands not the pray; this was the message Frederic wanted to impart to Matt.

Don't be reactive. Be proactive. Be brutally decisive in dealing with your adversaries was Matt's take of the directive. This time he would not be a bystander and just watch his cohorts extract vengeance and information. This time he knew his role would be different. It would be one of an executioner.

As he perused the pages in front of him he knew his vacation had come to an end. The good guy image that he truly wanted to live by had dissipated and the old Matt Papaz would shortly surface. He still had to take BiBa to LAX, Los Angeles International Airport. It would be her trip home and his trip to places and situations he had lived through before.

At the concierge desk Matt arranged tickets for BiBa to Las Vegas and a delivery service to pick up the Jag at the airport. The car would be delivered to her home in Las Vegas that afternoon while she was in transit.

After checking out and getting the keys from the valet in front of the hotel, BiBa would be back in the driver's seat on their way to Los Angeles. Matt suggested the trip was less than two hours and they would have time to stop off at Laguna Beach for lunch and a last stroll on the sand. They could bask in the beautiful weather and break up the monotony of being in the car again. It was evident Matt was not a commuter type person. The fifty minute drive from La Jolla to Laguna brought them to an eatery called The Restaurant across the Street from the Laguna Beach Hotel.

After a small meal they decided to walk along the beach to Las Brisas Point one of the most beautiful vistas on the California coastline. From there they walk back to the car and resumed their trip to LAX. It seemed as if this conversation for the day was perfunctory, no emotions, no shared feelings, they were both afraid to discuss what was on their minds. The chatter was pleasant but there was the ever imposing elephant in the corner, Matt's clandestine life. It had to be brought up.

Matt finally said, "The quiet is deafening, I feel like I owe you an apology again. Look, all I can say is I've never been so smitten with anyone in my life and you have to trust me. I'm not a psychotic sociopath or someone who would be a danger to you. There is a cliché, I don't know maybe an adage, and it goes like this, the truth always surfaces. It will hopefully surface sooner rather than later. When this is over you will really know who I am and I know you'll be comfortable with it. I want to keep in touch with you in a safe way, but it can be dangerous. When I'm gone I will try to keep in contact with you. I will have to use a different name and correspond with you by some outside channel. Heck, maybe I'll use Frederic as a go-between."

Matt knew all of Frederic's correspondent to the hotel had been on secure lines and were not traceable. "I promise I will let you know how I am. When I correspond please don't be put off by generalities and oversimplifications."

She leaned across the seat and said, "That's all I need. You'll hear no more from me except be careful and whatever you do, do it well and get back to me as soon as possible. I can go through this once but this can't be your usual way of life. If it is I can't be with you. I can't stand the thought of you leaving me again and again. It's not permanent, you leaving me all the time is out. Once I can deal with."

He reiterated that this was a situational ordeal. He didn't want to go into details, he couldn't, and he didn't want to say anything he would have to live by in the future.

She said, "One final thing, you don't have to be anything more than general in your communication. Just let me know you're going to be okay."

For one brief second he got serious and said, "You know I really am a tough guy. I can take care of myself. I promise you, you will never see that side of me. This is all another life and when I get back I'll be yours."

-----o-----

The air became fresher and the sky became clearer as if a million pounds had been taken off their backs. Matt thought to himself, the conversation had been brief but cleansing. All BiBa had wanted Matt to do was acknowledge her hardship. That was enough for her, simple acknowledgment. It took less than fifty minutes to arrive at LAX and parked the car. Her bags were left in the trunk. They boarded the shuttle going to their separate terminals to check in for their flights. Matt intentionally stayed on the shuttle after she got off at terminal one where she would take a Southwest Airlines flight back to Las Vegas. As he said to himself, from this point on, she can't know about my comings and goings. Her parting kiss felt like magic to him. No matter what it would take, no matter what the carnage, no matter the circumstances, he would live to revisit this moment.

He awoke from his whimsical trance of what must have been only a few brief moments as the shuttle driver said, "Terminal four, British Air."

He exited the bus and went straight to the first class/ business-class station. He handed the attendant his passport and his electronic ticketing receipt. Matt Shaw had no luggage. He was only carrying one of his IDs, some papers, and his credit cards. He had dispatched the other set of IDs at the hotel's business center where he carefully placed them in a shredder.

Clutched in his right hand was the manila folder with the Leopard Directive inside it. Frederic's written brief had been clear on what he had to do upon embarking to Johannesburg. He was assured safety and anonymity as Matt Shaw, novelist and professor of literature at the University of Southern California. He was now a writer with portfolio. His genre was international mystery novels and he currently was working on his new book the Leopard Directive. The briefing calculated Matt's chances of being stopped and formerly interrogated at less than one/one hundredth of one percent, but he still needed a cover for the directive existence if stopped, hence the directive had a red stamp on the front of the envelope that said draft. It was a first draft complete with errors, malapropisms, and misspellings of an international adventure mystery scripted in the aftermath of 9/11 dealing with drugs and terrorism. Who would ever think he thought.

He boarded the plane with group one. The seating assignment was affixed to his first class boarding pass. His eleven hour flight from Los Angeles to London, the first of two legs, would take him to Heathrow Airport. Once on the ground he would have two and one-half hours to disembark the plane and change terminals for his ten hour flight to Johannesburg. Matt was now in what he called a compartmentalized zone focusing solely on matters at hand. His life depended upon his ability to block out all adjunct matters and only gravitate his thoughts toward Mustafa Al Bin. His reflections of his past life, Costa Rica and even BiBa and Las Vegas had to be sequestered in the deep recesses of his consciousness. He had no margin for error. For him clarity of thought was obligatory. His life and others depended upon it.

-----o-----

Once on board the British Airlines flight to Johannesburg via London Matt immersed himself in the intelligence and position paper Gisele generated. He familiarized himself with the schematics of the prefecture and the surrounding police buildings. He reviewed the summaries of the antiterrorist unit's activities and its pursuant interrogation of the robbers. Viewing the list of the actual terror squad members who had participated in the torture and killings of the disposal company's workers involved in the Baragwantath Hospital theft gave him no new insights into the whereabouts of Al Bin.

He went over the invoices from the Disposal Company and Radiology Department waste materials bundled for transfer to toxic dump sites. He found himself where he had begun, no greater understanding of what had transpired in Johannesburg. He turned his attention to a list of the thieves and their families. Posthumously it was evident the disposal company employees had been bribed to steal the radioactive waste and sell it for a mere pittance. There was no one on the list of the now deceased robbers who had the ability to act on their own.

Matt's focus and ability to cut through large amounts of material and condense it into usable data was a testimony to his engineering background. His analytical mind filtered information into simplified general categories. He always looked for the lowest common denominator or the lowest hanging fruit as a baseline for his analysis. Over thinking a problem led to failed results, he thought to himself. The simple truth was he would not find anything new or any major leads from interrogating the police. Going to Johannesburg would only serve as a statement. He would, in effect, be sending a message by his actions on the ground in South Africa.

He wrote down the phrase, 'you don't fuck me for free.' Its expression would be the product of his mission to Johannesburg, retribution, pure and simple. Whoever was behind the foiled plot to have Al Bin seek out nuclear waste would pay a heavy price. His analysis was a simple input output matrix. The cost of going to Johannesburg was his time, lost opportunities, and the implied vulnerability of coming into the light. He thought long and clear about the benefits and came to the conclusion, when he finished the job he had to have some tangible expression that would make his adversaries take note. It was to be a statement. Not one on paper or electronically generated, but a statement.

The best result of his mission to Johannesburg would be a trail that led to Mustafa Al Bin. The worst result, and he thought that this would be the case, would be a declaration of don't tread on me.

His analytical sense was that his journey would bring to bear the latter and not the former. He knew he would be meeting with his friend Kasogi in less than a day and hoped their collaboration would bring some clarity to their efforts in Johannesburg. As he disembarked the plane at London's Heathrow Airport and transferred to another terminal for the remaining ten hour flight he felt fatigued. He started to look forward to the bed and soft linen sheets in first class. He took an Ambien, a sleeping pill that was his mainstay for deep uninterrupted rest. It would work its magic in less than an hour and he would be under blanket, as it was called, as the plane took off for South Africa.

Seven hours into the flight he awoke and was physically refreshed but he was emotionally entangled about the thoughts of his future. Ambien had a way of imposing sleep but with Matt Shaw it did not put him into REM, a deep therapeutic sombulecent state. He was still trying to clear his soul of past indiscretions when he woke up. Sleep would not afford him a clean slate to work. He felt conflicted. In his personal life he was a step closer to finding a companion or mate in BiBa. But he had no path to dealing with his omnipresent double life. How would he explain his past to her when his mission was over? Even if he could marshal the resources to extricate himself and his friends from the Mustafa Al Bin situation he still had to reconcile a future with BiBa based on a lie.

He had thoughts of feeling sorry for himself, but as he always said, things will work out and you have to play the cards you're dealt. It's how you deal with the results that determine your viability he thought to himself.

A strange sensation overcame him as he analyzed the situation. He was problem solving like an engineer about his future with BiBa but there was no emotional input. He questioned how he could go from a mathematical or engineering model-based image and impact questions of the heart.

His mental restlessness only exacerbated his doubts about the future. Would he have to cross the lines of civility and kill people to deal with the Al Bin crisis? Who was behind the plot? Who and why anyone was coming after him and his co-horts. These and many other thoughts were swirling in his head. BiBa, Al Bin, and the future were almost too much for Matt to assimilate. An overhanging variable in all this was how he would deal with the terrorist and how far would it stretch his humanity. Would he cross the line in seeking Al Bin and be so damaged it would affect his ability to find a new life.

After three years of limited peace would the new conditions and elements he had been thrown into create an environment changing him forever? Would the pursuit of Al Bin create a new face for Matt Shaw? He kept thinking 'good men sometimes become an instrument for horrible acts as a way of protecting their way of life.' Would that be his fate? Would he morph into a person capable of callused murderous acts and become psychologically unfit for someone like BiBa.

The last three hours on the plane reflecting on his future were long and lonely. He would look to his friend Kasogi for guidance and counsel not only in his quest for Al Bin but in his quest for a new life.

-----o-----

PART III

JOHANNESBURG, SOUTH AFRICA

The thoughts running through Matt's mind were mostly astonishment. Arriving Johan-nesburg's Tambo International Airport or JNB, he was amazed at the changes. It had been four years since his last visit but, everything was strikingly more modern and first world. After clearing customs, walking through the airport retail center, he reached the main lobby and saw one of Kasogi's men with a placard saying Matt Shaw.

His flight arrived twelve hours ahead of Alverez, Bill, and Malique who were staying separately in the city's Sandton District. Matt would not have contact with them until later that night. During his forty-five minute limousine ride to the Westcliffe Hotel he sat in the back seat preparing himself for reunion with his old friend.

After entering the hotel and making arrangements at the registration desk, he was taken directly to Kasogi's suite by his driver/bodyguard. Matt had eagerly awaited this reunion for more than three years. Their relationship was father-son or mentor-pupil but both men outwardly viewed it as equals among close friends. Matt looked to Kasogi for strength and wisdom as well as fraternity. He had what he called unrequited love and respect for his friend and mentor.

Kasogi looked at Matt quizzically and said, "At first sight you were correct when you told me I would not recognize you. Even your voice seems a little deeper and of course your weight must be much to endure."

He extended his hand and leaned over and kissed Matt on the left and then right cheek, as all Middle Easterners customarily do. Kasogi was a large Egyptian both in physical stature and length. He was 6'5" tall and weighed close to two hundred fifty pounds.

He continued speaking, "After describing yourself to me I thought I would need some time to get reacquainted with the looks of you, but I now see the deep honor in your eyes. It is as if time stood still. Eyes don't lie my friend. I would recognize you anywhere. How are you? I've missed you. You know you are like a son to me, I miss your strength and your courage."

They talked for more than an hour of what the Egyptian considered womanly chatter, but for some unknown reason it felt natural for Kasogi to express emotions and a longing for the past with a friend of such deep loyalty. It was strange to him. There were no other men in his life that gave him the feeling of being comfortable enough to discuss his frailties and sensitivities. Their three years of estrangement melted away. It was as if they had never been separated by great distance or time.

They ate at the hotel. During the course of their meal Kasogi received a phone call and announced to Matt they were going out for a reconnaissance of Johannesburg, in particular, the zoo. He said their source of information at the disposal company projected a second attempt to steal the hospital's nuclear waste as early as the following night. They had little time to waste, as he put it, so they were going forthwith. It was a short distance from the Westcliffe Hotel to the zoo located in Herman Eckstein Park.

Matt queried him, "Why the zoo and what is its importance?

Kasogi said, "If the terrorist squad interrogation is not fruitful, I may have to feed one of the men to the lions to make the others more talkative."

The lion, as Matt was to find out later, was the leopard, proverbially the most feared hunter of all South Africa's big cats. These predators had their own compound within the zoo area called the big five collection. The big five were the most coveted animals in all southern Africa. The lion, leopard, rhino, Cape buffalo, and elephant made up the quintet. It would be important for Kasogi to know the zoo logistics if and when he had to feed one of his captors to the great cats. After zoo surveillance they traveled in the moonless night for more than twenty minutes to Soweto's Baragwaneth Hospital where Kasogi might have to ask questions, as he so nonchalantly put it.

Alverez, Bill, and Malique with the help of Kasogi's Arab contingent and the ANC mercenaries would act as an army allowing Matt and Kasogi freehand as if they were a government force within the confines of Johannesburg. Money gave them the power to buy information. The small army they assembled would give them authority to implement any measures necessary to find out about Al Bin.

In the course of their drive-by surveillance Kasogi laid out a plan whereby Alverez, Bill, and Malique would meet his Arab assassins at a rented flat in the city's Sandton district.

He said, "Bill will stay at the hotel and monitor intelligence from there. After our men and the ANC have secured the precinct, you and I will follow. I feel more comfortable now that I have seen the city layout and the police station. We can go back to the hotel now, tomorrow will come soon enough. If you're not too tired let's have a drink to discuss our future plans and be like old women and talk about our pasts."

Matt responded, "Yes, when we get back I think I could use a drink."

Kasogi said, "I just have a couple more things to say before we go back. Let me lay out some of my thoughts for tomorrow night. You and I will go to the prefecture after our men and the ANC have it under their control. While they are taking command and readying things for us, we will still be here at the hotel playing cards. I've organized the game to be in my suite and last until two o'clock in the morning. We'll have an alibi until then. We will be playing cards with some of my South African business associates, non-Arab businessmen of stature, who can vouch for our whereabouts up until 2:00am."

"Kasogi, you've thought of every eventuality."

"When the game is over you will go back to your room. If everything works out properly, it will be about 2:05am. I have arranged for two of my men to be in our rooms and call for room service. In a separation of less than five minutes each man will call for food and drinks. Going to your room and going to mine. They will look enough like us that in the dark when they open the door of our respective suites the bellboys who deliver the food will think it's you and I. Our men will make sure they get generous tips fortifying their remembrances of us being in our rooms after the card game. That is our alibi or fallback position if necessary. I am sure it won't be the case but you never can be light of foot when in danger."

"It certainly gives us good back-up particulars."

"We will leave the hotel using the service entrance; a cab will be waiting for us. One of my men will drive and take us to the police station. The drive is less than ten minutes. Tomorrow night we will have two SUVs waiting a block from the station to take all the interrogators to the zoo. We will only take the five who questioned, tortured and killed the robbers. They will be blindfolded and severely beaten before they enter the vehicles. That should put the fear of death in them. Once we are inside the zoo, we will walk them to the leopard compound. There the options for the truth will be evident, even for the black African ones. Those cowardly bastards will understand one of them will be thrown into the cage, toyed with by the leopard like a house cat toying with a mouse until the final violent death moment. It won't take long for those remaining to understand my ways. It will be very effective."

Matt just listened. He would follow the lead of his trusted friend. He had an intuition some sense of fate would make his role in the antiterrorist squad interrogation more than Kasogi had planned. Being fluid and nimble in the danger-house was a trait seemingly embedded in Matt's DNA.

Matt questioned, "Why the zoo? Why is it so instrumental in the torture of the squad?"

Kasogi assured him, "Tomorrow night it will be abundantly clear how effective throwing a man into the cat's compound will be a way of loosening one's tongue."

The conversation in the cab was as brief as the ride back to the hotel. It was evident Kasogi's plans were being implemented with exactitude. Once back at the Westcliffe all discussion of the next day's activities were set aside as the two men made small talk over drinks.

In less than thirty minutes Matt excused himself by saying, "My friend, I will see you tomorrow morning. We can talk about specifics of our business in a less public place."

He was hiding the truth of their Johannesburg plans as if they were under surveillance.

He continued, "I need to go to bed I'm really tired. The jet lag is finally hitting me. I think maybe at 10:00 or 10:30 I'll meet you for breakfast. I know by then, you will have been up for hours, Johannesburg time is close to Cairo's. But I need as much sleep as possible; tomorrow will be a long day."

Both men got up. Matt gave Kasogi a tight hug and said, "It's good to see you my friend, even in the worst of circumstances. It's always good to see you. I look forward to tomorrow morning."

Matt's mind was racing because of the jet lag. Once again his life was in turmoil. He could only equate the Al Bin threats to the Porter situation three years earlier. His state of mind was different but the eminent threat was the same. Three years earlier he had concentrated solely on staying alive, only one consideration, self-preservation. However, in that instance, his failed marriage and distance from his children made the ordeal tactical not emotional. This time was different, it was emotional.

As he lay on his bed, talking to himself, "This is different, Shit, I can't believe it. I'm fighting for my fucking life and my focus keeps shifting to BiBa. The last thing I thought about in the Porter fucking mess was my future and my ability to have a normal life. Shit, the last three years have been just a fucking diversion. I've been with a lot of women and really can't remember one of them. I am rich and powerful and don't have a god damn thing. This BiBa stuff is out of control. I've only known her for little more than a week and I'm thinking about her when my life is in danger. Am I some kind of moron? I must be a weak dumb fuck. What is wrong with me? This can't be good for me!"

Matt's little voice in his head would not let up. "The killing thing is different this time. Al Bin might take me to places I don't want to go and I promised BiBa I would tell her everything when this was all over. I told her I would contact her in the distant future and it's only been two days and I need to hear her voice. I feel like a f'n pussy."

He tried to clear that little voice from his head but he had no place to either run or hide. He had to stop thinking. He had to slow down. He felt he was losing control. That voice kept talking to him, it was almost deafening. His mouth was dry and his stomach was churning.

He even uttered out loud, "I've got to stop thinking. I've got to stop thinking."

He did not know if it was the jet lag or if it was his fragile emotional state. All Matt Shaw knew was he could not turn off his mind. He walked over to the bathroom, opened up his shaving kit and pulled out two Ambien sleeping pills. He prayed in the proverbial sense for his head to clear so he could sleep and be able to attend to the work ahead. He wanted the Al Bin situation and BiBa to recede into the shadows so he could sleep. The pill's effectiveness would take hold in a half-hour.

-----o-----

He wanted a resolution to his emotional problems so he could recede or fade into the shadows and sleep but more importantly some day have a normal life; hopefully one with BiBa Lamanas. He had to rein himself in from contacting her. He felt like an impetuous little hormonal teenager not a man who must be up to the task of life and death. His return to some sense of sanity was imperative. Compartmentalizing data and dealing with it in a cold calculating manner was a must if he were to survive.

After taking the pills and still unable to rid himself of conflicting thoughts, he tossed and turned for thirty minutes, then he decided to get up. He walked over to the small bar in his room and poured a drink. He was hopeful the interaction of chemicals and alcohol he had ingested would put him into a somnolent state. He knew if he had a drink he would feel a little groggy in the morning but a glass of Neil Ellis' Groenkloof Sauvagnon would be a perfect complement to the chemical-alcohol cocktail he needed so desperately. It took another twenty-five to thirty minutes before Matt Shaw fell asleep.

After the self medicating concoction, Matt Shaw awoke at 9:00am with the groggiest cobweb state he could ever remember. He navigated himself into the shower and stood under the plate sized nozzle affixed to the glass ceiling of the glass enclosed bathroom area and turned on the three nozzle set centered in the granite wall structure making a water combination from a high and a perpendicular angle toward his body. Standing and sitting under the running water for almost half an hour, his mind slowly cleared bringing him into a comfortable awareness of the day's activities lying ahead. The little voice torturing him the night before had been extinguished by two sleeping pills and two large glasses of wine. He thought to himself, "The twenty minutes I've felt like shit this morning is a cheap price to pay for a clear head."

His yearning for BiBa and the appointment with his undefined nemesis had been tempered by sleep.

-----o-----

He finished dressing, went to the restaurant and met Kasogi where his friend laid-out their day. They greeted each other. Kasogi noticed Matt's transformation from a bud to a flower as the Arab adage went.

"You look rested. Your mind seems less cluttered than last night. Today will be leisurely my friend," he said. "I have arranged a trip to Soweto and Nelson Mandela's house. You will also visit the Naledi High School where the riots of 1976 took place. The blacks, mostly Xhosas, Nelson Mandela tribe, were marching from the school to the Orland soccer stadium as a protest to apartheid. The national party's paramilitary forces slaughtered scores of innocent peaceful marchers."

"Most South Africans feel this was 'the beginning of the end' for white rule in South Africa. Being in Soweto during the day you'll get a sense of the enormous problems here in Johannesburg. You will see as we say, poverty blending itself into sands where no man wants to place his foot. You'll see what money can do for a traitor like Al Bin. Throwing so much money around, to get the hospital's nuclear waste is not clear to me. He does not need to spend so much. It's excessive, but we will find out soon enough how to trap him or at least how to follow him because of the money trail. Human waste like him always makes mistakes. I'm getting away from your day, excuse me my friend. Let me get back to the rest of your trip. From Soweto you'll travel to a small animal reserve called The Farm and have lunch. If you like you can ride in a van through the reserve and see some of its wildlife. You will be getting back to the hotel late in the afternoon. You'll have time to rest before a leisurely dinner." Kosagi continued.

"Now, for the card game, it starts at 10pm. I've told all the players the game will be capped at four hours to accommodate my American friend who suffers from jet lag."

Matt chimed in, "How thoughtful."

"They won't mind because they will have at us when we're in Sun City later this week. Our game stakes tonight will be a buy-in of twenty thousand US dollars. No limit. Everyone will be more interested in your play than your money. Sun City is the big game for Africans of any race. The buy-in is two hundred fifty thousand

American dollars. Tonight they will slow play us and be very cautious, that's not their nature. When we play with them in a big game they will be aggressive and try to overpower us, actually you, with their money. They are better gamblers than card players. Though they're not Arabic they have the instincts of men with no fears except for some God and he is not allowed at the table. They will play safe tonight not to show their intentions. I think you would say 'no pressure' tonight."

"After the game, as I told you last night, we have work to do, we both know, man's work. It will be very precise. My men with the help of Alverez and the Africans from the ANC will have taken over the police station scripted to the minute.

As we say, as it is written it shall be done. The game will be a diversion and an alibi for us. When you and I get to the police station you will see. I have my ways. You'll have to have the stomach for it. Don't let my tactics with the terror squad effect your outward appearances. Play tonight in Soweto like a high-stakes card game. Let no man read your face.

Don't go off tilt no matter what happens. The fate of our adversaries was etched in stone when Al Bin crossed the line in the sand and came after us."

"Once we have secured the terror squad I will deal with them, they are mine. I will be aggressive and decisive. You will see my manner once we get to the zoo. What I do at the zoo will not be a bluff, it will be a statement of my intent to the interrogators of the hospital robbers."

Matt's Soweto tour later that day was low-pressured. He went back to the hotel, took a short nap, cleaned up, had dinner, and was at Kasogi's suite by 10pm. Time at the table rushed forward as if the kidnapping and interrogation of the police was a common event in the Matt Shaw life. He felt neither anxiety nor any need for rehearsing his role in the events that were taking place. His coolness and nonchalant preparation for the night's activities was in juxtaposition to his complete meltdown the evening before.

He was ready at 2:10am. He only needed ten minutes after word from Kasogi. The phone rang and as prearranged he met his friend at the hotel service entrance. They entered the cab for the short trip to the prefecture; however, the zoo was the new destination, unbeknown to Matt. Alvarez with the Arab contingent and the ANC mercenaries had taken command and control of the station at 1:30am.

The police were taken in the SUVs as the station was turned into a black hole. Its communications were down, the remaining men were bound and gagged and a trail leading to Al Bin for the forced entry was put into place.

Kasogi made the decision for Matt and himself to meet the contingency at the zoo. The cab drove up the M70, which linked Johannesburg to its outskirts and went directly to Herman Eckstein Park housing the animal sanctuary. The moonless night made taking the zoo by Alvarez's men an easy operation. They disarmed all electronics and security surveillance equipment, rendering the guards and security force at the zoo useless. Operation Leopard had begun.

Matt and Kasogi arrived at the zoo, where Alvarez, his men, and their captives were waiting. The police officers had been handcuffed with a light plastic restraint, gagged and blindfolded. They were all beaten severely at the police station but were ambulatory enough to walk over to the Big Five Exposition. Their destination was the leopard compound within the zoo's predator section. The five men had been pushed and shoved expediting their arrival to the leopard compound where their blind folds were removed. Construction equipment, tools, makeshift outhouses and scrap material piles lay next to the construction site. A large swath of the zoo was cordoned off so patrons could still view the animals in their artificial settings.

Kasogi and Matt approached the big five compound and noticed the zoo was in the throes of restoring the prized animal holding cages, where their mercenaries were holding the antiterrorist squad who had interfaced with the robbers. Along the way Matt had picked up a shovel as if it were a walking stick. Neither Alverez nor Kasogi were alerted to Matt's picking up the shovel. He used it as an appendage, as both men headed towards the leopards. No one took notice of this unusual act. It seemed natural and innocuous. He followed Alvarez and the captives using the shovel as a cane. It looked ordinary for him and not out of place.

Once they congregated at the compound, an area of more than one acre cordoned off from the walking path by a deep ravine, the five frenzied antiterrorist squad police officers were again at the total mercy of Alvarez and his men. The leopard compound was an island of trees and savanna like vegetation encircled by a trench acting as a barrier between the cats and the visitors who looked down from the path above.

The captives, five men, ranking from detective to lieutenants were tied at foot and wrist. There were outward signs of brutality inflicted at the station. Blood from a deep gash in one captives' head left him almost lifeless and had visibly shaken the other four. The apparent disposition and terror in the men was gratifying to Kasogi. It was a state of hell for the outnumbered and brutalized police. All fifteen members of the Arab contingency and the ANC were now wearing masks. Matt and Kasogi wore sun glasses to help hide their identities. The dark night skies coupled with the leopard complex black background foliage made it impossible for the bludgeoned and terrorized police to see who their malefactors were.

Kasogi said something in Arabic to two Egyptians of his task force. They randomly picked out one of the five horrified, bludgeoned men and held him by his feet. They pulled him to the parapet overlooking the compound and dangled him over the three foot metal rail that acted as a secondary barrier between the tourists and the cats. The two massive men hung him over the leopard's cage rail as if he were a rag doll.

The animals below started to parade with anticipation. The leopards slowly walked to the site under the man hanging in air and quizzically viewed the activity playing out above them. The largest leopard, one hundred eighty pound feline, roared a resonating sound as if it knew feeding time was near. The cadence of their pacing sped up. The decibel level of the quiet night reached a higher pitch as the leopards roared for their unexpected treat.

Kasogi instructed his men in English, so the captives would have a clear understanding of his intentions, "Drop the man," he said.

Before the Arab foot soldiers could react to his orders Matt broke in and coldly commanded, "Put him down. He's mine, put him down."

Before Kasogi could dispatch an order, Matt slowly looked at him and said, "He's mine. Tell your men to pull him up and stretch him out over the large rock." as he pointed to a granite boulder next to the pathway

The sheer power of his voice and strident instructions alerted Kasogi that Matt's inten-tions should be heard. He ordered his men to pull the man from the railing and follow the demands of his partner. His deference was instinctual; it would turn out to be the correct decision.

Before his intentions were fully understood Matt pulled the head of the shovel from the ground and wielded it as if it were an ax, striking the captors arm above the elbow. In trying to sever the man's right arm with the blunt instrument Matt had to strike his captive five successive blows to separate his arm from his body. He coldly picked up the blood-soaked appendage as his victim tried to scream. The Arabs held his mouth shut as well as possible muting his utterances of pain. In a matter of seconds he fainted from the heinous violation to his body.

Matt walked up to the four other captives while holding the blood palpitating arm of their comrade and said, "First the arm, then his leg, then the other arm, and than the other leg."

With that statement and a few expletives he threw the arm down to the circling leopards. He looked at the four men and said, "These animals need to get used to the taste of human flesh so we'll do it slowly."

The scene of the police officer's remaining arm palpitating deep crimson blood had traumatized the remaining captured police officers with thoughts of their impending deaths. One passed out, one shit himself, and the other two were frozen with fear.

Matt instructed the two Arabs holding the slumping victim to place the remaining stump of his arm in a deep pile of sand that lay next to the walking path encircling the leopard compound. His hope was to coagulate the blood and revive the officer for interrogation. The grotesque, savage act held all the men, captors and captives, silent with anticipation.

Matt looked deep into agonized eyes of his victim and said, "Don't fuck with me. I want the name."

He looked at the other four men as one of them shit himself and said, "First your friend limb by limb. The animals will have a great desire for human meat. Then it's your turn. My friend here, pointing to Kasogi, has only to give the word and we'll rip off his leg. His fate is in your hands. It's just a matter of time before we get one of you to cooperate. If we have to kill four of you to get one of you to give us information about Al Bin so be it. I'll get what I need. It's just a matter of time. Just as an extra measure we have knowledge of where you live, your family and friend's whereabouts. What's most important to you? All of you will die and everything of value in your miserable lives will be taken from the face of the earth. I will just say it once. You need to tell us about what happened at the hospital the other night. Our men found no interrogation records at the station. We need to know where your notes are, any videos, or recordings of what took place before you killed the hospital intruders."

Before the men could utter a word, he wielded the shovel savagely again, this time with greater force and accuracy, severing the man's right leg. He threw the second appendage into the leopard's compound. The noise of the animals fighting for the newfound food, the sweet taste of human meat, caused one of the four captives to vomit. As the regurgitation rolled down his chin he urinated on himself.

Matt looked at the other captives and said, "You will never leave here alive unless I get a name. He is useless," pointing to the man with a severed arm and leg in a bloody pool twice his body size.

As he pointed to one of the other captives, he looked at Kasogi and said, "Tell your men to bring him over here. That one. Yeah, that one."

He lifted the shovel with his right hand and used his left hand to pull the gag from the man's mouth.

"You have until the count of three or I takeoff your fucking head. Don't tell me something I don't want to hear, give me a name."

He started to count. He got to the number two before the man yelled, "It's Mustafa Mohamed, his name is Mustafa Mohamed. Don't kill me, please don't kill me."

As he pointed to the construction waste that had been raked into a pile near the leopard compound, Matt looked at the Arabs holding the mutilated man up and said, "Find something to burn in the shit heap. Burn what's left of his arm. It'll cauterize and stop bleeding. We don't want him to bleed to death. That's way too easy for this piece of shit."

The horror of the human violation was an indelible sight. It generated information as to the whereabouts of men who were acting on behalf of Al Bin or his agents. The sobbing frightened, past the point of submission, men divulged information about a Hawala in Johannesburg's Lake

Bruma region, who had transferred funds to Mustafa Mohamed, who transferred funds to the robbers who had tried to steal the hospital radiation department nuclear waste. It took less than fifteen minutes to sanitize the crime scene and leave a message for the Johannesburg police and the world's security apparatus. The captives were tied to the rail overlooking the leopards. The bloody body of their own comrade, his arm and leg severed and thrown to the leopards was a warning to anyone who stood in the way of Matt Shaw. The captives would have to wait till morning light before they were found by the zoo's security guards. Four men whole in physical stature but who would never be the same and one double amputee were left for the police to find. A clear message had been dispatched, don't fuck with us and don't side with Al Bin.

Second or third person information was better than no information he thought to himself. With the same exactitude beginning the mission, the team exited and left their zoo carnage.

The operation Leopard team vanished from the animal sanctuary and dispersed into the megalopolis. Matt didn't know why he did what he did. He thought to himself, his actions were better than murder. It was instinctual; it was a reflexive action he had no control over. He could live with this kind of violence. He could rationalize it. It was better to torture than kill he thought to himself.

As the SUVs went off into the black night Matt looked at Kasogi and said, "We have made a statement tonight my friend."

-----o-----

Matt and Kasogi got what they came for; a complete dominance of Johannesburg's police department. They set a seriousness tone as players in the game of international terrorism. The world's major security agencies would have instant acknowledgment of the police department's elite terrorist's squad abduction.

Alvarez's men had left behind limited electronic surveillance as clues to their identity and activities. These clues would be troubling to the world's security agencies. Alvarez was ahead of the curve on accessing information he allowed the world community. He controlled the agenda for the abductors search. The Johannesburg antiterrorist squad was thought to be a sophisticated task force but Operation Leopard opened the spy community eyes to a new threat. The prefecture kidnapping was a brazen violation to the security establishment and it would have far-reaching implications. The event in Johannesburg was reminiscent of the lawlessness in Mexico before the pseudo-legalization of narcotics. The world would want to know who was behind this hideous mutilation of the police department's Special Forces.

The operation rendered some important information. It revealed the name of a Hawala banker who financed the botched robbery at the hospital. The brutal nature of the antiterrorist squad interrogation was sufficient enough for lieutenant Mumba, one of the abductees, to give the name of Mustafa Muhammad. Mohammed was a smalltime banker who had an exchange in the Rose Garden District of Johannesburg where the tourist markets for handicrafts flourish.

He helped facilitate the transfer of monies for the attempted robbery at the hospital and the execution of the apprehended thieves. No higher departmental people at the prefecture were made aware of the robbery particulars. Knowledge of his involvement stopped at a low level of the police apparatus where the terrorist squad could extort money from him with the threat of torture and arrest. The bounty from information was one of the major perks of being in the Johannesburg police establishment. Its reputation for corruption was well-founded. Central command of the city's police department knew nothing of Mustafa Mohammed.

Kasogi passed the information on to Frederic from the car and within thirty minutes a profile of Mohammed was sent to the Westcliffe Hotel. Matt, Kasogi, Alvarez and his men back at the hotel looked over the communiqué developed by Gisele.

Mustafa Mohammed was not a player of significance. His only use would be identifying people higher up the unofficial ladder of Hawala banking world. Kasogi dispatched Alvarez and three other men to pick up Mohammed and interrogate him. It was clear they could use any methods of interrogation and that Mohammed was expendable. All they wanted was a name. Mohammed's activities were confined to the tourist craft market at Rose Garden. The money transfer from Cape Town to Johannesburg came from his cousin Tarek Azizi who was the largest Hawala banker in southern Africa.

Over three hundred, million dollars was funneled through his network on an annual basis. The unofficial banking world of Hawala was a paperless exchange of money most often between family members, business associates or a loose organization. A merchant or cousin would access funds from one city (lender) and deliver it to a third party in another city (borrower) at an interest rate of two to ten percent depending on creditworthiness or risk. There was no paper trail or formalized bank of mortar.

There was only an unofficial pledge securitized by one's word and ultimately his life or limb. The Hawala business relationships were based on generations of understanding business dealings held sacrosanct by all parties. All bankers were held neutral and safeguarded by both sides – borrower and lender. The bankers, in this case Azizi, were not subject to robbery or threat because even the criminal element needed their services. Azizi was responsible for all funds transferred from Pakistan to South Africa on behalf of Al Bin who was acting as a surrogate for unknown entities.

Alvarez's men would change the Hawala dynamic of doing business by going after Azizi directly. Traditional safe-guards in the money underworld exchange and laundering no longer afforded him protection from Operation Leopard. The brutality at the zoo and the impending interrogation of Azizi would cause panic and make those responsible for untying narcotics legalization think twice and change the course of their actions.

The ride back to the hotel was quiet and reflective. At the hotel Matt was almost psychotic about his role in all of this. His coolness and total disregard for human suffering paid dividends at the zoo by giving them Mohammed, but the gravity of his own depravity and the heinous acts he committed earlier that night were unfathomable. Usually life's changes came in incremental steps, why was this a quantum leap? His pursuit of All Bin had blacked out all human feelings and that was the choice he would gladly accept if possible.

He told himself, "I will deal with the emotional bull shit later. I must try to put BiBa and this dark side on the back burner."

To be able to emotionally function, in his new life after the Porter Incident three years earlier, he had to develop a plan and expedite it. Reaction to his surroundings was the only control he had of his life. He never knew where he was going, he only knew what he was running from. His only hope was when this was over he could forge a new beginning with BiBa whatever that meant.

-----o-----

Alverez, Bill, and Malique commandeered Mustafa Mohamed in his car as he drove home from the marketplace. Al Bin's banker was now in their custody. He would be shown no mercy, a tactic that would later be called the Matt corollary. Kasogi was comfortable with the inter-rogation methods for Operation Leopard amplified by Matt's actions at the zoo.

Muhammad would be given no choice but to divulge the name of his business associates and be disposed in the same fashion as the antiterrorist police officer at the zoo. He would be tortured until he divulged all pertinent information, killed a slow death, and his body cut into pieces then thrown to the leopards. These great animals had acquired a taste for human flesh. Mohammed would be the second of many installments for the pride.

Gisele contacted Frederic and asked him to alert all parties for an open ended audio conference. She had developed a new search engine for mining information about Al Bin and dirty bombs. To her amazement the algorithms came up with indisputable data which had to be shared posthaste. Gisele wanted her didactic findings and their implications discussed by all parties bringing in as many fresh eyes as possible. She did not want to present a directive but instead she wanted to throw out ideas for discussion because of her data's gravity. She wanted a flow of ideas. Her reasoning would be clear to all because of the consequences to the players involved.

Frederic set up a secure telephone confer-ence call for the next morning. He called Matt and asked him to interface with Guzman. All other players were in South Africa except himself (Florida), Guzman (whereabouts unknown), Pedro (Mexico), and Gisele (Paris). Gisele would preside over the call. At 8:30am South African time she conducted the conference call.

Matt, Kasogi, Alverez, and Bill were all sitting in the hotel's business office conference room. The other participants were at terminals with untraceable lines in disparate places around the globe. It was symbolic; they were spread to the wind as Kasogi described it.

"Our enemy is like the Locust," he said to Matt, "they ravage from high. We only see its carnage not its path. Al Bin is like an insect or even a desert snake; he is like a common asp. Our enemy flies, it crawls, it tries to destroy others to feed its own hunger. Men like Al Bin are vermin. Men who work with vermin are cowards. We will find who is behind this, they are cowards my friends."

-----o-----

Gisele opened the call and greeted everyone.

"The information I will share with you is confirmed but its interpretation is up for grabs. I will present this Intel the best I can in an objective narrative and try my best not to be biased or editorialize. I don't want my conclusions, of what I think is transpiring to affect your thinking."

She laid out the intercepts, the banking activities, and the e-mails and said, "I'm going to ask each one of you to call me one by one on a direct line. Where only I can hear, to tell me what you think. I will share these findings with everyone after all of you have said your piece to see where we are. That way, no one can influence your thinking. What is going on is so unbelievable I don't trust my intuitions and I think if we all put our conclusions into a pot synergistically our thinking will be clouded."

A picture was laid out of dealings in the magnitude of three to four hundred million dollars. Its source was publicly held tobacco companies. British American Tobacco, Phillip Morris, Reynolds Tobacco, and Experia were acting as a horizontally integrated monopoly and investing their money's in offshore Cayman Islands accounts with fictitious corporate registrations. They were expanding their purchases of large land tracts to be used for tobacco production as well as the future legal production of ganja, marijuana and cocaine. Their present activities a form of tacit collusion was illegal in the United States but has a gray area in the WTO. Their future foray into new research and development of psycho active drugs was also unearthed by Gisele.

Guzman was the first to react. He said, "I cannot divulge my whereabouts or financial holdings because it might put everyone in jeopardy but I've noticed in my new home country the demand for farmland with high nitrogen and phosphorus levels at higher elevations is being sold at abnormally high prices."

"Also," he noted, "the demand for particular petrochemicals, have been driven up for no apparent reason."

He continued, "Gentlemen I am no longer in the narcotics business but I keep a keen eye out for my brothers in Mexico. It is an old habit not easily broken. Maybe it's the tobacco company's money. There's so much of it, this has to be the reason. I can't believe they would make a play like this. They must have strong ties to someone in government. It's almost as if we're looking at the drug traffickers in Mexico for five years ago as a model for corruption. The tobacco company's actions show big balls, they're not doing this on their own."

Before anyone else could add to what Guzman said, Gisele interrupted, "There's another shoe. Let me drop another shoe." she said. "My analysis puts Al Bin in the public light thirty days ago. All the world's spy agencies have the same information and processing matrixes for calculating risk and imminent dangers and he did not come up. They should've picked him up just like we did and they didn't. So we have to ask ourselves why not? Why are we pursuing a phantom? They're showing no interest in him whatsoever. We're not dumb gentleman, so I asked myself again why our decision making process is different than Homeland security or the NSA and I came up with an interesting observation. I found, all bureaucrats or non-political appointees saw Al Bin as a major threat. They took him seriously and advocated his extermination. But, let me stress something very important, all political appointees of less than three years, the present administration, showed no outward interest in Al Bin. In fact they were strongly adverse to his interrogation or apprehension. So I delved deeper. I looked at the State, the Defense Department, and the National Security Agency and here's what I found. I found that any political elements with government grades of above G-17 sided with the faction wanting to apprehend Al Bin was purged almost as if this was the old Soviet Union under Stalin.

I looked at all the men left standing after the purge and looked at all the men they cast aside by the purge and an important distinction became abundantly clear. The clicks that remained at the State, Defense, and the NSA all had tacit political support from Senator James Richardson of Texas. He is a conservative fundraiser with power over the appointment process. His prowess is well documented. With a little deeper investigation I unraveled his ties to tobacco. With major corporations, in this case the tobacco companies, being allowed to give as much money in political campaign funding as they see fit, with political protection as if they were individuals, and with free speech immunity it was evident they bought Richardson."

"We have electronic intercepts of some of his conversations with the tobacco companies. If you look at the documents in front of you it is clear who is orchestrating these terrorist threats against the United States. It is treason, clear unadulterated treason by a small group of tobacco CEO's for corporate gain. You know and I know it's a direct frontal attack on you and your arrangements for legalizing the narcotics industry in exchange for global security from terrorism. They are trying to flush you out and have you held responsible for the terrorist attacks and at the same time prop up their profits by criminalizing narcotics sales again."

The room was still, Kasogi decided to venture an opinion first. "It is evident these industrial tyrants want to change the rules of the game," he said. "It is also clear to me no good can come from their actions as it relates to us. It is as if we are hung on a line to dry like fish in the marketplaces along the river Nile. All our agreements with the freedom fighters and religious holy men in the Middle East are about to unravel because of these scum. All our supplying arms and legal protection agreements allowing our brothers free sanctuary for drug selling concession for not spreading their terrorism to Europe and United States will be off the table if these men have their way with us."

Alvarez jumped in, "Bill and Malique and myself have noticed how much turmoil the old guard has been facing the last couple months. We haven't been able to figure out why. This clears up a lot. Tobacco is betting Al Bin can destabilize our alliances if he detonates a bomb and changes the world to bring us back to where we were. Our forces could have held off these young *wantabe's* anytime in the last three years but the politics for change and the support of guys like bin Laden and Mullah Omar have deteriorated greatly because of their repressive and corrupt ways. It's a new ballgame now and we better do something about it because, if tobacco and Al Bin are successful we're dead men. The way things are right now we don't have enough men and resources to stabilize what's going on in Afghanistan and Pakistan. To be honest with you we never envisioned our alliances falling apart, certainly nothing like this. It's like a house of cards. I know. I feel like we're on a banana peel. I don't know," as Alvarez looked at Bill and Malique, "how we're going to stop these guys. Like I said, I didn't see this coming. For tobacco this makes sense, even if the attack on New York City is not pulled off. Just the threat of it is enough to make everything unravel. It is just fucking unbeliev-able how far these guys will go to make money. This is beyond crazy. This is beyond any level of greed that's imaginable. I can't believe this stuff; I have to get my head around it. I can't be the only one here freaked out about their play and how crazy they are."

Everyone felt the same as Alverez but let him express himself so they would seem more level headed. The room again was quiet as were the other participants scattered around the globe. Fear permeated the call. Gisele's revelations and Kasogi's and Alverez's assessments had struck home.

Guzman made a declaration, "I want to have someone killed as a show of force."

"Al Bin," he said, "has to be captured and killed as soon as possible. Whatever the price is, even if it means losing some of our men, it's the cost of doing business. He has got to be killed publicly. We can buy some time and stop an attack on New York as soon as we get him."

"Frederic," Guzman said, "Get Pedro whatever he needs to kill this fuck. It's got to be public and we have to make a statement to tobacco because guys like Al Bin are cheap and they will just keep buying them until they are successful. Whoever is pulling the strings has big balls and they think their power will protect them. They don't know shit; they are underestimating the price they will pay. Pedro will do it. His men will kill this little worm. It will take a little time and money, but at some point this Al Bin guy will show up. He's our link to tobacco so we have to use his carcass to make a statement. This is like Mexico in the old days; lots of people will die. Compared to what profits tobacco thinks they can make by this insane shit, the cost of pulling it off is small. What are we talking about twenty to thirty million dollars for them to resume selling tobacco without any real government regulation? Since drugs have been legalized, tobacco must have lost billions. They are so arrogant they don't foresee a risk. We have to change that. We have to let them know their fucking lives are at stake. We have to change the rules. Once we get Al Bin we behead him and send his body to the zoo and place his head in a corporate office of one of those tobacco fucks. That should change the game."

"Gisele," Guzman continued, "Get me the names of the three top tobacco executives and information on them. I want where they live, their security forces, their family members, their bank accounts. Anything you can find out about them. I want all three of them to be kidnapped on the same day and have their executions televised to the world. No mercy. If they're not the ones responsible for all of this, I don't fucking care. So what! The true bosses of this madness will feel our pressure and know our threat is real. No one fucks with us, if we have to go after government officials no matter how high up the same thing. No one fucks with us. We will coordinate all our activities like al Qaeda. Whoever is instigating this is sitting behind a soft desk. He's either at some corporation conference room or in some government office. They won't have the balls to know how to respond to what we are going to do. They will learn what real power is. Some of you may think I'm too strong about what I want to happen, but just look at what we did in Mexico. We controlled it. We terrorized it. No one did a thing. We will cut off tobacco's head and they will have no will. So, we first get to Al Bin and kill his fucking ass. Then we go after tobacco. Then we get to whoever we have to in government. We have no alternatives but to strike back with such force they will not know how to deal with us."

He continued, "The Hawala guy in Johannesburg will lead us to someone. We must follow up on whoever he gives us and if we leave enough dead bodies it will take us to Al Bin and then whoever is behind this."

Guzman had a reputation for being brutal and decisive. It was clear to all, his reputation was well-founded. His declaration was heard loud and clear. Everyone on the call expressed affirmation for the strategy Guzman laid out.

Matt's reflections back to the Porter Incident gave him more emotional stability. The group's ability to adapt, improvise, and overcome were extraordinary. It would give them the advantage in dealing with tobacco. Hearing Guzman put Matt more at ease and comfortable with his friend's leadership skills. After working with Guzman in

Costa Rica for the past three years he marveled at his friend's transformation from ruthless drug lord to a world class politician. He now understood the adage of one not losing their roots or core values.

Guzman had lost none of his rage and he was dangerously brilliant. Under the leadership of the ex-drug lord the members of Operation Leopard would be tactically superior because of their lack of mercy for their adversaries. Their amoral human capital made them formidable. With Guzman's leadership, Operation Leopard would set the rules of engagement and tobacco would be on its heels. Their offensive had to start someplace and at some place was the apprehension of Al Bin.

Guzman as all leaders rose to the occasion because he simply was better at it than anyone else. He concluded his remarks by saying, "You guys have this Mustafa Mohamed, right."

That was affirmed.

"He gave you a name in Cape Town, right. I want to be there electronically when you interrogate him again, maybe we'll find something more than a name.

After we get what we want kill the fuck and give his remains to the leopards at the zoo."

-----o-----

Matt left Kasogi in the conference room saying, "I'm going for a short walk."

He was trying to separate himself from the horror of the situation, again in a life-threatening drama, this time trying to define an enemy, not planning an attack on the nefarious, John Porter. Pushed emotionally to his limit, he wanted to pity himself. The last three and one-half years were unquestionably more than anyone should have to endure.

He asked himself why this situation was so much more difficult than his last encounter with injustice. He previously had given up his wife, his children, his friends, even Frederic, and he had surgery to alter his appearance, moved to Costa Rica, bonded with people that previously he had defined as scum of the earth.

He had been able to cope with the last three and one-half years until this incident. Now he felt paralyzed, all because of BiBa

Lamanas. Even though he had only known her for a short time, their bond was totally consuming. He recalled every minute of every intimate situation, every conversation, her attire and mostly the incredible sex. She was the reason he was beside himself almost to the point of uselessness. He had to break his covenant and call her. He had to hear that voice if he was to function in the future. His barbaric actions at the zoo and his falling into depression when not physically surrounded by his cohorts were all expressions of his losing emotional stability. She was the only person who could bring them back to a place of safety. She would create clarity, would give him a reason for moving forward. After walking around the hotel grounds in a stupor he finally arrived at his suite. He opened the door slowly, moved into the living room and picked up his laptop. He e-mailed Frederic.

Within five minutes the phone rang, "Well old buddy I expected this much sooner and I can't say I would not have done the exact same thing. I might have tried to call her sooner. It's all arranged."

Frederic told Matt he could call BiBa in two and one half hours. It would be 8am in Las Vegas. The phone would be absolutely clear. A call would be placed to her working number and she would most likely receive the call because it was on her business phone. It would not be traceable or tap-able and her phone would be electronically disabled when the conversation was over.

He continued by saying, "You have all the time you want. When she gets the call it will be from a Las Vegas number the hotel vendor uses. She should pick up the call and from there you're on your own. Okay buddy, tell her your old friend Frederic says hello. I think she fancied me calling her in the morning when you were in Vegas. Tell her if things don't work out with you I'm always available. I will be right there for her," and he laughed. "Listen, Matt, I think she's worth it, but you know we're not out of the woods. Shit we ain't even begun to see the trees yet. Something else I can't promise when you can call her again so have at it buddy. Really, give her my best. You too, old friend."

-----o-----

Matt sat in the living room area of the suite with the lights on staring straight through the window that overlooked the hotel grounds until he finally picked up the receiver of the hotel phone. He was in a lighted area staring into pitch black and wondered if there was any symbolism to his actions. His mind was racing with the anticipation of hearing BiBa's voice. At 10pm Johannesburg time he called. He had been given a set of numbers by Frederic and with the completion of the last digit the phone rang.

BiBa was walking through the lobby of the Encore Hotel when her phone vibrated. She looked at the LCD screen; it showed the words Reynolds Limo Service. She pressed the green button on the top left side of the phone and answered by saying, "Rey, are you calling about coffee that you owe me or are you trying to pad the bill again with a smirk in her voice?"

Instead of the anticipated response Matt said, "Sorry I ain't buying you no coffee I couldn't help it. It's me."

The phone went silent for a second and she blurted out, "Oh my God, God Almighty. Matt, is that you? I have missed you so much. It seems like forever."

"BiBa, I miss you too. I said I couldn't call and in reality I probably shouldn't have but I couldn't help myself. I really miss you and don't know if it'll make everything better or worse. I just had to hear your voice. I must sound like an idiot."

"Don't be silly." She jumped in.

"At our age we have said or heard, I love you, I miss you, can't live without you or something like that. Well, this comes from me and it's all true. Shit, I missed you. Worst of all seems like an eternity since I've seen you and it has been less than a month. I can't tell you anything I've done or will be doing. All I can tell you is how important you are to me. I really don't know exactly when this will be over but when it is I'll explain everything to you."

He lied to her again he said to himself. He would have to explain himself in the future but he would worry about that later. He continued, "As soon as I get out of..." he hesitated for a second, 'this shit I owe you the truth I know that."

She could not get a word in edgewise but finally said, "You just said everything I need to hear. I can't believe how fast the relationship has grown and how strange it is to say I love you, but I really do. You said you thought you sound like an idiot, how's that. I love you. I really think you're my soul mate, isn't that ridiculous considering how little time we really spent together. I'll be here when you get back and for now please don't tell me anything about what your doing, I don't expect it and I have this gut feeling that anything you tell me can only make things worse for me."

He said, "I never thought I would ever say this again in my life, I love you too. Shit we sound like teenagers but what the hell."

The pall of his depression started to lift. The fog of her not knowing if he were alive or dead or if she would ever hear from him again cleared. The only thing that remained was a sexual tension of epic dimension hanging in the air.

The conversations developed into little passwords like, "BiBa I miss you, I love those beautiful blue eyes, and I miss your soft skin."

Her saying, "I feel so safe in your arms and even if you think you're out of shape or a little overweight," with an anxious laugh, "I don't and I miss lying next to you."

These were no more than deep expressions of carnal desire. They both felt it and they both longed for being in each other's arms.

"Matt," she said, "I have to go in a couple minutes. I'm in the hotel lobby and my guests have spotted me. I can hold them off but I really must get off the phone soon. I know it's inappropriate, but I miss you and I love you. It feels like, I haven't talked to you forever."

The conversation lasted for three or four more minutes. Matt said, "I love you. Be careful and I promise to be back as soon as I can."

Later that day after BiBa had rehashed and reconstructed the conversation over and over she asked herself, "Why did he say, be careful?" She shrugged it off, thinking she was over analyzing everything.

"Hell she said to herself," he just called me. "What more can I ask, he called me and told me he loved me."

-----o-----

Gisele appeared on the screen.

"Gentleman," she began, "Everything is fluid. I have all of you leaving Johannesburg later today."

"Matt, you will be flying out at 4:30pm this afternoon." "Agnon you and your men will be leaving at 6:30pm"

"Bill you will be on an 8:00pm plane but you won't be in Cape Town very long; so don't get settled. You are all obviously arriving in Cape Town at disparate intervals."

"Matt a limo will be waiting to take you to the Alluvia Winery in Stellenbosch. They have a guest house for you and your MO will be that of a wine merchant from the United States."

"Agnon we have you and your contingency staying at the Intercontinental Hotel in Cape Town itself. The hotel grounds are at the Victoria and Albert waterfront."

"Alverez, you and Malique will be working with our ANC cohorts in the Khayelitsha slums next to the airport but you will also stay in the waterfront area but not at the Intercontinental. The ghetto where the ANC is working is much like Soweto. They have contacts there and their headquarters won't be as bad as we make them out to be. The card game we had scheduled for Sun City has been changed to Cape Town. As luck would have it, Azizi is a card player and has agreed to participate in a high stakes game later in the week. Agnon we used your name to entice him. He feels honored to have been invited. This time of year, his usual recreation is being at his Portofino villa. He is the only Arab member of the Portofino Yacht Club, the most prestigious in Italy. He usually brings his African harem with him while his wife and four children stay in Cape Town. She is in France with her three youngest children, Mohammed the oldest son is staying home with protection from the family security force. Azizi will hold off leaving South

Africa for a week to play poker with a player of Agnon Kasogi's stature. We will use his staying in Cape Town to our advantage."

"I don't want to get ahead of myself, so here are some of the basics:

A card game in Stellenbosch, Agnon you and Matt are both scheduled at the table,

Kidnapping and killing Azizi's son Mohammed,

Blowing up Azizi's prized possession, his 241 foot yacht, 'The Banker,' moored at the Portofino Yacht Club in Northern Italy."

"All of that comprises the first phase of our operation. The second phase is investigating his gambling relationships in the United States. We have sketchy information. He is a big player in Las Vegas at Caesars Palace Hotel. We have reason to believe some of his gambling friends, as he calls them, are members of big tobacco. Our intelligence capabilities using the N.A.S.A. databases are limited, so as we speak, we're trying to break into Caesar's Palace information systems."

"By killing his son and taking away his prized possession, we hope he will become vulnerable and make a mistake. He's arrogant and what speaks to that point is more than his son's life he prizes his yacht."

"Now, more specifics, Matt, you are breaking away from Agnon. He must stay in Cape Town proper because in Stellenbosch where the game is to be held he would be viewed as a persona non grata. Stellenbosch is still steeped in deep Africana politics and anyone other than whites, European, or known Africana would be viewed as a threat. If he comes in to play cards, that's one thing, staying there is another. As I said earlier, you are staying just outside Stellenbosch at a wine estate. Its name is Alluvia. We have a five-bedroom guesthouse for you, it's excessive but it speaks of high roller."

"Agnon, you and your Egyptian contingency will be staying at the five-star Intercontinental Hotel in the waterfront district. Your reputation precedes you so you will not need a cover. We have four rooms for the other members of your party. If you think it would be better that each one has their own room, we can accommodate that. I did not know how you wanted your relationship with your men to be viewed."

Kasogi replied, "Let them share rooms." It spoke for itself. "Alverez, you and Malique will be staying at the Commodore Hotel at the other end of the waterfront."

"Bill you will be there too, but you will be separate from them. Your cover while you are in Cape Town is that of a tourist."

"Alverez, you and Malique will be looking for African art for some wealthy minority American clients. When each one of you gets to your respective rooms we have electronic packets of materials and collateral information to bolster your cover. Let me summarize our activities in Cape Town."

"Alverez, Malique, you are responsible for getting to Azizi's son and killing him and his bodyguards. I'm emailing you information, including architectural plans of Azizi's estate; it is just outside of Haut Bay. I am also sending you information about his security force, and detailed maps of Table Mountain to show you where to take Mohammed's body and dispose of it to maximize Azizi's torment. Our information should make it an easy task for you because his bodyguards have a reputation of being relaxed in preparation and cowardly when pushed."

"Bill, you will be free lance on the Cape but we have other plans for you, Guzman will fill you in later."

Guzman interrupted, "Senorita Gisele, I don't want this Azizi fuck touched. I want electronic surveillance on him at the game. When we kill his son and blow up the yacht I want to see his reaction. Then when he starts to understand the fate of his miserable life we will have him by the balls. I will take over from there. Yes, I want someone to interrupt this card game and give him a video of us killing his son and taking his security guards. At the same time I want him to see his fucking yacht being blown up. We did this sort of damage to our enemies in Mexico. We let them see that we are capable. I want him to know when we did it and how his fucking son and boat were taken from him. Up to this point he has no idea how much his involvement with tobacco would cost him. All he knew was he was making profit by washing their money. I want him to know how dangerous we are and there's nothing we won't do to him or the rest of his wealth or his family. I want him to shit on himself with fear."

"Alverez I want his son's death to be brutal. Kill him, cut his head off, leave his body some place with maximum exposure, Gisele you figure out where. It sounds like table Mountain, I don't know much about it but I will leave it up to you. I want his son's head thrown to the leopards at the zoo there in Cape Town. That is our calling card. Bill your job will be that fucking yacht. Make sure whoever blows up his boat is seen wearing a leopard shirt, our calling card. There should be no mistake as to who did this to him. I want him to get this information at the card game. I want to see it on video so I can read his eyes and know how much he knows. I want to see that fuck's face and know how alone he feels in all of this shit. If this devastates him as much as I think he will be all alone. He will give us anything we want."

"Gisele, you haven't said anything about Al Bin being in South Africa trying to get his hands on those medical materials. What's going on there? You said he'd paid hospital security people for a second attempt. Where are we?"

Guzman sounded different to everybody except Matt. He had learned his political skills well as the President of Costa Rica. He still had the attributes of being brutal of mind. His brief tenure as President made him polished and definitive. Matt new of his foul aggressive mouth but Guzman never resorted to it in any Cabinet meetings. Here he was his old self, the former Mexican drug czar, but more articulate when you filtered out the profanity.

She responded, "José, we appreciate your strong words and we are in total agreement but you are a little ahead of me. Here's where we stand. I said everything was fluid. It appears a second break-in at the hospital has been shuttled even though Al Bin has done nothing but throw money around. The Johannesburg terrorist squad killing has put a chill on everything. We can't put our fingers on exactly where, but we think Al Bin is still in Pakistan somewhere in the tribal territories. We know he is not in South Africa and we have no reason to believe he's coming here. Someone is calling him off. The actions at the zoo changed everything thanks to Matt's interrogation methods. We think our tobacco adversaries were taken back by the brutality of all this and they're a little bit on their heels. Our Intel tells us they are sending messages to Al Bin to stop the operation on the dirty bomb. At least for now, that is. We also have information there are no other operatives seeking materials to make mass destruction weapons. As I just said we feel they're on their heels."

Guzman re-entered the conversation, "Those fucks don't know what they've opened up. But they'll find out soon enough."

-----o-----

Guzman was in his element. The skill set he had acquired while becoming Mexico's most feared drug lord and led him from the Tijuana streets was consistent to what lay ahead. From a fake death four years ago, his new identification and metamorphosis into the President of Costa Rica added maturity and discipline to his decision making. As he had done on numerous occasions during his presidential tenure, he put his agenda on hold, took the usual working vacation and moved the seat of government from the capitol to the Pacific side's Papagayo Peninsula.

He would be in contact with Gisele at all times overseeing every operational detail of apprehending and interrogating Azizi's son and afterward the card game in Stellenbosch.

"Gisele," he said, "I need your eyes and ears. We have three distinct operations and only a week or so for preparations. There is no time to waste. I want Matt to the card game. He will make all the plans."

Gisele replied, "That will help."

Jose continued, "He will bring a woman to the game. I need you to set up the women with a camera, a small button-hole type camera. She will need a clear, total view of the table. All she has to do is make sure there are no obstructions between her and Azizi. I also want to make sure one of the women Azizi brings to the game will work for us. Whatever you have to do to turn her, do it. Just have one of the ANC solders impress Azizi's whore that if she's not cooperative her face will be cut up like a fucking pig and if she has any family they will die. All she must do is pass a video to him displaying how we can cause him more pain than he wants to endure. I want the video passed to him in full view of all the players at the table. Matt will have to object forcefully. Only giving in to the interruption by saying this must be a matter of life and death for someone to break into the game."

"Matt has to make it look real and make everybody believe how pissed off he is about the interruption. Tell him not to let the woman give Azizi the video until a hand is finished. The longer he has to wait, the more pressure on him and the better for us. Also, I want the video she's giving him to be in a packet or case with a leopard design."

Gisele replied, "I know just the package to provide."

"Good," Jose continued, "After we do what we have to do in Cape Town one of the ANC soldiers will bring a tape up to

Stellenbosch. He will bring it into the game and give it to the whore."

"Gisele, the next thing I want you to do is have Alvarez and his men split up. Have Bill, he's white, go to Italy. His color won't set off any alarms there. He can oversee the destruction of Azizi's yacht. I want it blown up in the afternoon so there'll be as many casualties as possible. Get me all the information you can about this Portofino place. I want to know so we can hire an Italian army, even if it's Mafioso. They will go in under his direction, in a small boat, and place the explosives a couple days before we blow up the God damn thing. I want all his men looking like a crew of the ship and I want them wearing something leopard, you know, like T-shirts or hats or something."

"You said Azizi's yacht is over two hundred feet long we'll need a lot of C-4 so you have to arrange for that also. Like I said, they have to lay everything out a day or two before the actual explosion. We want to make sure the explosion is timed exactly on the minute they kill his son. I want both of them done at the exact same time. You calculate the time differences between Italy and South Africa. Make sure all communications are silenced to Azizi so he will not know the fate of his son before or during the game until we give him the video. Do you have any thoughts on how to make his world silent until the game starts?"

"Yes, I do," she said, "leave that entirely up to me."

"Gisele, now we have the matter of Azizi's son. Let Alvarez and Malique take care of it, they're black as far as I'm concerned. I'm sure in South Africa they are not looked at as being white so they will stand out and seem menacingly, distasteful to the whites. That's okay, they just have to be careful. Let them run with the ANC team. Figure out where you want them to stay. It'll probably have to be with the blacks, they'll understand, it's professional, not personal."

Gisele said, "The five ANC soldiers are willing to manage the operation from the sprawling Khayelisha slum. The main township had a mandate for fifteen hundred people, migrant black mineworkers, in the 1950's. Today, it is a city unto itself. More than four hundred fifty thousand people living in some of the worst South African slum conditions. These shanties, mostly corrugated metal with tin roofs, some might even be cinderblock, have no electricity or running water. Education is lacking if not nonexistent, the ghetto has the highest level of violence in all South Africa, and worst of all are its health conditions."

"Nothing has changed in the sprawling slum even after Nelson Mandela's triumph over the Africana National Party in the early 1990's. Over eighty percent of all black South Africans live in poverty," she said. "Jose forgive me, I'm on a soapbox. I am so angry about the discrimination, just thinking about it set me off. You're saying Alvarez and Malique are black and are to be treated that way. I know you didn't mean anything by it but my blood boils just thinking about how badly some people in South Africa are treated. We don't have much discrimination in Europe, except against Arabs and they are not looked at as being black. Sometimes some are looked at as being terrorists. Well, maybe I'm exaggerating. Arabs and Romas women are discriminated upon, they really are second and third class but nothing like what goes on in South Africa. Sorry, let me get back to Azizi and his son. I know that was really out of character for me. I promise I won't do it again. Excuse me, where were we? Oh yes, the team will be led by Alvarez and Malique."

Guzman said, "I want a team led by them. I want you to send electronic surveillance equipment, maybe heat seeking sensors, or ultrasounds, night vision equipment whatever they need to penetrate Azizi's compound. I don't want any mistakes in identifying his son. If you have any pictures or any speech recognition information, make sure they are used so there are no mistakes as to who we capture and kill. If you need more men give the ANC whatever they want."

She said, "Our information suggests the son's apprehension should not be overly complicated. He is capricious and undisciplined, so is his security task force. Don't hold me to it. I'm just talking off the top of my head. I'll have precise figures for you shortly but to get into the compound, secure his guards and kidnap him should take less than three hours."

Guzman replied, "I want him removed from the compound and killed in public. I'll leave it up to you."

She said, "We can take them up to Table Mountain. It will be late in the afternoon and there are numerous hiking trails. I have first-hand knowledge. I was in Cape Town just three years ago. From the bottom of the mountain where the tourist tram starts to the top of the plateau, it's about twenty-five hundred to three thousand feet. They can kill him and throw the body off from up there. It will land at the base of the tram and have the greatest impact."

He interrupted, "I want his head cut off and they will take it to the fucking zoo and feed it to the leopards. I want all of it on video. Azizi can see his son executed, taken to the top of the mountain, beheaded, his body tumbling down, for what did you say three thousand feet, and his son's head thrown to the leopards at the zoo. However, Azizi must be kept in the dark thru all this until we give him the video at the card game."

She said, "He has an office in Cape Town not that far from the waterfront where Kasogi is staying, from there to Stellenbosch is less than an hour."

"When he's at the Villa where the game will be held all cell phones will be seized as per arrangements and rules of the game. A total communications blackout for all participants and their entourage's, of course will circumvent that, our people will have full electronic capabilities. I estimate that our window of silence will be about two to two and one-half hours before the game starts and however long you want to wait after the first hand is dealt. We might have as much as five hours to coordinate taking his son and the total destruction of his yacht once he actually leaves his office in Cape Town. I think what will be best is to stream all the video onto an iPad we give his companion and she'll walk up to him and tell him it's imperative. He must look at it right that second. We can convince her of what she must do and the consequences of not following our script to each letter and point. You said Matt will jump in and deliberately cause as much disruption as possible. I think that's a good strategy. It will hide any inkling of our involvement."

"José, I know all of this is the first blush for you. I, that is, we, don't have much time, but it sounds well thought out and I can manage to get it done with precision. I like your plans. Now my job is to coordinate this, of course I will line up all necessary assets, men and materials. I'll get back to you with more specifics and a timetable. Do you have any other requests for me?"

Guzman had just taken command control. He reiterated his instructions, "We only have a week. So, there is no time to waste. First Matt handles the card game. I need you to set the game and make sure we have complete control over it and its surroundings. We must turn one of the whores Azizi brings as an escort to our side. All she will have to do is bring him a package with a CD or DVD player concealed in it; you said they are about the size of an electronic notebook, right? She has to convince him that he view it right then and there. That fuck will see his son and yacht destroyed in front of his eyes. I want it done right in the middle of a hand;

it must be done in front of all the players at the table. As she approaches Matt will have to get up and object, and I mean strongly object, to her interference in the game. I want Azizi's emotions all over the place before he sees the video. I want him to be pissed at his whore for disturbing him, and I want him to be pissed and self righteous at Matt's objections. The bigger deal Matt can make out of the fucking whore the better. The CD she hands him has to be in a leopard package, a case with leopard design. You'll figure out what I mean. I want it to be our signature. You have to put a lot of pressure on this whore before hand to make sure she does everything by our script. Have some of Alvarez's AMC men impress upon her that if she does not cooperate they will carve her face and find all her living relatives and torture them before they are killed. She will cooperate. It's very important after he receives the camcorder that she walks away as fast as possible. I want a straight line to his face. Gisele, you need at least two people in there with camera feeds to you and me. One being held by whoever Matt brings, and the other one being used by one of Kasogi's men. I need straight sightlines to Azizi's face to read his intentions and fears. I will leave all the particulars up to you."

"The next thing is, we have to pull off the Italian operation. Bill will head it up. You said he was on his own, I sense you want him in Italy. He won't set off any alarms because of his skin. I know he has expertise in explosives. It shouldn't be too difficult to blow up the fucking yacht. I want it done creating the most attention and greatest amount of destruction. It's my understanding it's moored no more than fifty feet from some restaurants, so blow it up in the afternoon to cause the greatest amount of casualties and fear. Give me all the information you can about this Portofino Italy place. I want to have Italian soldiers, we have mafia friends that owe us some favors, and I want them to look like a crew from another yacht. I've been going over some maps and we will have them all stay in Santa Margarita and go into and out of Portofino by rented boat. I want the boat they're renting to have a false name. Put the name on the side as well as the boat back. Call it the Leopard or something. Have the crew ware some type of leopard T-shirts. Make sure they're seen walking around Portofino. There are a lot of surveillance cameras in place near the yacht club which is close to restaurants and stores. Make sure the surveillance pictures are of our men in uniform. Leopard T-shirts and white baseball caps would be perfect. You said his yacht is over two hundred feet long then we use C-4. That's what we used in Mexico. They're going to need a lot of it. Can you supply everything they need?"

She said, "Of course and more." She followed up, "if you are not set on C4 we can get grenade launchers or surface to surface missiles, we have access to anything you need. I mean anything."

He said,"I want C4. It has a signature all the intelligence agencies will try to track it. Try to get some that can be traced to the Middle East. Some that was manufactured in Russia. That should throw them off for a little while. If we do this right it will really fuck up their investigation. It's going to be important you coordinate the explosion on the boat and the killing of Azizi's son at the exact same time. We need both of them videotaped with the time streamed on the recording devices so there is no mistake in Azizi's mind of what he just saw. You also need to coordinate information blacked out so he will not have heard any of this before the game. Keep him in the fog. He must be kept in the dark until the game. Can you do that?"

Gisele replied, "Leave it to me. I will coordinate all the time sequences so he knows his son and his yacht were, I will use the word terminated, at the same moment. I have the technology and the reach to keep them in the dark until we are done. I assure you, it is not difficult."

Guzman re-entered the conversation, "Now we have the matter of Azizi's son. Like you said, let Alvarez and Malique handle this. They are black as far as the South Africans are concerned, so we'll have them work with the Africans. Let them run with the ANC. Alverez and Malique will get Azizi's son. I have a list of some technical equipment I think they will need. If I omit anything you fill it in. Get them some heat seeking sensors with ultrasound devices to identify whoever is in the compound. I know this can be tied up to voice and visual recognition software, so just do it. We don't take any chances of a mistake. If your preliminary reconnaissance is correct we will need four or five ANC soldiers and a couple of well-equipped SUVs. Find out what type firepower they want and leave it to them. Be in close contact with Alvarez he might have some specific demands. The information you sent me suggested Azizi's son is undisciplined and either drunk or on drugs most of the time."

"Right, his guards keep him supplied."

"That's to our advantage, so I think his kidnapping shouldn't be a very complex operation. From what you've sent me his compound's security force at any given time is no more than ten men. They don't sound very professional. See if you can get some more information on the type surveillance equipment and automatic weapons they have on the compound itself, what you've sent seems sketchy. The security system must be at least fifteen years old, so that doesn't sound like much of a problem. I figure once near the estate, the whole operation, actual reconnaissance, overwhelming the security and kidnapping Azizi's son shouldn't take more than three hours. Looking at the maps you've given me it doesn't look like more than a half hour drive to the Table Mountain Tram. You better check for traffic. This will be done in late afternoon so see if you can come up with a reasonable amount of time to get there. Only one road in and one road out of the tram area goes to the top of the mountain. It looks like we'll have to park and walk him up to the ticket area where the tram is. Make sure they park facing downhill towards the highway. From the parked SUVs it'd be a maximum ten minute walk to purchase tickets and wait in line to get on the tram. All the tourist information you sent me says the actual ride up the twenty-five hundred feet granite face of the mountain is twelve minutes. He's going to have to be drugged. You look into the best drug that leaves him out on his feet but still functioning enough not to cause attention. Maybe we'll have to put him in a wheelchair to get him to the top. The tram is big enough so cripples in wheelchairs can go up for the view. I looked at the material on the hiking trails. The Lion trail is perfect. It starts by the tram ticket office and circles to the mountain top. It takes the average hiker about four and one-half hours. What makes this trail perfect is at the top it's so steep they need ladders for the last two hundred feet. Just before they reach the plateau top is a deep cornice they have to climb. The overhang is so steep the ladders in some parts are almost horizontal. This is perfect because from the bottom of the mountain where the cars are parked and the people are waiting for the tram you can not see above the cornice. That's the exact spot where we chop off his head and throw the body. All anyone will see is a body tumbling down the twenty-five hundred feet sheer vertical drop from the highest point of Tabletop Mountain. I looked at the weather condition information you sent me, there's no chance of high winds or fog in the ten day forecast so it's a go. There is no chance of it being closed."

"Getting in the compound, taking and killing his son should be relatively easy but you have to keep Azizi in an electronic freeze. He has to be in the dark. No cell phone. He can't be close to radios or TV. That also goes for anybody on his security team. Gisele, he's got to be in the dark for almost five hours. That's up to you, whatever you have to do, get it done."

She said, "From his office in Cape Town to Stellenbosch is about an hour and a half with traffic, which in Cape Town will be the case. We can disable his cell phones if needed. The reason I'm saying it is he's constantly on the phone so we're thinking of either tying it up with some innocuous calls generated by us or coming in with some radio news leads about some electronic storms that will interfere with cell phone performance. We can do something that won't catch his attention. He'll be irritated as hell, but we'll do something. We will also set up once he gets to the game site he and all other players will have to give up use of their cell phones. Our information is he never calls about his son nor does his security keep him in the loop about his son's activities. He hates his son. He thinks he is gay and a real embarrassment to Azizi. We will monitor all this. It won't be out of place for him not to receive calls from Portofino, so we will tie them off at that end and he will be out of their communication loop, nothing special there. If they try getting hold of him after we destroy the yacht all the calls will be rerouted and directed to us. We can hold them off until after everything in Stellenbosch is completed. We might have as much as five hours to coordinate all of this. Let me just summarize all the parts; the kidnapping of his son, taking him to Table Mountain and decapitating him, throwing the body down the trail and finally transporting his head to the zoo to be fed to the leopards. While all this is being done in Cape Town the complete destruction of his yacht will be synchronized in Portofino. Everything will be recorded by two video cameras both here in South Africa and Italy and we will have a live stream, both you and I, in real time. Making and editing the video shouldn't take much more than a half hour maximum. We will stream it to the game's site where we will have two iPads available to download the videos. None of the electronic video data can be traced. We will have secured untraceable electronics the whole way. Once everything is downloaded we'll get the iPad to one of Azizi's companions. She'll deliver it to him right in the middle of the game and you'll have direct view of his response. Jose, this is all first blushes and I'll have to work out the details but this is pretty much it. Do you have any other request of me?"

Guzman thanked her and said, "It sounds reasonable but I'll have to go over it again as well. Get back to me as soon as possible, Gisele that means no later than tonight or tomorrow. We only have six full days to pull this off." He sounded like a commander-in-chief.

"Gisele," he said, "I need your eyes and ears. You have identified three different operations that need my direction."

-----o-----

Matt prepared himself for the forty-five minute ride from the hotel to the airport. At 3:20pm a limousine was waiting at the hotel registration office where his bags had been taken from his suite fifteen minutes earlier. The three-quarter hour ride and the VIP line through security had him on a small Boeing 737 at 4:30pm, the prescribed time for the flight from Johannesburg to Cape Town. Boarding was uneventful but he was astonished at the lack of security for domestic South African flights. He only had to show his ticket and was not asked for an accompanying ID nor was he asked to submit his lap top computer for x-ray. South Africa lacked all protocols for airport security existing in most of the developed countries. It further amused him the x-ray scanners were not sensitive to his 44mm Panerai watch, he always joked that it was the size of a dinner plate. The general security readiness at South Africa's largest airport was nonexistent.

"It certainly will make it easier to transport materials and sensitive electronic equipment to Cape Town," he said to himself.

The hour and fifty minutes flight went by quickly. The sunset landing in Cape Town was almost magical. As the plane approached the city it banked left and opened up to the flickering Metropolis lights and then to the dark blue Indian Ocean. The setting sun, with Table Mountain as a background was an unexpected view from his window seat. He disembarked and his bags were tended by a waiting porter. Matt Shaw, the gentleman vintner from California, was whisked away in a curbside limousine for the ride on the N2 Freeway to Stellenbosch. The elapsed time from airport to the Alluvia Winery was less than forty minutes. He was met at the registration desk by the proprietor and his wife. The traditional Africana greeting was a glass of Pinotage Rose and local Stellenbosch cheese. After fifteen minutes acquainting himself with the estate owners he and his bags were taken to his villa in a small golf cart. His accommodation, as owner Hans Vickenloof called it, was a five room two-thousand square foot villa edged by the Idas River that runs through Stellenbosch Valley. After showering and changing into more comfortable clothes he walked ten minutes back to the winery's main office and asked how he could get into town. He said he was hungry and asked where he could have a light dinner of Africana fare.

Mr. Vickenloof said, "It's my pleasure. I shall drive you into town and there are a number of restaurants or pubs I recommend where you can have good Africana food representing my Dutch heritage."

He told Matt, "You can catch a cab without any trouble. Here is my business card. They will bill me. If you'd be so kind, give them a handsome tip. Be sure to call the office tomorrow morning when you get up. We will have breakfast for you either here in the winery or if you wish it will be sent to your room. Anytime you would like is fine with us. My wife is very accommodating. She loves to cook for all our guests. By the way, one more thing, there are numerous antique and artifact shops in the village and the stores are open very late every night. The River's Edge on Van Reibeek Street is the best. Don't worry I'm not sending you there so I will get a commission. They have the best representation of Africana and Old Dutch antiques anywhere on the Cape. If you're considering purchasing anything hold off.

I will negotiate for you tomorrow or anytime during your stay. Of course I can negotiate a much cheaper price and we will send it parcel post back to the United States. Sometimes foreigners are taken advantage of, that's our Africana way."

Even at eight hundred dollars or six thousand, four hundred Rand per night Matt was not expecting such civility and personal attention from its Africana counterpart. He said to himself, "I guess it's because I'm white. Well, the money prospects and purchasing a lot of his wine might also have something to do with it."

The next morning Matt went over his files and operational assignments from Gisele and Frederic before calling the winery front desk. A vintner/retailer from the Napa Sonoma California wine region of California his cover was to purchase South African wines for investments as well as retail purposes. Gisele already had buyers for specific wines so the Stellenbosch operation would be a wash as a financial transaction. Gisele had set up a line of credit with the Standard Bank of Johannesburg and a mailing address for any South African purchases Matt would make. To keep consistent to his cover he had a Napa County California address. At breakfast Matt told Hans Vickenloof that he wanted to see his operations and sample some Pinotage Rose he had the previous night.

He said, "If it tastes as good as my recollection, I want to purchase a thousand cases at the online price of ten American dollars and I do not need to use arbitrage to get a lower price point. Hans, we don't need to negotiate a price. I will take a thousand at ten dollars per bottle, but, there's always *a but,* I want you to act as my buying agent for the rest of my stay here in Stellenbosch and when we go up to the Franschheok Valley wineries. I am confident you'll get me a good price. I want you to negotiate for a foreign anonymous buyer, that's me. I am just with you as a guest of the winery and in no way shape or form do you want me to be privy to any of your negotiations. I am not that buyer I am just a guest at your winery. No introductions, I don't want them to know who I am. I will give you a list of what I want and the prices I am willing to pay. If you can purchase them for a lower price which I know you can the difference is yours. I will pay you seven dollars US a bottle for Rheinagu Merlot. If you can negotiate a cheaper price then the difference is your profit margin. My calculations are you can probably get it for four dollars, fifty cents per bottle. You'll have to do the calculations from dollars to Rand but it will work out handsomely for you. I know there are some winery co-operatives who set export prices. I just have a suspicion you're part of the organization. You don't have to say yes or no. You don't have to explain but my offer will benefit you, I'm planning to buy anywhere from two to three thousand more cases. Having you act as my agent will be better for me because there's no way I can get the price I'm willing to pay on my own. Here is a list of a few other wineries I want you to do business on my behalf. He handed him a quasi-invoice and a list of wines from the Warwick and Blyerskloof wineries. If my calculations and your skills as a purchasing agent are correct, you can make another fifty to sixty thousand dollars American and I will have a South African partner. I know foreigners are not treated as well as Afrikaners are in this part of the country. I can't negotiate these prices on my own so we are both winners. Call Standard Bank Johannesburg; even better, have your banker here in Stellenbosch call Standard and see if I'm bona fide. I want you to set everything up net/net. All charges and fees will be port to port, South Africa to the US. They will be inclusive of all taxes, duties, customs, freight forwarding, or any other expenses. Do we have a deal?"

Hans Vickenloof looked at Matt Shaw and said, "You must be part Africana and held out his hand."

Vickenloof agreed to the win-win deal Matt proposed.

"I'll have my representatives at Standard Bank look over all the contracts and shipping agreements." Matt stated.

"From what they've said, they will be able to cut you a check by tomorrow. Tell them where you want the funds transferred. One more thing, I don't know much about South African tax laws so I'll give you the option of sending your money in any currency anyplace in the world. Tell Standard what's best for you and they will expedite it as quickly as possible."

-----o-----

He shook Vickenloof's hand. "Now, how would you like to be my guide and take me to some of the best wineries here in the valley? I'd like to be just a tourist; I would like to go to Franschheok. I've heard so much about it. Everything I've read seems like it's a replica of the Moselle Valley in Germany. I would really appreciate your company."

Vickenloff said, "Sure it would be my pleasure but do you always do business like this?"

Matt replied, "Yeah pretty much. If I do my due diligence it's like the old adage 'practice is harder than the actual game'. When the final decisions are made its easy. I've done all the work the business is the simplest part. You and I know it is just numbers and we're both good at that. This is going to sound foolish and maybe old-fashioned but to me it is a business relationship. And I have an intuitive feeling about you and your wife. I'm impressed with the two of you. I like to keep it on a personal level. Like I said; it's a win-win situation."

Considering Stellenbosch during the day he felt a sense of California in South Africa. He could not wrap it around his head but much of Stellenbosch Valley reminded him of Napa Sonoma and the Mendocino county region in northern California. His cover as gentleman winemaker on a South African buying excursion for his vineyard's large retail shop was a natural role for Matt.

He never envisioned the civility and beauty present in this region of South Africa with its notorious reputation as being the center of the Afrikaner movement. The Stellenbosch people's outward appearance was impressive and startling he told himself.

"Hans," he said while they were driving to Franschheok, "I don't want to get political but we've been to Stellenbosch and driven almost thirty miles east. We're now in the center of wine country here in Franschheok and I haven't seen many African blacks. It's beyond my comprehension but I don't think I've seen fifty black people all day. Maybe one out of ten people are real Africans everybody else is white. What's up?"

Vickenloof said, "This is the old South Africa. Not much has changed here in the Cape since the National Party took over in the early 1950s. That's why this valley is so beautiful and so safe. The blacks know their place. They work for us and go back to their homelands every night. It's too expensive for them to live here and then he smiled, that's part of it and maybe it's because they're still not safe. This is our country, they know their place. They all live near Cape Town in Khayelitsha; you drove by it when you came from the airport. That's where they belong."

Matt did not push it; he acquiesced to Vickenloof's political beliefs no matter how repugnant they were to him personally. He felt he didn't need any problems. He didn't want to offend his newfound friend he might need him someday, he thought to himself.

Driving through the little Dutch town of Franschheok Matt was amazed at how provincial it was. It was no more than twenty square blocks, its population was approximately three thousand people, but its tranquility and peacefulness were eerie. It was too perfect, almost a place out of a novel. The curio and antique shops, restaurants, parks and church in the town center reminded him of Disneyland. It could not have been more visually beautiful. Vickenloof said, "My friend, this is the real Africa. The Dutch brought way of life to our wonderful land four hundred years ago. Lives were given for it. I'm glad you appreciate how beautiful it is and how lucky we are to be Afrikaners. Let me take you to the crown jewel of all wineries here in the valley. It's hard for me to say this, because I'm envious. You'll see. We modeled our winery after this one."

From city center to Franschheok Winery Estate was a fifteen minute drive. The winery had its own restaurant with a Michelin five stars rating. The chef was from the famous culinary Cordon Bleu in Paris. There were ten villas nicer than this in Stellenbosch, but Vickenloof was right, the estate was a testament to excellence. Matt was taken back by its seclusion and beauty.

His first thought, "We must have the card game relocated to the estate."

It could easily be secured by their ANC partners under the direction of Alverez. He could be in the valley two hours after his work at Table Mountain. The winery would be a perfect environment for the high rollers attending the game. The measures needed to protect the players and implement the Azizi operation would be easily manageable in this isolated environment. The participants at the game would be impressed by the winery's opulence and intimacy, befitting their wealth and power. They would all be allowed to bring their own security guards and have the protection and cooperation of Alvarez's men. With Matt's request of anonymity through his facilitator Hans Vickenloof, the winery would acquiesce to his request of providing his own security, ergo Alvarez. It would be easy for Matt as the anonymous facilitator of the game to change location for security purposes. Convincing the other players that safety comes first would be a non sequitur. Matt would contact Gisele and Frederic, have them work out details of switching the game location. He knew money had its way, for a price the restaurant could be converted into a gaming parlor and the estate's villas would house each participant and their security forces. A large enough remuneration to the winery owners would be persuasive in having him cancel all previous guests' reservations and open the estate to their card game.

Gisele would fabricate an excuse, something in the nature of winery electrical problems and pay the injured reservation holders compensation lessening their aggravations and inconveniences. The scripted telephone call or e-mail with apology and substantial monetary compensation would be forthcoming in twenty-four hours.

Matt was convinced no other location in the South Africa's Cape Town region would be as strategically safe as the Franschheok Estate. Soon as he got back to his room he placed a call on a secure phone to Gisele and asked her to work her magic.

Gisele and Guzman's directive placed Bill and his men in Santa Margarita, Italy in two days. The Operation Leopard's force stayed at the Grand Hotel six miles from Portofino. His cover was businessman vacationing after a trip to Tuscany where he purchased olive oil for a super market chain.

Bill's expertise in explosives would be tested. The sinking of Azizi's yacht must be a spectacular pyrotechnics display. The visual destruction of the two hundred forty-one foot technological marvel needed to mirror motion picture special effects images. Guzman wanted the video to be taken from Azizi's villa located directly across the Portofino yacht club dramatizing the breadth and scope of Azizi's adversaries abilities and be an extreme personal violation stripping the Arab banker's will. The villa had its own dock opposite the yacht club but Azizi, per Arab ostentation, preferred his prize be moored in front of the prestigious club in one of five major slips. The yacht's gangplank laid fifteen yards in front of the village's three major restaurants. The yacht club's marina configuration was its five major slips of two hundred or more feet and its three hundred buoys encircled by a walking path with upscale boutiques and restaurants frequented by the European upper crust. The marina was one of northern Italy's smallest but was ultimately the most prestigious, rivaled only by Porto Banus, Marbella, Spain. The mooring was a monthly expense of fifteen thousand US dollars. The yacht, 'The Banker', had a crew of twenty-one, its electronics cost more than seven million dollars, and most of all its parking in Portofino was a display of pure arrogance. The extravagant monthly yacht mountainous cost plus the one hundred twenty million dollars for its purchase were definitely a statement made by Azizi.

Guzman's own statement, the destruction of Azizi's prized possession, would be a greater insult than the killing of his son.

Bill and his men would take control of the villa, video the explosion and subsequent carnage of the crew and tourists frequenting the restaurants.

Guzman said, "I want it to be seen by the world. Send video copies to all the major news agencies. I want Al Bin to see it." he said to Gisele. "The greater statement comes by the more people who die. We have a rule in Mexico; make sure we have two cameras so there's no possibility of mistake."

He did not use the word redundancy but his paramilitary history demanded all contingencies were covered. Bill and his men would board the yacht two nights before the operation setting the explosives and pyrotechnics. Their small forty-two foot catamaran leased from Moorings, the largest yacht rental agency in the world, would be moored at one of the yacht club's outer buoys. The name "Leopard/Cape Town" would be affixed to the boat stern. His men would be seen at the Trattoria da Pino restaurant fifteen yards from 'The Banker' gangplank. They would be wearing leopard shirts and white baseball caps. The three mafia men would act loud and disrespectful so people would notice their drunken state. By calling attention to themselves they would later be considered prime suspects in the sinking of Azizi's yacht.

-----o-----

Alvarez and Malique were presented a precise operational plan. They would receive electronic surveillance equipment at the ANC's headquarters. The sprawling Kayelistaha Township had no formal paved roads and therefore the consequence was a system of cart commerce. The Cape Town ghetto dirty arteries were filled with potholes, strewn with litter and animal dung. Most roads were impassable by automobile. Humans were pulling carts with commercial articles promoting business in stand after stand at every pedestrian cross road. The population density in small makeshift houses made a community whose people's belongings were outside when weather permitted. A cart with electronic equipment could easily be camouflaged as boxes of over ripened fruit being sold as a last resort by white farmers to blacks.

Two carts hauling a load of indistinguishable cardboard boxes with local farmer's trademarks were innocuous in the township. The electronics equipment would be delivered to the ANC stronghold late in the afternoon with no assumption of irregularity. With equipment in hands, Intel included real time satellite pictures of Azizi's compounds, maps of Table Mountain and its hiking trails and a precise script for the video interrogation of Azizi's son.

Alvarez and Malique did a dry run. They drove to the seaside community Hout south of Cape Town where the compound stood on a strategic cliff overlooking the Indian Ocean. In a rented Toyota SUV retrofitted with surveillance equipment, Alvarez read over the directive he would follow during interrogation of the twenty-six-year-old Mohammed. They drove past the estate gate to see if the equipment was functional. Next they drove to a bus stop near Table Mountain, left their vehicle and took the bus, as many tourists do. They stood in ticket lines and purchased tram tickets. Next they went to the mountain top and did more than an hour's reconnaissance. After retrieving their SUV, they drove to the zoo.

All recon was recorded. It would be reviewed numerous times before entering the Azizi compound.

In two days Alverez, Malique and three ANC members wearing all black; ski masks, shirts, pants, and shoes as camouflage would take command and control the estate. It would be an easy task for Operation Leopard's mercenaries because of the unprofessional and cowardly nature of Azizi's men.

Alverez, wearing blackface makeup to hide his olive skin and Latino features with two Arab, twenty-five-year-old ANC operatives, would stay in the vehicle and be used as needed to get Azizi's son on the tram to the top of Table Mountain. The total number of men for the operation was seven. Once the compound was secured, a camera on tripod would stream the brutal interrogation of young Aziz. His knowledge of the money transaction and how Al Bin procured dirty bomb materials in South Africa would be made apparent.

Malique using a hand-held camcorder as a redundant piece of equipment per demand from Guzman would also capture the action. After the interrogation, including bludgeoning all body parts except the face, Azizi's son would be given powerful tranquilizers, Thorazine and Risperdal, to make him more manageable during the journey to Table Mountain and his ultimate death. The estate's ten men security team would be gagged, bound and given the date rape drug Rohypnol, gamma hydroxy butyrate, which would render them without memory of the events after their cowardly surrender.

Azizi's son would be in a manageable state of consciousness and ambulatory enough to be taken to the top of the great plateau overlooking Cape Town. Zombie like, with the two ANC Arab medical attendants and five African looking assistants, he would be placed in a wheelchair and treated as if he were a special-needs person on an institutional outing with entourage. The two Arab members acting as medical personnel would be wearing black slacks and white long-sleeved shirts encrested on their shoulder a Cape Town General Hospital's Neuropsychological Center logo. The seven people contingency and hostage would wait in line, get onto the tram and ascend twelve minutes before they reached the three thousand foot Table Mountain top. Exiting the large sixty-five people occupancy tram they would venture onto a walking trail having a three hundred-sixty degree view of the peninsula. This would be familiar ground to Alverez and Malique because of their prior visit. From the tram's exit the party would move past the structure housing restrooms and venture another one-hundred yards towards the walking trails emanating from three thousand, three hundred fifteen feet below near the visitor's entrance level.

A ten minute walk would take them to the famous Lion trail that serpentines the face of the granite mountain. The degree of difficulty in trekking this trail was rated five because the last two-hundred-fifty feet were vertical necessitating climbing ladders over the dangerous cornice or overhang.

With cameras in hands per Guzman's orders Malique would hold Azizi's son's face down to the ground and Alverez would sever his head with a nine inch hunting knife. The brutally murderous scene captured on video would be transmitted to Gisele. His head would be held up to the camera dripping blood. Then his body would be thrown down from above the mountain top cornice coming to rest near the tram stop. The gruesome details of the headless body tumbling to ground's end would be taped from an adjacent trail below the cornice by one of the ANC team. From below at the entrance level to the tram where people were purchasing tickets for a ride to the mountains top it was impossible to see above the cornice, so Alverez and Malique's act of violence and their identification would be shielded from the hundreds of people who saw the headless body tumble three thousand feet.

After doing their debauchery at the isolated Lions Trail end, the seven assassins would have enough time to change their clothes in the restroom area, separate into smaller groupings and take different trams down to the mountain's lower station. In the case of Alverez, he would take off his blackface, change into jeans and a T-shirt and proceed to the bottom on his own. Arrangements for two cars at the foot of the tram had been made, which would give the seven men team three vehicles dispersing to different parts of the city. As laid out by Gisele, it was tram operation protocol not to stop because of an accident. The tram area and the viewing areas atop the mountain were equipped with cameras but the city did not have financial resources for real time video viewing personnel.

Any analysis of what transpired on the Lions Trail hiking route would be conducted many hours after members of Operation Leopard left the city. By then all vehicles would be wiped clean and set afire. Before the teams left the city by train, car and bus, Alverez would be on his own heading directly to Franschheok.

-----o-----

Gisele communicated with Kasogi late the next morning.

"Agnon," she said, "I hope your accommodations are acceptable. I know the waterfront Intercontinental has been a hotel choice of yours so I respected that. I am booking rooms for your men and a suite for you. I'm letting you know,

Guzman and I have communicated with everyone."

She then spelled out the next couple of days. "There has also been a location change for the game. Matt's reconnaissance shows the Franschheok Winery would be tactically better than having the game in Stellenbosch. Because of its secluded location and its upscale lodgings he determined it was a better fit for our needs."

"I'm sending you more information. I think you will agree, we developed a scenario for the game and how we're going to approach Azizi. Besides being a participant, Matt calls you the game's heavy hitter, you're only responsibility will be to play and bring your usual man attendant. He will be a very important piece in finding what Azizi knows."

"He will wear a button camera with a wide-angle 12mm lens so Guzman can get a read on how Azizi reacts when he finds his yacht was destroyed and his son was killed. I'm asking you to talk to your man and make sure when one of Azizi's escorts presents the video, there are no obstructions between him and Azizi. Jose wants not only to see his face but wants to look at his body language. Matt will be bringing a woman as escort. She'll also have a button camera. That way Jose will have many views of our Arab banker friend."

"Everything is in place. We will have ample security thanks to our ANC cohorts. To make up for the fact that all the players will bring their own bodyguards or security forces our African ANC brothers will act as members of the winery's staff. Everything will be swept by our men, and all electronic devices brought to the winery except for ours will be rendered useless. We have ways of circumventing the effectiveness of their equipment and they will not be mindful of the uselessness. I don't have the expertise to understand exactly how all this works but our people tell me we will effectively have total electronic control. We'll have enough men posing as staff members and will have men placed in strategic areas in the winery itself. We will have total control over any eventuality."

"Alverez will be there after his Table Mountain work so everything is under our control. Malique will stay behind in Cape Town and clean things if need be. Alverez will personally see that you and Matt are completely safe. We will also keep your personal security detail in the loop as much as possible. Azizi will have no knowledge of your involvement or Matt's."

"I'll send you more detailed information in the next couple days. Do you have any questions for me or any special needs? Agnon, anything you need is just for the asking."

He said, "No, I have some business to take care of while I'm here. My men will get me anything I need and I will keep busy until I hear from you."

-----o-----

Seven days in Cape Town brought the results Guzman and Gisele anticipated.

Matt said, "It's amazing what a little money and mayhem can do."

The death of Azizi's son and destruction of 'The Banker' were enough for Azizi to understand his plight but not the causality of his pain. The video delivered by Fatma Mubarack, one of many whores accompanying him at the winery, took his soul developing an understanding of his own mortality.

The electronic feed gave Guzman an unobstructed observational platform of Azizi's physical and emotional response to the world crashing down upon him. His expected behavior was predictable. Guzman's interpretation was that Azizi did not have specific knowledge of how the transferred money would be used in South Africa. He had no outward knowledge of personal wrong doings. His financial conduit role for American gambling acquaintances or any business transgressions over the last decade were not unwarranted in the shadow economy where he functioned. As a Hawala banker he placed monies at the disposal of nameless, faceless, innocuous people and its consequences was not his concern. His world of generating a spread between moneyed persons and their designated recipients was not personal, it was always business. He had no clue as to why his wife was in jeopardy.

The video delivered in spite of Matt's aggressive response to the women's intrusion and Azizi's reaction was viewed by Guzman. Matt's reaction as if he had been violated by Azizi's whore played well with the other players. His collaboration in the plot was completely obfuscated by his theatrics. Pain was written all over Azizi's face.

Guzman had seen many men broken; this was not a man who possessed a secret. In his role as brutal interrogator he knew the truth lay in a man's eyes. It was despair, the deep dark complete despair held the truth. Azizi's look was of a man who had been striped naked by the evil one man can do to another. His face was contorted and showed unmistakable horror that could not be duplicated by even the most artful actor. The events leading up to Azizi's pain were more than he could endure. He froze at the sight of his yacht and son. He was paralyzed by the brutality on the electronic device he was given. He dropped the iPad player and stared into space as if his neurological synapses had ceased functioning. His massive jaw jettisoned forcing his head to bow. The air dispelled from his lungs and he shrank as if a pin had pricked a balloon. Sitting slumped at the table with his head down and his eyes deeply recessed into their sockets he was transfixed on the horrors presented him. His world crashed down with such weight it ripped out the very fabric of his being.

Kasogi jumped up and hastily walked to the other side of the table and tried to console Azizi as if they were more than just participants in a game of chance. He placed his arms around Azizi's rounded shoulders and waved for his men to assist him. The game's fallen participant would be taken back to his villa by a contingent of Azizi's and Kasogi's security forces. Kasogi staying at the table called for a recess to all gaming activities and gave players the choice of continuing the hand or terminating the card game and tabulating its outcome at that very moment.

The depth of Azizi's response to the video led to a total secession of card playing but opened up an endless conjecture as to what happened. The men now standing were verbalizing and gesticulating what they thought had just transpired. After almost ten minutes their collective adrenaline rush dissipated and a critical mass of comatose took hold. They began to understand the gravity of Azizi's depression but not its cause and a sense of fear permeated the room. The fellow players at the table had virtually become paralyzed by a fallen comrade's pain. They could not understand what befell him or what he viewed on the video but they wanted to leave in mass.

Before any of them could exit the restaurant, the ANC soldiers overwhelmed all bodyguards and bound and gagged everyone in the room including Matt and Kasogi. They were all taken back to their rooms where they were stripped and beaten and relieved of all of their valuables. The episode played out as a mass robbery.

Matt and Kasogi were taken to their rooms in the mass roundup and collaborated the story that they were all robbed and beaten. While in their suite they were in contact with Guzman and theatrical makeup was applied to make their plight similar to the other participants.

As make up was being applied to Matt's face and body Guzman told him, "It is now time to press Azizi. The ANC placed a video feed in his room. They will set up teleconferencing with that fuck," as he called him.

"He should be tied to a chair and a laptop placed on a table." Guzman said, "I will see his face but the screen on his side will be black. He will only be able to hear my voice. It will be computer enhanced, that will intensify his fear. I'll get as much as I can from him. He will have no will. We'll use him to set up a game in Las Vegas. We'll contact his banker and tobacco friends as if nothing had happened. They don't know what goes on in South Africa. Gisele's intelligence says none of the players here tonight except for Azizi have ever had contact with the Americans."

"You will take him with you when you leave. You'll hold him for a few weeks. By then all our American friends will be in Las Vegas waiting for their host. They will be invited to Caesar's; it's the usual place for their game. The host, this time will be Azizi, picking up the tab for everyone. So they will be there. Once they are all at the hotel and assembled they will be anxious to play. We will figure out a way to hold off the start of the card playing for an hour or more after they have assembled at the table. They are serious players and this will cause some of them great stress. Maybe we'll figure other ways, worse ways, to annoy them. I haven't read them that well yet, but I will figure out what offends them the most while they are waiting for their dead friend. We'll have someone come in the room or maybe a television monitor, or something. But it will be dramatic. We'll show these tobacco fucks Azizi being tortured and giving up their names for funneling money to Al Bin. We will place them in a position they've never been in before. Trust me, we'll get something."

After questioning Azizi in his villa, Alvarez directed the ANC to vacate the winery. Gisele placed a call to the Franschheok Police Department. With electronic triangulation she had the call emanating from the Anglican Church in the center of town. The 911 call in Africana dialect tipped the police off to suspicious blacks descending upon the winery hotel.

The small rural police station's men with backup from Stellenbosch would assemble two kilometers from the winery. In less than twenty-five minutes fifteen police officers were ready to enter what appeared to be an abandoned property. They found a situation where all the apparent perpetrators of what appeared to be a well orchestrated robbery had gone and left badly beaten and injured hostages. All the game's participants, minus Azizi, were in their villas handcuffed to the four poster beds furnishing their bedroom suites. They were gagged, their hands tied behind their backs with handcuffs affixed to the bedpost so they were facing the bathroom doors. The rooms were trashed and all their personal belongings were strewn onto the floor. The room's furniture, mirrors, and light fixtures were destroyed.

One commonality was apparent as the police opened each room. A leopard glove was left on each king size bed. In the seven villas each scene was similar; severely beaten men tied to their beds in a sea of chaos. One room, that of Azizi was trashed, the bed had a leopard glove deposited on its quilted bedspread, but an Arab imposture was tied to the bedpost.

The ANC mercenary who was paid handsomely would be led out of the villa by the police and seen by the other hostages. His face was bloodied so severely his resemblance to Azizi was a non-factor. He gestured to the men he had been playing cards with who were all assembled in the winery courtyard.

As he passed the group he grabbed Kasogi's hand and said, "I'm okay, my friend. Thank you for taking care of me. What happened?"

A police detective pulled on his arm and said, "You will have time later sir. You need to be taken to hospital."

The ambulance responsible for Azizi was controlled by Alvarez's men and took their victim to Stellenbosch University Hospital for a quick checkup and release. Azizi was gone. By the time the police arrived he had been taken to the ANC headquarters in Kayelistaha Township near the airport.

The Franschheok magistrates interrogated each participant of the card game and their bodyguards. Three players and nine guards were taken to hospital. The others including Matt and Kasogi were allowed to leave the premises on their own because the severity of their injuries didn't appear to warrant medical attention. Police questioning of the victims found all their stories were similar. An electronic dispatch to Cape Town authorities for the apprehension of the winery black staff was sent out. All the ghettos and shanties surrounding Cape Town were subject to a brutal lockdown by regional police working in concert with police Chief Wilbert Smith of Franschheok.

-----o-----

Azizi was held hostage until Las Vegas arrangements were made for the high stakes Texas hold-em game. In the next two weeks a computer program translating spoken words to individual speech patterns, in this case Azizi's, would contact the table players apologizing for his cowardly reaction after seeing the video telling them of the family's kidnapping and being held for ransom. Alvarez developed an elaborate scheme. To clear Azizi of any culpability in the robbery, a high stakes game was setup in a safer environment.

The new game would consist of the same players together with Azizi's tobacco acquaintances. He told the other Franschheok players the robbery was a plot to stop the game, giving their captors an advantage while stealing everyone's valuables. He profusely apologized and said he would try to make it right because he somehow felt responsible.

Proclamation to each player was that he, Azizi, was picked and he did not know why but he felt the need to apologize for it. His conversation with each of the players left the impression Azizi was alive and well. The incident was portrayed as just the rich man's price of not properly attending to their own security. He would see them later, and it would be his pleasure to host the game in a more secure public place. He would only live two weeks longer. His eventual death and decapitation would take place in the cellar of the ANC headquarters.

The basement was staged to look like a Middle Eastern jail. In the center of the ten by ten feet room was a metal chair where he was tethered until his death. The plastic restraints on his ankles and his wrists were tightened to such an extent his appendages would become gangrenous. His allotment of food and water were only generous enough to keep him conscious and aware of his pain. Upon the wall opposite a large leopard logo was a mirror so he could see his image and the degradation of each additional minute of his life. The black ski masked men routinely force-feeding their captor sitting in his own excrement in solitary confinement was on a continuous video feed that would later be edited and sent to Las Vegas.

The ANC followed Guzman's directions. Even Africa's most hardened revolutionaries who had faced the full brunt of apartheid were repulsed by the vicious treatment their captor who was an unwitting participant to tobacco's assault on the legalized drugs' world order and quasi-governmental relationships safeguarding the Western world from terrorism.

"People must pay a price greater than they can sustain," Guzman said.

The reach of Operation Leopard and its brutality would be unpredictable because its men under the direction of Guzman would not adhere to civilized world conventions.

Their direct attack on adversaries and mercenaries was an extraordinary response to the unmitigated depravity of a terrorist dirty bomb in New York City. An attack taking thousands of lives and making ten square miles of New York City uninhabitable for hundreds of years merely for profit was beyond even the scope of a hardened murderer like José Guzman. He had a history of successful tactics and strategies in Mexico. He was sure the tobacco decision-makers would not be prepared for his heavy handedness. He felt if he struck with excessive force and discriminately went after tobacco's executives he would hold off Al Bin as a threat on American soil.

After the game in Las Vegas and the proof of Operation Leopard's resolve, tobacco would either surrender or move to plan 'B'. There was always a plan 'B' for cowards.

Matt made a decision not to return to Stellenbosch and asked Hans Vickenloof if he could assist him. His call for help didn't take the Africana by surprise. News traveled fast on the Cape. He told Matt he had heard about the incident and needed no further explanation.

He said, "I can imagine how bad it was. The blacks are animals. You are lucky they didn't kill you, usually they do kill whites after they rob them. The police will make the winery staff accountable. All Blacks know each other. We have our Africana ways of finding the truth. This cannot be tolerated in a white man's country. A lot of blacks will suffer but the police will get to the bottom of this."

Matt thought to himself, how the authorities would respond to all of the black staff at the winery being held hostage in one of the wine cellars that proved their innocence. He did not respond to Vickenloof's comments.

Vickenloff was on a soap box, "The blacks think the courts in Pretoria will protect them, but they won't. We will get revenge for this. They came from Kayelistaha and they will see white justice for what they have done."

He told Matt, "Have inspector Botha, he's a big fat policeman there at the winery, bring you here. I'll take you to Cape Town if that's what you want. That's the least I can do for a fellow white and business partner of mine."

Matt was appalled at what he had heard but he had to back off from his personal convictions to keep his cover. He felt like he was in 1950's Alabama. He wondered to himself if there would be a mass lynching. The whole incident, the robbery and police interrogation, took six hours. He was taken by his African business partner to the Intercontinental Hotel at the waterfront in Cape Town after the police finished with him. He arrived an hour and one-half after Kasogi.

Being at the same hotel after the apparent robbery would not set off any alarms. After he said thanks and usual salutations to Vickenloof he went to his suite and e-mailed Gisele to set up a communication with Guzman. He didn't know what to say but the extreme prejudice used against their adversaries seemed to be building with each incident and even though he was a complicitor, he felt it was excessive. He wondered if José was pulling all the strings because he liked power and brutality or if the vicious response to tobacco was a direct offshoot of his own zoo actions.

He had clearly lost respect for himself in Johannesburg and he was losing respect for the man he had called brother for the last three years. He had to clear the air. He had not known what to expect when Jose told him and the others he would take control over all the operations.

-----o-----

He now knew the depravity and brutality of Operation Leopard's collective actions were over-the-top and he must do something about it.

"José we have to talk," Matt said. Before he could say another word

Guzman interrupted, "Listen very carefully my friend. I know you are not sure of my ways and you don't want any more of this. The killing is too much for you. You want to stop or at least not be part of it. But this will not be. We have no other choice. These fucks brought it on themselves. They are willing to kill thousands of people for money and for some reason you think we should show them mercy. They would kill you and me in an instant. Just think about it. They issued an order to kill thousands of people in New York City, and you think I'm out of control? I am not questioning your loyalty, I am not even questioning your courage, but I am telling you we have no alternative. I told all of you once before, this is what I do. I do it well my friend."

"Never question my motives or my ways," he continued. "They are cowards who have never seen death. The truth is they are animals and you must know I am not the animal. I'm reacting to them the only way I can. Soon they will react to us. You forget. You're blind to what will happen to all of us if they're successful. They're trying to unleash the American government and all its power against us. They're willing to kill thousands of people for profit. In Mexico we had to war on each other because that's how we protected our families. We did not kill innocent people for money. The killing and the torture came with the products we had to sell. We had no land, we could not get work, the only thing giving us our meager livings were drugs, and they wanted to use it against us. You don't respect how we lived in Mexico. You don't respect the rules. It was the only way we could live because the whites and Europeans took everything from us but drugs. They raped our families, they took our land, and they took everything from us. The killings and the torture come with our way of life. We are not animals. They forced us to live this way. It is no different with tobacco. They are the fucks and deserve to die. What you see is death people bring to each other and you hate it. Trust me, we have no other choice. The corruption and violence in Mexico ceased when we took over. The corruption and violence all over the world ceased again when we took over. You saw what we had to do before. We have no alternatives but to do the same today. Our enemies are bigger and stronger so we have to be harsher. More violence, more blood, more whatever we have to do. There are no rules except to adapt and kill them before they kill us. These tobacco fucks are willing to kill for money. There is nothing worse. What we did in Mexico we did for our survival. We had no alternatives. We had to do what ever it took to protect our families from the filth and death we were left to live in. These men behind their tobacco desks only have greed as a motivation. They are corrupt in ways we can only counter with unimaginable violence towards their leaders, their men and their families. I will not give you a choice my friends, you are part of this. Their killings are the price for our safety. Don't say anything else to me."

Matt held his breath for a few seconds. "Jose, I know you are right. It's hard for me I did not grow up like you. I have been by your side for three years and I would give my life for you but this is hard for me. I feel like I'm caught up in a different world and don't like what I have become. I look in the mirror and hate myself."

Guzman responded. "It is better than being dead. You have said what you wanted to say to me. Leave it at that and don't bring it up again. You are in this and there is no other way. If you weren't my brother I'd have you killed. Trust me, I love you like a brother, but there is no other way."

This was a side of José Guzman he knew existed. He knew his Mexican friend was right but the words chilled him to the morrow of his bones.

The phone went quiet and Matt immediately got back on his computer and e-mailed Frederic. "Contact me. I am at the hotel. I have to talk to you. It's important."

His cell rang in less than three minutes. "I know you just talked to José, what's up?"

Matt said, "Yeah you're right, I just talked to him. I told him that there was just too much violence and maybe it was his way but it wasn't necessary. I got aggressive and basically said we are killing people to feed his ego or image or something. I told him we have been like brothers for the last three years. During that time he had never, not once, displayed any of these brutal tendencies. I knew his history but I truly thought he had changed. I thought he had grown but shit, he was so cold and matter-of-fact that he frightened the hell out of me."

Frederic replied, "He just reacts to threats by using extraordinary violence. He does whatever he must. That's how he survives, you know that. That's why he was so feared. He's calculating and never careless. He would never put you or any of us in danger unnecessarily. He is not doing anything to you, they are. You are pissed at the wrong people. You're overreacting. We have to be aggressive to deal with these tobacco corporations. We don't have a choice. Guzman knows we have to use terrorist or guerrilla tactics because of tobacco's financial and political advantages. We don't have a choice. I am sorry I'm being so blunt. Don't think I haven't thought about it. Don't think this has not affected me also. It's tobacco making us killers not Jose, not you, not me. After the incident at the zoo in Johannesburg I told myself I had to man up. I'll tell you the same thing. Just man up! You have come too far to be a pussy. I've not been in the field like you. I can't imagine what it was like cutting a guy's arm off, but I have given you guys everything you've needed so I am part of this too. It's just as if I swung that shovel or killed Azizi's son. It all had to be done and what makes it worse is there is a hell of a lot more. Guzman is right. He is cunning. He is adaptive, you and me and Alverez, have to be the same way. Just remember we didn't start this shit or set the rules. Tobacco did. We have no options. Talking anymore isn't going to make either one of us feel better or change our attitudes. Just remember we did what we had to do, so don't get soft now. There will be a hell of a lot more. It's what it is my friend. I'll talk to you later." The phone went dead.

PART IV

LAS VEGAS, NEVADA

Five hours later Frederic placed a conference call to Matt and Kasogi. "Gentlemen now that we've concluded our work in South Africa I'll be setting up operations in Las Vegas. The Cape Town authorities are searching for the bandits who pulled off the winery robbery. At this point, the regional police have labeled five African members of a Kayelistaha street gang as prime suspects. The Franschheok and Stellenbosch Police Department's are convinced it's only a robbery with drug connections to Azizi's son but they are baffled by the leopard gloves. They think it's a copycat crime. For the moment they are convinced it has nothing to do with any criminal activities in Johannesburg. We'll leave it at that, no interference on our part. This makes it cleaner when we set up a game in Las Vegas. We placed a little money in Cape Town and have some controls over the press. They are reporting substantially the same story. It's coming off as a brutal robbery of whites by blacks with a drug history."

Continuing Frederic said, "Let me change the subject and talk about Las

Vegas. Matt, we have you staying in South Africa a little while longer. You'll be there almost a week and a half more. We're having you go to Durban and shop for African artifacts and antiques. From there you are going back to Johannesburg staying at the Westcliffe again and purchasing more artifacts. I will send you an itinerary including a list of galleries and art to be purchased."

"I have a feeling you are in need of a vacation, so from there you will be going to a game reserve called Mala Mala. A private jet will take you there, it's only about an hour and a half and they have their own runway on the eighty thousand acre parcel. It's the nicest wild animal reserve in South Africa. It's for photography only no animal killing safari licenses allowed. There are eight cottages on the property but they're more like homes. It's probably two thousand square feet, elegant English furniture, sunken tub, a Jacuzzi on the outside patio overlooking the Crocodile River. It's rated the number one tourist destination for high-end tourists. The place is called Mala Mala. You will be staying at the Rattray camp.

It's named after the family who owns the reserve. Their attitude is you should be treated as one of their own personal guests. Therefore, you'll have your own attendant. These are licensed guides but he will be with you at breakfast, lunch and dinner. He will attend to you as if you were a guest in his own house. The place only accommodates sixteen people but the staff of thirty-four gives you a better idea of how luxurious it is. You're going game riding into the bush mornings and the afternoons. It will be an unbelievable experience. Before you leave Johannesburg, I've arranged for you to be supplied with a professional camera, a Canon 1 D. Marc 3, and a whole bunch of professional lenses. We'll have somebody come to the hotel and teach you how to use it."

"Why are you doing this?" Matt demanded.

"This is kind of a payoff for your nonparticipation in the Las Vegas operations," Frederic replied.

"Oh, well. I guess I can handle it."

"It's hard for me to bring this up but, Guzman and I feel you are too close to

BiBa and we don't want any personal feelings getting in the way of what must be done in Vegas."

Frederic changed gears, "Now for Vegas, we're setting up the card game without you. The invited players consist of Agnon and Abdul Al Nori, he is the shorter of the two Al Nori brothers you met at the Franschheok game. We're also inviting Stephan Denton he's from American tobacco, Stephan Players CEO at Reynolds, and Howard Auckland from BAT. Three more guests from Iran, they are Azizi's cousins, will be there. We have Azizi hosting the game which means he will pay the expenses of the other players. That's how these guys set up their games. It's all provided by the host, even the flights."

"Now the hard part, I'm just going to give it to you as straight as I can. Our intelligence from Homeland is touchy, it's really thin. The Las Vegas hotels have much better information than we do believe it or not. We need to break into Caesar's IT systems and don't know if we have the ability to do it. As of right now we haven't been able to compromise any of their mainframes. We need help, here's where it becomes difficult. We need BiBa and you can't be involved."

Matt broke in, "What in the hell are you talking about? This is fucking absurd." Holding back his anger he continued, "I'm trying to be real objective about this. There has to be a lot of hosts or hostesses who have the same fucking information. Why her?"

Kasogi just listened and did not enter the conversation.

Frederic replied, "All we need is a password. I will have an encryption expert talk to you when you're not so pissed off. We don't want to be intrusive. We don't want to mess with her at all. We just need some simple information from you rather than snooping around and using problematic resources getting it from her. You say why her? I know you're not going to like this, but after looking at all the hosts at the different hotels for the biggest players her name came up as having the most clients and the best information on them. Look, we just need to know simple things, nothing deep. We are just searching for a password so we can sneak in and look at her files. Stuff like, if she ever had a dog. What was its name? Did she ever mention a cat? You said she was athletic, what were her jersey numbers? She's got a six digit password it is three thousand times harder to access it than a four digit password. Our encryption expert has to start somewhere and we would like that somewhere to be you. We just want your help to protect her. I know you're pissed but hear me out. We don't want to set off any alarms by hacking into her laptop or the mainframe at the Encore. Looking into these tobacco guys through her files if we have to go through some of our backdoors could set off some bells. We don't need it. She doesn't need it. So if we can do it more straightforwardly by figuring out her password then she's out of the loop and she's protected."

Frederic took a deep breath, "Hell, remember, if you screw up with her I'm next in line. I don't want to mess this thing up for me. Look I'm just kidding and you know I wouldn't do this unless we had to. If you have some other suggestions let me know. We don't want to involve her in any way, not just for her but obviously for you.

We just have to have the information on these tobacco high rollers. We don't see any other way. I keep saying we, it's Guzman, Gisele, and me."

This whole time Kasogi was silent.

Frederic addressed him, "Agnon you will have to be in Las Vegas in two weeks. We're setting everything up through Azizi's accounts for you as well. You'll be one of his honored guests at Caesars. I hope the two weeks we give you will be enough time for all your personal or business matters. We'll have a private room that we rent for twenty-five thousand dollars a night on the fifth floor of the hotel. We'll have the hotel talk to each player and their security teams to make them feel more comfortable about the arrangements. We will be working through a man named Ralph Wyzell who is head of security. He'll tell them he heard about South Africa and guarantees player safety. By now the word has gotten out about what happened at the game in Franschheok. The gambling world is a small one. We will need to use Azizi and the robbery to our advantage. Like I said before South African authorities have classified what went on as a robbery. Azizi will host the game as a way of apologizing, it was in his country. We will set it up as his way of dealing with his kid's drug-related death. You know Arab macho. Life must go on. None of this thirty day grieving, which would be the case for most Muslims. The gang wanted to use his son as leverage for the robbery. The kid had a history of drugs and being out of control so Azizi won't be held responsible. Hosting the game so quickly after his son's death is a way for a disgusted father to move on. Kasogi, if you and Al Nori will be at the game the rest of the players will feel safe. The tobacco guys, especially Stephan Denton will be chomping at the bit for this game. They think Azizi and his Iranian cousins are easy pickings. Look, all these guys know each other. The Arab, Azizi and his Persian relatives are big losers. They can lose five hundred thousand to one million dollars in a night so Denton and his friends will be there. They're that greedy. Even if they felt unsafe, which they don't, they'll throw caution to the wind. They're not only greedy they are too lazy when it comes to easy money to tie things together. So a robbery and drugs will be the cover. Our limited or even poor intelligence on the tobacco executives suggests these guys might not be the ones responsible or privy to the industry's plans to set off a dirty bomb in New York."

"Without BiBa's intelligence we're just not sure. We do know someone has aborted the attempt. Guzman thinks the game is an imperative. Even if these guys aren't the right guys whatever we do to them will get back to the right people. Now, it's our turn to take the initiative."

"Matt, you've been quiet. I know this is a lot to digest. You've got to know I wouldn't involve BiBa if there was another way. Sorry you can't be in Vegas and I'm sorrier we need information from her. You've got my promise; if we can't determine her password then we'll stop there. Guzman feels the same way."

-----o-----

Walking down the steps of the Gulfstream 4, Matt noticed the difference in temperature from the much cooler Johannesburg.

The guide, Stephan Botha, waited for his guest in a converted open air land rover. The vehicle was retrofitted with steel bush guards over the headlights and extra plating on its sides for protection from rhinos and Cape buffalo.

After introducing himself Stephan said, "There's only one rule we have in Mala Mala and that is your safety and your comfort come first."

He handed Matt a small thermos filled with coffee and continued, "It's either this or we can make some tea. I have a basket in the back of the vehicle if you'd like some cookies or biscuits."

Matt answered, "The coffee is fine."

"If we go straightaway to the main house it will take 45 minutes but I think we'll be lucky enough to encounter some wonderful rhinos near the river." Stephan suggested as he adjusted the earphone connected to his cell.

"There are only a few dirt roads on the reserve, so you'll have to accustom yourself to our driving through the bush. This Land Rover is little over ten thousand pounds. We have the ability to go over shrubs and trees and not get caught in gullies or valleys. We can climb at almost forty-five degrees. The vehicle will not stall out in the river unless we are in over 3 feet of water. We can pretty much do anything we want."

Stephan continued, "You may have noticed I'm getting calls on my cell. There are eight guides in the bush in every hour of sunlight. We're in total communication all the time. That allows us to know where the animals are, we don't waste your time finding them. Also it gives us a measure of safety that should make you feel more comfortable. Let me talk a bit about myself, I know I'm young, but you're in good hands. My father was a guide and I have been in the bush since I was nine years old. I also went to college and got a degree in tourism to help me get my license as a professional guide in a much shorter time period. I guess you noticed the single shot rifle on the hood. I am designated as a special marksman. I've been in the bush for more than thirteen years and I've never had to use my gun. That's a last resort and it sure as heck won't happen while you're here. Never underestimate the animals, they are wild and dangerous. If I left you out here you wouldn't make it. Clear and simple, you would die. If we approach all the animals slowly and follow the simple little things I ask of you everything will be fine. We just can't make unexpected movements or noises. We blend into the environment and that gives us the ability to virtually sit right on top of them. You'll see, before we get back to the main house and get you in your room you will be so close to the rhinos you will feel you can stick your hand out and touch them."

Trying to talk and listen at the same time Stephan was getting word from another senior guide. He had located a rhinoceros herd fifteen minutes away on an embankment on the Crocodile River which ran through the Mala Mala Reserve.

"Matt, may I call you that?"

"Yes, of course."

"Please call me Stephan. If you have any questions just fire away. I know I'm young for having been out in the bush for so long, but I'm 28. Just listen to me and I know you'll have a great time. You'll be safe. Within the next five minutes it's going to be pitch black. Then you'll see a mass of stars you've never seen before. With no moon the Milky Way is probably the most impressive sight you will ever see in your lifetime. Wait a couple minutes, you'll see. We'll be driving down the river bed getting to the rhinos. It's the dry season so the river won't be very high. We can drive right down its middle. There are no places deeper than maybe a foot and a half. You might see some small crocs or hippos don't worry about them. We'll come back and see them in the daytime. They are no threat at all."

At the airport, Stephan had picked up Matt's luggage and camera gear and thrown it in the second row seats directly behind him. The rover had three rows of ascending seats which held two passengers across. The back row was about three feet higher than Stephan's position as driver on the right side.

He said, "Viewing from the back is best because you're higher but you'll feel safer near me. When most people see the rhinos," he started to laugh, "All macho goes out the window. I'm not saying you're macho but their proximity and huge size is really threatening the first time you see them. It is especially important you feel safe and comfortable, you're here to have a good time, for most people this is a once in a lifetime experience. So if you are not in the right frame of mind you are not going to appreciate it. I guess I'm being overly verbal but find a place were you are comfortable. You can make up your mind when we get to the embankment, maybe ten minutes away. The rhinos are virtually blind so fifty feet from where we see them you can change positions. We are up wind so they can't see or smell us. You can make your decision then."

Matt decided to sit in the front, saying, "I will sit up here. I trust that you're not crazy enough to jeopardize yourself. I think I'll feel safer up near you and that big gun tied to the hood makes me feel better. When we get there I will need help with my camera. I just bought it in Johannesburg and the truth be known it is way out of my class. When the trip was set up I was told you would help me. I don't remember a damn thing. I'm leaving it in your hands. This way if my pictures aren't very good we know who to blame," he smiled.

Stephan said, "This will be your lucky day, let me change that, your lucky night. You'll see. Trust in me everything is easy. Just a couple words and then I'll keep my mouth shut. Matt, when I ask you to do something sometimes we won't have time for me to explain. I won't be telling you to do something unless it's necessary and of course the most important thing is our safety. In about a minute and a half I'm going to flash a halogen spotlight in the deep shrubs just on top of that embankment. We've been driving at a really slow pace but the animals are aware of us. As long as we don't change the outer sightline of the vehicle or the noise level as we approach the herd we will be fine. They will be drawn to the spotlight. Clear and simple, we sit here in the water. They are on the embankment and I put the spotlight in front of them and they will follow. They will come as close to flash light as they can; they think it will lead to food. They will come down right to the rover. Just to make you feel better since

I'm on the right side I will have them come to me. The big adult males will come down the embankment to within virtually a foot of the rover. It will take maybe two minutes because I'll move the spot light very slowly. Let me have your cameras. I'll set it with a real high ISO so you won't need a flash. This way you won't startle the animals. As long you move slowly you can take as many pictures as you want. Just do it slowly. Those are my directions. This will end up being the most unbelievable thing you have ever done. Are you ready?"

As the rhino family followed the halogen spotlight down the embankment Matt was amazed at their surefootedness. They broke through the twelve foot high reeds as if they were toothpicks or straws. He couldn't get over the deep resonating barks that emanated from the rhinos mouths. It was almost as if dogs were grunting a deep sound from the center of their stomachs. The rhinos were just foraging for food. They were grazing, eating the succulent green grass that sprouted from the river's edge. As they came closer to the vehicle Matt noticed how massive their hind ends were. What came to mind was a gigantic pit bull, an animal that seemingly was just all muscle, sheer strength that foretold brute power and danger. These black rhinos weighed over three thousand pounds, they were agile and fast, he knew Stephan was right in saying he would die if left on his own out here.

-----o-----

For more than twenty minutes Matt and Stephan took hundreds of pictures. Living in the moment, Matt Shaw forgot where he was. His world was focused in his professional camera viewfinder. Myopic as it seemed, it filtered out all the problems he had been facing for more than three years. What he focused on was the majesty of these massive animals. As soon as Stephan pointed a light towards the embankment the rhinos followed its yellowish white spot and migrated back into the pitch black night.

"Well, how was that? You just get off a plane and..."

Before he could finish Matt said, "Shit that was great. I can't believe how big and how f-ing close they came. This is more fun than I ever expected, I don't really think I have the words to describe how frightened I felt. That big bull's horn couldn't have been more than a foot and a half from your door, shit that was exciting. When it first started coming down the hill I white knuckled it but, I couldn't hold on to the railings inside the truck tight enough, man they scared me."

Stephan assured him this was just one of many incredible sightings. He said, "Let's get back to the main camp and get you to your room. We will discuss this tomorrow."

As they drove in the moonless star-studded night with only the aid of the halogen spotlight Matt realized Stephan was so familiar with his surroundings he didn't need a GPS system. He was amazed at the young man's knowledge of his environment.

Matt had to question him again, a man's question. "I'm going to ask you a stupid question again. If you threw me out of the Rover you don't think I'd make it back do you? Even if you pointed out how to go you don't think I could make it back. I can actually smell the dinner cooking at the lodge, its mind boggling you don't think I can make it back a couple miles."

Stephan just looked at him and said, "You better stay with me. It's no place for people without any particular skills or expertise and that's exactly what I have. The bush is a killing-field, everything is eaten by the predators and night is a time for hunting. I'm sorry to say you need me. You would not make even a mile. He pointed towards the right, you can't even see it but there are a pride of lions on the other side of those small trees. You could never make it past them. I think you noticed, you see no electrical fences around here, the compound doesn't have an electrical fence. The animals roam in and out where we stay. So even within our own eating and sleeping area it is dangerous. Lions and other big cats have wandered into camp but we have guards and procedures to protect you. On your own you might make it a couple hours, but for sure you wouldn't make it the whole night. Any time in the Bush I have the rifle with me. Since we left the runway it's been on the hood of the rover, but you'll soon see as I get out of the rover I carry it. I have not had to use it because over the years I not only live with the animals I've studied them. I know them well enough not to initiate any threats causing them to respond by attacking me or my guests. If any of what we call the big five smells a human that could cause them to attack. These are mere defenses for seeking food. I am here to protect you and really there's nothing to worry about. I've been well-trained. My college training and obtaining proper guidance certificates took twelve years. I mentioned I've lived in the bush since I was a kid so most of this is old territory for me. With all that said we still have to be vigilant. Never let your guard down never put yourself in a threatening position to the animals. You're probably thinking I'm over dramatizing things talking to a tourist like this but it's what I do. I'm sure in some respects if you told me what you did I would be just as smitten by your field of expertise. By the way, you never said what you did for a living."

When they arrived at the main house three attendants were waiting with washcloths and a tray of hot tea or coffee. The main house structure was not what Matt had envisioned. It was post-modernistic, much like the architectural design of homes in Palm Springs California. He walked to the double doors leading to a large entryway. Inside the buildings front area was a lounge decorated with paintings of wildlife, animals and hunting parties with porters. A library one would find in a gentlemen's club in London adjoined the room.

A man dressed as a guide walked out of the library and introduced himself. "I'm William, one of the eight guides on the property. While Stephan takes your luggage and your cameras back to your room I'll show you around. Let me take you out back."

As they walked through double glass sliding doors onto the patio overlooking the Crocodile River, he pointed to his left and said, "This is the dining area, next to it is what we call the study, but it is a bar. Later I will introduce you to Charles, he's the bartender, and he's at your disposal twenty-four hours a day."

Looking across the way, "That's her kitchen," as he nodded to the head chef, Mobica. "The house is yours. Mr. Rattray feels all our guests should be treated as if they were actually staying at his home in Cape Town. Whatever you see is for you."

As he walked around the elegantly decorated main house, William pointed out, "It's our job to make this the best experience of your life. Stephan is not only your guide. He is your 'Man Friday'. We have eight, what we call rooms set up for two adults. There's no one on this property less than eighteen years of age. So when we are at maximum capacity there are sixteen guests and thirty-four attendants, we call ourselves family members. Any one of us can meet your needs, it doesn't make any difference if we are white or African we are all here for you. Stephan probably told you already, we only have a few rules here on the compound and he's right, your enjoyment and your safety. I only have one more rule. On the compound, please treat our people with respect and dignity. We've never had a problem with anyone because being in the Bush makes everyone understand their place in the world.

When Stephan returned, he found Matt in the bar and ordered a ginger ale.

Matt looked at him and said, "This is nothing like what I expected. I've only been here a couple hours and from the plane to here I've never before experienced anything like this. Now that I'm in this main house area I can honestly say, if my house were this nice I'd be a lucky guy."

Stephan said, "Wait till you see your room it's much nicer. Many of our guests spend more time in their rooms than they do in the bush. You will see. Besides being luxurious we have every type of technology that anyone could ever hope to have. I'm your guide and I'm a naturalist so I prefer being outside and that's why I think most people want to come here, but your rooms have the best flat screen TVs, iPod, lap top as well as desktop computers, printers and fax machines, and of course your own private line. We have an IT person on the staff at your disposal twenty-four hours a day. I think you remember when you walked in you saw a really great looking library, it's not all books we have an extensive set of software that's at your disposal. Most of it is for photography, the newest professional Photoshop software, Aperture, things like Lighthouse, any software you need. Let's finish our drinks and I'll take you to your room you can clean up I'll have someone bring you back here for dinner."

He sat and talked for another fifteen minutes mostly about the itinerary for the next couple days Matt decided it was time to see his room.

-----o-----

The five-minute walk on a dirt trail from the main house to his room was different than he expected. Matt experienced different sound on foot than being in the Land Rover. The trail's closeness to the Crocodile River and the grunts of hippopotamus in papaya reeds waving in the wind were less subtle than he thought would be the case. His heart was pumping a little faster than normal. He almost felt like he was in survival mode.

As they walked the trail to his house he again scanned the skies and was taken aback by the beauty of the Milky Way. The calls from the bush and the river were those of the prey huddling in great numbers for protection from the predator. They walked up to the door of what Stephan called the room. It was a freestanding house and as far as Matt could tell it was probably a little over two thousand square feet.

Stephan said, "Sorry I put your stuff in the main sitting area. There's no need for keys here. You will always be brought to and taken from your room by either me or an attendant. I think you understand why. It is better not to venture out on your own. When we get inside you'll see that the deck area is safe, we don't have any fences around here but you're right in the middle of the bush. I'll leave you to yourself. Whenever you're ready just call me. He handed Matt a cell and said, just dial one. Mr. Rattray thinks it should be enjoyable for the guest to figure out all the gadgets. Later if you have trouble I'll show you anything you want, I know it seems backwards, me not telling and you asking about all the rooms' amenities, but you'll have a lot of fun with it."

The house was unusual. The main door they had just walked into brought them to an entryway with access to the main house from both the right and the left. It was as if it were a large mud room in a Swiss Alps cabin. Beyond the walls of the entryway was a massive fifty by forty feet bedroom and sitting area with wall-to-wall glass sliding doors open to the river and an unobstructed view of the wildlife below. There was a voice activated Bose sound system in every room. It took Matt almost ten minutes to realize the blackout drapes were also operated by verbal command. The bathroom area had a massive shower, six by six feet, also a steam room. There was a sauna, a sunken tub and toilets and bidet. The floors in the main area of the house were deep and rich mahogany. The surfaces in the bathroom were the finest granites from Italy. All electronics were from Japan. Like all adventures in life there would be a learning curve for these technological living quarters in the middle of the bush. Matt cleaned up and made a call to

Stephan to be brought back to the main house for dinner. He would get settled in later and put his clothes and his belongings in the many drawers, cabinets, and closets of his living quarters. Having dinner with Stephan and the six other guests and their respective guides was relaxing. There was no pretense of one's accomplishments to be able to afford such an expensive outing. The conversation was one of animal sightings during the day and plans for the next morning. Everyone had a similar experience of exhilaration coming through the gates of Mala Mala. If one guest sited an elephant coming into the compound another saw the pride of lions, one of the guests saw leopards walking on the road. Matt recounted his stories of the rhinoceros. Each person animatedly told of their encounter with the big five. Each account brought greater anticipation for tomorrow's game runs from all the men in the room.

Matt did not know if it was coincidental or typical that the only tourists were men, but in reality he did not care. After about an hour and a half of eating and conversation he said he felt a little tired and would retire for the night. Samuel, one of the attendants at the bar, said he would walk him back to his room.

At 7:30am the next morning Stephan called and said breakfast was waiting per their conversation the night before. Samuel will be at the door in five minutes.

As Matt walked into the main house lobby Stephan grabbed his arm and said, "We're really lucky this morning. A female leopard, a big one, just brought down a zebra. If we leave right now we can see her trying to put it in one of the trees for safety. It's only a couple minutes away so when we get back you can still have breakfast."

They jumped into the Land Rover and drove off the dirt road, which encircled the main house, and plowed through shrubs and small trees for less than five minutes. At the base of a Rhus Leptodictva tree, a leopard had its prey's neck scruff held firmly in its jaws climbing to a branched fork attempting to protect its kill from other area predators. It took almost fifteen minutes to place the dead zebra carcass in the fork between the two limbs.

Matt was astonished by the lack of blood and almost sanitary environment of the kill. The leopard's power, pulling its pray weighing one hundred and fifty pounds vertically for fifteen feet, was impressive. The time-consuming ritual of taking its prize out of harm's way from its competitors and the idea of survival of the fittest were symbolic. His life during the past three years was strikingly symbolized by this scene. Fate would have it that a leopard sighting would be his gift from Frederic.

Stephan set up the camera and said, "We can stay here as long as you like."

He took out his own equipment and both sat less than fifteen feet from the cat and its prize. The leopard now proceeded to eat, as all big cats do, from the hind end of the animal to the front as it hung lifelessly from the tree. She would feed on her meal for three to four days before hunting again.

Stephan interrupted his picture taking by saying, "Leopards are the most efficient of all predators we have here in South Africa. What's interesting is sometimes they kill not for food but to intimidate their prey. We think sometimes they kill to sharpen their skills; the females kill to show their cubs the ways of survival. All other big cats are only known to kill for food not to put fear in other animals or kill for sheer entertainment. The leopard is the ultimate predator not only in terms of skill but in terms of kill ratio. It has the highest number of kills per attempt of any predator. We only have scientific observation obviously but most biologists concur. The leopard has this rare quality of killing for fun."

Matt almost dropped his camera. The image of Guzman orchestrating death and mayhem against his adversaries now became clear to him. What he had seen and participated in over the last two months since the attempted terrorist strike by Al Bin was against all he stood for as a person but now it seemed more acceptable. Literally one event changed his mindset. The leopard started to put things in a more proper perspective. From the very depths of his emotional base Matt now understood. Guzman was correct. Kill a few people put fear in many and take command of the situation. Kill with the highest priority of putting fear into your enemy. The strategy of tilting the field to the predator's advantage was so ingrained it was passed down in the genes or DNA of its predators.

At Mala Mala, Matt saw survival of the fittest at its best. He wondered if Frederic intended he learn this lesson here. He would question him about it later. It was clear Guzman was in his element, to question him and his tactics was inappropriate. He and Stephan watched the leopard for almost an hour. The images were etched in his mind. He had a physical reminder of operation Leopard. He had taken over two hundred pictures before they ventured back for breakfast.

The rest of his stay at Mala Mala followed a similar itinerary as his first night and morning. He saw elephants, buffalo, lions, more leopards, more rhino and an assortment of smaller mammals, birds and reptiles. Late in the afternoons and nights he spent time in the study talking with Stephan and the other guests. Five days on Safari went by quickly. It reenergized him and gave him a better understanding of his friend Jose Guzman and what had to be done. He flew back to Johannesburg and then to Miami where Frederic was awaiting his arrival.

-----o-----

Matt was picked up at MIA, Miami international Airport, and taken to a townhouse in South Beach. Immediately after unlocking the door his phone rang.

Frederic was on the other end. "Good having you back old buddy. The driver said he just dropped you off. I'm going to see you tomorrow. We will meet at the Sports Club of Miami. It's the nicest gym on South Beach. Let me fill you in on the particulars. I have a racquetball game set up at eleven o'clock. When you get to the club go to the registration desk and tell them you're in town for a couple months. You can purchase a temporary membership. After filling out all the paperwork they will give you an ID card. Take it to the challenge court for racquetball. I have it set up that we will be on the same court. It's a good cover. I know you're fat but I guess you can still move around some."

"Okay sport," Matt said, "I lost some weight in Africa so not as fat as you think. All you have to know is I will be there. Enough of this stupid smack. I'm really looking forward to seeing you. But that won't stop me from kicking your ass."

Frederic said, "Yeah I know, we'll see tomorrow at eleven. And by the way, Guzman said he needs to talk to you as soon as possible, it's a private matter. Use this number, 866 437 9900, it's a clean phone. I'll talk to you tomorrow."

Anxious to hear from Guzman after their man up conversation a few days earlier he knew he had to initiate a conversation. His reactions to their little talk while he was in Africa pressed heavily on him. He dialed Guzman's cell, "José I just talked to Frederic. He told me to call. How are you my friend?"

Guzman said, "Matt Shaw is dead. That is why we need to talk. He hesitated for a second and continued. We had to kill you off in Argentina. It happened that you had to die in the hospital. We could not hold off all the rumors about your illness. The press was investigating why you were still getting treatment out of the country. I did not want to take a chance you would see your death in the newspaper. I know you still follow what goes on in San Jose so I figured I'd better talk to you. I had to make a decision and it wasn't a very difficult one, you're dead."

Matt thought to himself, was this Guzman's way of telling him something. But before he could respond Guzman continued, "I never apologize to another man. It's a sign of weakness but our friendship has softened my ways. I was too hard on you the other day. We will go after those tobacco fucks but I don't want you to think I see you as disloyal or a coward. I respect you. You are a brother to me just as much as Pedro is."

Matt interrupted, "Jose I was going to call as soon as I got to Miami. Our conversation has weighed heavily upon me. I saw something in Africa and it made me see things differently. I'm not just saying this, but I know what you have to do is right. I know killing a few to control many through fear will tilt this war to us. I just have to take it from my mind and understand it in my heart. You were right. You don't have to say it, but I was acting like a pussy. I've been reacting to what I did at the zoo in Johannesburg. I was forced to do something that sickens me but in reflection I had to do it. It was the right thing. I only did it because I thought maiming somebody was better than killing somebody. I couldn't believe how it tortured me. I didn't know how to face the consequences of such a horrible thing. I figure saving the guy's life would be easier for me to handle, but it was so fucking off the charts I couldn't get over it. This whole thing, Al Bin, the bomb, and all the other stuff is just fucking crazy. Talking to me the way you did and seeing something in Africa made me understand this shit a lot better. I respect you and I'm aware what you do is something left to people with a particular skill set. Someone used that phrase and it speaks directly to you. You're the only person who can lead us through what has to be done. I don't want to say too much more but you are the only one who can lead us. I'm glad to be your brother in this. I will never question your decisions again. There's no one in the world I respect more than you and there's nothing that means more to me than our friendship. You were right. I was acting like a pussy. Enough of this, it's good for me to clear the air I have thought a lot about this conversation. I'm glad Frederic told me you wanted to talk to me. It's always good to hear your voice."

Guzman was quiet on the other end and finally said, "I am also glad to hear from you, my friend."

The conversation ended. Both men were more comfortable with what they had to do.

With his death in Costa Rica, Matt would have to create a new life. His role as Chief-of-Staff to the President of Costa Rica was no more, but life would move on. If he wanted to be with BiBa when this was over, he would have to build a new persona. This was an opportunity, not an obstacle to his future. The bridge would be crossed at a later date. "I cannot see nor talk to BiBa until the crisis is over," he told himself.

Hardly ten minutes in Miami and he was both physically exhausted from jet lag and emotionally exhausted from his conversations with Frederic and Guzman. All he wanted to do was settle into his apartment. He did not know how long he would be in South Beach nor what was expected of him. He would find out tomorrow morning at the Sports Club.

He got up at 6am and took another shower. After dressing he ventured out of the townhouse looking for a coffee shop. He was staying at 17th and Lenox Avenue. Walking south on 17th he passed the convention center and the Jackie Gleason Theater. Within fifteen minutes he reached Collins Avenue and the Atlantic Ocean. He found the neighborhood Starbucks and ordered a scone and a tall coffee. He sat outside and watched as people were waking up to the morning with a jolt of caffeine. It was good to be back in the United States even though he was on the east coast, he thought.

He was looking forward to seeing Frederic so much so he contemplated throwing the game to make his friend feel better. Matt was much more athletic and somewhere deep down in the recesses of his mind he felt a loss could be attributed to his extra girth or jet lag. Somehow it might be a payback to Frederic for his trip to Mala Mala and their friendship.

------o------

After finishing his cup of coffee he walked on the beach for almost an hour before he decided to return to the town-house. Once inside he made a phone call to the Sports Club and asked if they had a boutique or shop where he could purchase athletic gear. He needed shoes, shorts, T-shirt, and a racket. He would arrive at the club at 10:15am. The Sports Club of Miami was the sister club of the one in Los Angeles. It was the most exclusive and upscale sports facility in Florida. As a non-member the entry fee was fifty dollars for the usage of the gym and its racquetball courts for the day.

The huge complex reminded him of the Hollywood crowd in West LA. It was ostentatious, its members were there for social reasons to be seen not to work out, and most importantly it was a happening. The women were Miami's finest, attired in the most expensive upscale fashions. The meat market, as he called it, was reminiscent of the plastic social climbing crowd of Los Angeles. The women were beautiful, the men were buff, but it was hard for Matt to identify with the young crowd.

After paying his fees and walking over to the boutique, where he purchased his clothing and equipment, he found the men's locker room and changed. He was early so he decided to work on the Nautilus machines and stretch a little before Frederic got there.

Precisely at 11 o'clock Frederic arrived and the two met at the challenge court. Frederic introduced himself as if they were not acquainted. They ventured into the twenty by forty feet wooden floored box with cement walls and twenty feet high ceiling.

As soon as the door closed Frederic said, "I thought you would look a lot fatter," and laughed. "Don't use those extra pounds as an excuse." as he gave him the little blue ball.

"I don't need to hit or get warmed up. You serve."

Matt smiled and all thoughts of mercy on his friend changed instantaneously. He proceeded to win in a punishing way. He intentionally extended points and played to Frederic's backhand. The final scores were 21 -- 9, 21 -- 7, and 21 -- 18. He let Frederic feel a little better in the last game by tanking some shots. He didn't have the heart to be ruthlessly competitive and pour it on his old friend.

They walked out of the court and in front of four new players who were now waiting for their turn to play Frederic said, "You're new here, right? Matt, it's traditional for the loser to buy beers. How about it? After we clean up, it's my treat. I will meet you down at the main restaurant in the lobby."

The club had different showering areas for members and nonmembers. After cleaning up the two met in the trendy restaurant. Matt arrived first and sat at a table facing the check-in desk. The sight of so many beautiful women and their outfits was not lost on him. The huge open area that constituted a restaurant was impressive not only for its size but its decor. In most cities this restaurant would have a five star rating, Matt thought. "It's in a sports club. I can't believe how opulent it is," he said to himself. The 'people watching' was more popular than weights, or exercise classes, or anything else the club had to offer. He felt he was in Santa Monica, California or Malibu. Too many rich people with egos he thought to himself.

Frederic approached the table and placed his athletic bag on the floor. "Great game," he said, "you kicked my ass. You have to give me another chance."

He lowered his voice and said, "It's good to see you old buddy. I really mean it. I know we've had little contact but man it's good to see you."

The decibel level in the large room because of its granite floors and modern furniture made general conversation difficult unless you leaned towards the person to whom you are speaking. Any ability to over hear anyone or tape their conversation was virtually impossible. Electronic taping devices were rendered useless by the overall volume of background noise.

"No business," Frederic said, "we will just play it safe even though no one can really hear us. Save business for the phone or e-mail. When we talk we'll have to bring Gisele and maybe Guzman into the conversation so we'll have to set up a video conference call."

"Man it's good to see you," Matt said. They talked for twenty minutes discussing everything under the sun except terrorism and politics.

Frederic led Matt to the membership office and introduced him as his new playing partner, a Californian who would be staying in Miami for a couple of months. A two month membership was purchased with full club privileges for one thousand dollars and a fee of two hundred fifty dollars per thirty day period. When finished the two men walked over to the sign up desk and reserved a court for the next eight Tuesdays and Thursdays at 11am. They walked out of the club together, Frederic went to his car in the parking lot and Matt walked over to the taxi stand.

He opened the back door of the yellow cab and said, "It's a short way but take me to 17th and Lenox Ave. Thanks."

Back at the townhouse he couldn't rest so he communicated with Gisele.

After his e-mail she called on his cell. "It's clean, they can't trace this call and they can't listen. I hope you had a good flight and are well rested. I was going to wait for another day before a called but I felt you are as anxious about this whole affair as I am. I have some news I will share with you. Later I will fill in the others. Everything in Las Vegas is set up."

Matt sighed, "How's that?"

"We just have to concentrate on the simple logistics of expediting the three tobacco executive's apprehension. It should be simple. I won't bore you with any details. That's not why I need to talk to you. Everything at Caesars Palace Hotel will play itself out. There are other things troubling me. I have some conflicting intelligence. It's about the tobacco executives. As of right now we cannot pin down exactly which ones are using their national association to funnel money to Al Bin. That is nothing new, but the amounts coming out of the American Tobacco Institute are less than the total expenditures for the terrorist plot. The Institute has indeed passed money to Al Bin and his associates in Johannesburg using Azizi as their banker. There's a caveat, always a problem. The money for the operation the institute appropriated isn't enough. We have calculated the total cost to this point as a little over $27 million. We have a donut hole between tobacco's contributions and expenditures needed for the operation. This is pure conjecture on my part but there can only be one source for the monies needed. I'm reticent to say it but the other contributor has to be Homeland Security."

-----o-----

"It makes no sense to me at all. We only have partial information from dubious sources and at best it's not clear. I guess I'm afraid to say it but right now everything points to either Homeland or the CIA. The Las Vegas operation is extremely important. We need to interrogate Denton, Player, and Auckland to find out what they know. We're especially interested in Howard Auckland. Again, we don't think any of the three are players. Just knowing they are in or out will make it much easier for us."

"I don't anticipate their actual involvement but as Guzman says, 'if we kill them we will get the others to talk.' We think the key to tobacco's involvement is an executive committee at the American Tobacco Institute. None of the three in Las Vegas are on that committee. They are all on the board. We don't see any connection of the general board and Al Bin so they might not be privy to the operation. Someone on that executive committee is orchestrating this terrorist plot."

Matt listened intently as Gisele continued, "Our information brings us to the conclusion that some or at least one of its members directed oversight of the monies and resources to pull off something like the New York bombing. If we had not acted, we think an attack would have occurred because all U.S. security agencies were co-opted by these guys. Guzman thinks the only way we can squeeze whoever is head of this is by putting the fear of God into him. By the time we get done in Las Vegas just the mention or thought of a leopard will be enough to paralyze him. I can't get my hands around how Homeland might be involved but it's clear the Institute has only partially funded the operation. We are looking at political connections from the far right for the missing monies. The influence of Texas politics runs deep in all the anti-Muslim sentiments in Washington."

"Maybe Homeland has collaborated with tobacco, that's were we're looking. You know how a terrorist event could galvanize America against the Muslims again. Tobacco could win by criminalizing drugs again and Homeland would increase its influence in DC. Like I said, I can't get my hands around this. We're mining as much information as we can even if it means grabbing at political straws. The only positive thing I can present is it isn't as critical as it was a week ago. Al Bin is under the radar. We think he's in the tribal territories in western Pakistan but we're not sure. He could be in Afghanistan. He's just under the carpet. He will surface at some point. We don't know if it's him or his handlers but he's making all the right moves. Originally we thought whoever set up this plot to use him as a straw man used him because he wasn't very bright. We might have to rethink that. Every bit of our Intel suggests otherwise, it's hard to conceive why he is so elusive. It can't be his making as far as I am concerned. We have another theory. It might be some rogue operative in some little innocuous agency or commission that is being paid by some private contractor to cause as much havoc as possible so they can get contracts and privatize our efforts against terrorism. They had great influence in the Iraq war and want to get back in the game. Again, I don't know. I'm just throwing ideas at you. Every one of these scenarios has been downloaded in our mainframe and with our new software we are trying to calculate probable outcomes. It's like solving a math problem. There are some extraneous roots or unpredictable outcomes that might be relevant, I just don't know. I'm throwing all of this at you because we think alike. Having worked with you I'm sure you have pondered on all of this. I just need some input. I guess in a nutshell I'm trying to say I don't have anything conclusive right this second. I'd like to have irrefutable evidence as to who the principals are, but that's not the case.

Matt promised to give it some thought and Gisele ended the conversation, "Well, we still have Las Vegas and hopefully something will break there."

-----o-----

Matt's cell rang and the name Gisele appeared on the LCD screen. He engaged the conversation by hitting the green button in the upper left-hand side of the phone.

"Gisele, I didn't expect your call so soon."

"Sorry Mr. Shaw, my name is Jack Roper I'm an associate of Ms. Gisele and as we speak I'm sitting with her in her office using her cell. I am the encryption and password expert she mentioned to you last week. It's my pleasure to speak to you. She said you might be of some help in gaining access to BiBa Lamanas' password. I have some innocent questions for you, nothing invasive or offensive."

Matt agreed to the conversation. "Mr. Roper, I will help us much as possible. Go ahead. I will try to answer the questions as best and as truthfully I can."

"Mr. Shaw," Roper said, "most people choose a password based on two variables. Ease of recognition or past history. So do any dates or special events in Ms. Lamanas' life stick out in your mind?"

Matt informed him, "My history with her was brief."

"Okay then, did she mention any siblings or animals? Did she mention anything related to her social activities when she was younger, any nicknames?"

After about ten minutes, Matt's vague recollections of their conversations on the way to La Jolla and his and BiBa's short history was over Mr. Roper said, "Thank you. You've been a great help. Ms. Gisele wants to say a couple words to you."

"That wasn't so bad was it? We have the password. Roper says it's a collection of her parent's names and the simple number three. The password is Chris/Diana/3. We'll be in her account at the Encore in a few seconds. Hold on. We know the delicacy of your relationship with her and will not as agreed look into any of her personal information. Only her client's files will be within our purview. Matt, is your computer at your access."

He said, "Yes."

"Get into your Gmail account and access my last e-mail." He did, and within a second he was looking at BiBa's client information.

"The three of us will go over her accounts. Before this conversation is over we will set an electric alarm that someone is trying to enter her account. The way it's set up it will automatically change her password to a secondary password that she predetermined. I hope you feel more comfortable knowing it will be changed and we no longer have access. You have my word we will not let any cookies or Trojan horses into her account. As far as we are concerned it will be cleared. We won't keep any direct oversight of her electronic information. We have gone as far as we can making sure no one has the ability to tap her phones. We will do everything possible to make this a one-time occurrence and no further inquiries into her or anything remotely connected to her will take place without your concurrence."

Gisele continued, "Mr. Roper has left and extends his apologies for any intrusions. They began to look at the data BiBa had created on each of her clients. It was set up in an Outlook format showing information on Stephan Denton, Stephen Players, and Howard Auckland of the tobacco industry committee. After looking at Denton and Player it was evident her information held no leverage on either. Auckland on the other hand was someone who had more pressure points and was more vulnerable. All her files were set up as data entries. No summaries, no insights on her clients, all entries were professional and unbiased.

Gisele said, "I suppose she has all the important information in her head. It's clear we're not going to find anything about these guys from her. This limited information only eliminates potential surprises. I'm sending this to Jose; maybe he can make something more out of it. I know your relationship with her is important and it will be respected. As of this moment she is out of the game as far as we're concerned. Whatever else she has that is relevant or necessary for her work is no real use to us. By the same token, we feel she should be shielded. She can't be any more help to us. I'll get back to you as soon as we have some clear direction of what we will do."

After receiving the information from Gisele, Guzman placed a call to Alvarez in Cape Town, "How is our man Azizi?"

Alvarez said, "He is well enough for us to kill him at any time."

"Did you make the rubber impression of his face like I requested?" Guzman asked. "We need all the specifications sent as soon as possible so we can have a mask made. We won't kill him until the operation in Las Vegas is over. If there's a problem we'll still have Azizi. We'll not do anything until we're sure he has no additional value. He changed the subject, are things cooling off in Cape Town?"

Alvarez replied, "The manhunt for the Africans behind the robbery in Franschheok is real intense. Maybe a hundred blacks have been rounded up and beaten. The police are really tight with the Afrikaners but we are okay. No problem for us so far. Malique has everything under control. Our only concern is how long Azizi can make it. He is weaker every day. Let's hope we can keep him alive and we don't need him for anything else."

Guzman said, "Before we cut his head off, I want my voice to be the last thing he hears. We'll have Gisele set up a video feed so we can tape his execution when the time comes."

-----o-----

Frederic called Matt, "Tonight at 8pm there'll be a conference call. Everything is happening at once. A situation has come to Gisele's attention. Everything is fluid. We'll talk to you later."

Gisele had conference call command. She moderated the conversation. "Gentleman, as Mr. Roper further mined BiBa's files he found an IRS cookie. They monitor all the big players in Vegas for unreported income. Because of the Patriot Act, they don't have a problem with illegal surveillance of hotel personnel. If anything happened at a major casino to three of Vegas' highest rollers, it would set off law enforcement alarms throughout the community. Ultimately, with co-mingling all the security agencies' information bases, they could bring us into the light. They would leave no stone unturned saving the casinos' reputation."

"What this really means is that the named Mr. Matt Shaw might emerge as a

Leopard Directive

person of interest. Matt they could find out you were having a relationship with a hotel host and somehow tie it to South Africa. We combed the police records in Cape Town and they had your picture at the kidnapping in front of the wineries reception building. Matt Shaw of South Africa, the name you used, could be linked to Matt Shaw of Las Vegas and that would open up BiBa and you for investigation."

"If they start looking, your cover could be blown. We created a deep history for you but if it came to intense scrutiny we just don't know. If they fixate on you because of your proximity to Azizi everything could unravel. We just can't take that chance. Even though BiBa is not involved her relationship with you would be problematic. It's apparent we must change tactics. We can't kill all three tobacco executives to make a point. Does anyone have anything to add to this conversation," she asked.

Everyone was quiet. Guzman finally spoke up. "We will only target one of them, the Ackerman guy. After they are all in Las Vegas we will just go after him. We will set up conversations from Azizi to each player. He will say his doctors will not let him attend the game in Las Vegas, but of course he will still host the weekend, all expenses will be paid. Agnon, I want you to be in favor of continuing the game even in his absence. When it's over we can pay attention to Ackerman. It will be easy. We'll get him in a situation with a whore and he will stay in Las Vegas a few days after everybody else leaves. No one will put this together. After we interrogate him we will dispose of his body. Gisele, I'll work everything out later but in general he'll be drugged and so will his whore. We'll make it look like he had a heart attack on top of her. We have methods of giving him enough pain to get all the information out of him that he has the capability of knowing. Sometimes people know more than they think they do. We all feel these three guys are probably on the outside but we have to find out no matter what the cost. I know after we kill him and things quiet down we'll have to kidnap one of the tobacco CEOs on the tobacco Institute executive committee or whatever it's called. That's where we'll get the truth. By killing

Ackerman if we do it right it will put pressure on the people who head this terrorist operation. They might not immediately put together his death and our involvement but it will only be a matter of time. That's when we really apply the pressure. Matt felt a sense of fraternity with these men and Gisele for putting his personal life at the forefront of Operation Leopard. He sensed that data for anybody else except he and BiBa would be fair game. He hoped their protection would not jeopardize the mission. He felt he had to say something.

"I want to thank all of you, don't take this as a sign of weakness or acquiescing to the situation. We have been together for more than three years. I don't know what to say except I appreciate you having my back. It means a lot to me. We are family and as all of you know I would do the same for you. To protect me and BiBa is more than anyone could ask. We all know the loss of friends can be part of the price of doing business. I don't know what to say except thanks. I do want to apologize for slowing down our reaction time in dealing with tobacco's threat."

Guzman waited until he was finished. "Nothing else has to be said my friend. We would all do it for each other. We stick together. It might be this will put more pressure on whoever is behind a terrorist plot because the longer we wait, the more questions they will have, which could lead to their making a mistake. Bill I want you to set things up with Ackerman. Contact me with all your surveillance and give me all the information you can about the whore who will fill up his days in Las Vegas. After we deal with him hopefully we won't have to kill her, but if we do, we do.

Gisele said, "There's another piece of business. To make our communications with the players and Azizi more realistic we are finishing up what is called a hyper realistic body mask. It is silicon, it images the feel of real skin, it's flexible, and it's so exact the mask has pores. It even has real hairs placed on it one strand at a time. The colors are hand-painted by artisans and replicate the true skin color of Azizi. His wife wouldn't be able to tell the difference between him and whoever is wearing a mask. We'll have it tomorrow. So we can start making phone calls once all the players have assembled in Las Vegas. Between the mask and the computerized voice copying technology any conversation between the fake Azizi and the players in Las Vegas will be perceived as being real."

Guzman entered the conversation. "We will wait until after Las Vegas before we terminate Azizi's life. Just in case something unforeseen happens we'll still have him. We'll have our imposter communicate with each individual player giving a reason for Azizi not showing up in Vegas. It will be personal. There will be no suspicion because of his absence. We'll just make the conversation sound like he's too fragile after his son's death and he must follow the thirty-day mourning period for Moslems. He'll say something like I guess I tried to overextend myself dealing with my grief but it was unrealistic. When this is over I want his head cut off as he sits in his own shit on the metal chair in that cell in Cape Town. I want him positioned in the room so that when you cut his head off the blood will splatter onto the Leopard flag that's on the wall. The video will have my voice sentencing him to death for dealing with terrorist groups opposed to our world order. I want to warn all the Hawala bankers that if they process money affecting us their fate will be the same as Azizi and his family. Find out how many major Hawala bankers there are and make sure every single one of them gets a DVD of his execution. I want this to be an international Leopard warning. All these bankers speak Arabic so make it in their language but have English subtitles. That will make them think someone is superior to them. I want them to be careful as to the ultimate end of their money transactions. I understand that for however many years they have been doing business they have been looked upon like Swiss bankers with no responsibilities other than moving monies. That will all change."

-----o-----

Matt commented, "They've been looked upon as professionals, having no ethical position either side of the transaction. They are only money traders making no judgments about their commodity use."

Guzman countered, "No more! If any of their money touches us in any way there will be a price. Hawala families will die just like Azizi. This will shake their arrogance and their tradition of being safe. They're not above what the money can do. Their traditions of secrecy and safety will be no more. This will force them to be careful and not deal in the drug world. I know there'll be many unknown consequences of these actions but if we sit on the fence all of our narcotics relationships in the Middle East will fall apart and we will be dead men."

"It is a cost they will have to pay, if they want to stay in business." Matt continued, "If drug deals are hurt by a squeeze on this money market because they're scared of us we'll have to jump in and be bankers ourselves."

"Pedro will be perfect for that." Guzman added, "This is almost what happened in Mexico and Nicaragua when people who laundered our money cheated on us. I remember Ricardo said it's just the cost of doing business but Pedro and I hit them hard. For a few months there was no cash in the marketplace. The pipeline was dry. We consolidated and took the place of the Panamanians and Colombians and became bankers. It was the unintended consequence of protecting ourselves. The same logic rules here. We tell our suppliers and partners their Arab bankers are out. But financially consolidate and guarantee our suppliers and their buyers a fluid market. They just care about their profits and product. There is no loyalty. We make them the same arrangements, same percentages and safety in getting their money and they'll be ours."

"The worst case we lose a month or two profits while the pipeline is dry as we take over from these Arab bankers." Frederic chimed in, "we'll get the money back ten times over in our new business. There's lots of profit moving money around and it should be ours."

"Don't forget we have Arnouk that Turkish bastard. He's been involved in this kind of stuff in the Middle East for years. He ran the money room for National Security and our old friend Porter." Guzman continued, "The money matters will fall into place soon after we kill Azizi and the Hawala bankers see your video. They will either honor our threat or we will have a new business. We have to look at it as an opportunity."

Alvarez who was sitting at his computer in Cape Town said, "José when should we get rid of him. Gisele says you now have the plastic mask and we have a computerized print of his voice so we can imitate him anytime we want. Do you still want to hold off just in case there are some problems?"

Jose replied, "His last breaths are few. Unless you're under pressure because of the dragnet in Cape Town we should keep him alive. It's always better, you never know. After we conclude this call prepare for his death and have everything in place. When you kill him you should be able to get out of South Africa the same day. Be sure to be generous to your South African brothers of the ANC, we may need them in the future."

Gisele as moderator, "We will have a video link to each player in Las Vegas set up when they get there. That should be in no more than two days. The game commences the day after everyone's arrival. When they get to their room, each player will be greeted by a videoconference from Azizi. From that point on we'll leave it to Agnon. Agnon, we are asking you to take the position of continuing the game, but limit the tournament to two days not three. All the other players we'll want to continue except Nori, Azizi's cousin, he's probably closer to Azizi than we think. If that's not enough players, let the game terminate. Advocate playing the game even in the worst of circumstances but if you have to get another player back off. We still would have accomplished getting our three adversaries in Las Vegas. All we really care about is Auckland. We have to keep him in Vegas one extra day with or without the tournament. José and I have conferred and Auckland fancies himself as a ladies man. Bill, like we said earlier, it's your job to set him up. He usually likes multiple women but confine him to one. That'll make it easier for us to control the situation. His medical records show he has high blood pressure. After you drug him and his companion I'm sure your little medical kit contains something able to cause an untraceable heart attack. Its better if we don't have to kill her just make sure she doesn't have the capacity to remember anything other than being in bed with him. Try to set it up that when she wakes up he'll still be on top of her but dead. How long do you think you need to interrogate him? José you said you needed to be part of the interrogation, so later I'll let you guys set it up. We have connections with the Las Vegas coroner's office. But Bill, let me express it as strongly as I can, I don't want to use him unless necessary. Matt we will have you in Florida in a very visible game while this is going on. We're sending BiBa a new client, his name is Stephan Bradford, and he's a high roller. He will keep her invisibly busy for three days in Las Vegas, while we go after Auckland. Everything will be kept at Caesars Palace that's a good cover for her. We'll have redundant stories and alibis for each of you. You will be extremely visible and easy to trace. Our expectations are Auckland has no knowledge of the terrorist attacks but we can't leave loose ends. Bill will talk to him and find out what he knows and we'll go from there. If he knows something we'll be in a better position and if he doesn't it's definitely a warning to whoever's involved. One way or another, we will get to this executive committee, they're only seven members. We'll only have to apply unaccustomed pressure and these executives will break. It seems like we have a handle on Las Vegas. Let me change the subject again, we don't have a handle on Al Bin. We must get more information on where he is. He's underground somewhere in Pakistan or Afghanistan. When this whole thing is over we want to terminate him. I think maybe we have underestimated him and I don't want him to kick us in the stomach."

"Is everyone fine with all of this? If you want to talk to me or José just stay in the call. Alvarez, after you prepare Azizi and set up the video cast of his death tie me in to it. I'll make sure the video is edited properly. Then we will send it to our Arab banker friends. Bill, you set up the time and interrogation for Auckland and his companion. Malique you stay in South Africa and clean up whatever you must. We don't want any loose ends on any of these connections. The end-game is information. Either we get it from Auckland or we use him to obtain it from the other tobacco CEOs."

-----o-----

Each Caesars Palace game player received a video call from who they thought was Azizi relating his grief and doctor's orders to stay in South Africa for health reasons. His apology was tempered by the fact that all participants' expenses would be covered by his generosity.

The imposter playing the Azizi role ended each conversation saying, "I will cover expenses of the next game, future destination to be determined," then profusely apologized again. Agnon followed each call with one of his own seeking an affirmation as to the game's continuance. All the players, even Azizi's cousin Al Nori, said the competition was not only appropriate but they looked forward to resuming the no limit, high stakes game playing tradition.

Operation Leopard was now in motion. Electronic devices were placed in the three tobacco executive's rooms, whores were selected and prepared for their work, and an interrogation room was set up down the street at the MGM Grand Hotel. Medical cocktails for sedation and interrogation were cooked up under the supervision of Bill. Everything was in place.

Auckland landed at Las Vegas McCarran Airport at 6pm. His private jet made the three hour flight from Chicago and put down at the private North end airport complex. The 56-year-old CEO was met by a beautiful hostess and stretch limo.

As he walked down the steps of the twelve passenger jet, the hostess said, "My name is Laurie Wilson. May I take your hand luggage? We've made all the arrangements you requested. As a Caesars Palace favorite guest, I was told to inform you any request will be honored. We will be there in fifteen minutes, Mr. Auckland. We'll use the private elevators so you won't be inconvenienced. Your request for an escort tonight has been honored, of course, and she is awaiting your arrival."

She handed him a cell phone and continued, "I am on your speed dial. If you have any requests just press one. Your party has chosen Caesar's Palace and may I say we are very appreciative of you and your friend's patronage."

She opened the vehicle door of the limo that would whisk the tobacco executive to the hotel. When they arrived they were taken to the back elevators of the hotel for privacy. Ms. Wilson wished him a happy stay. "I will leave you on your own, again there's nothing too much for us at Caesars."

As customary with special guests of Las Vegas major properties, Auckland was taken to his suite by an entourage of young extraordinarily good-looking women. Once they reached his room door he told the women he no longer needed their services and began to pull his shirt from his slacks and started to unzip. Before he got to the expansive suite's living quarters, he called in his gruff narcissistic manner to his waiting whore.

"Get over here and help me get this shit off," he said. "I want a shower before we fuck."

Bill had informed her about the client's rough sexual habits and said, "For the money it will be well worth it."

She said, "I will set the ground rules for the amount of violence and abuse and physical punishment."

The last words of her phone conversation with Bill were, "It's no big deal. I'll have no problems with your friend. I assure you I can take care of myself."

In truth Auckland's bark was worse than his bite and he had no police record of physically abusing any of his sexual toys.

Bill finished the last part of the conversation by saying, "Whatever his verbal and emotional outbursts, it sounds like you can deal with it. I think he will just piss and moan a lot. However, if things get real rough, call hotel security. They know you're there. I have informed them of our arrangement and they'll make sure nothing gets out of hand. Look, I know this is your business so I will back off from here. I'm just a middleman getting paid to help a client."

The striking six-foot one inch African-American beauty who had been lying naked face down on the master bedroom king size bed of the complex got up and walked through the living area doors and found a disgusting looking, out of shape half naked man holding his penis with his pants down to his ankles. He was walking towards the master bathroom.

She looked at him and said, "Before you get that thing out and are ready for me, not only will you wash it, but you're going to hear me out. I will fuck you, blow you, let you put it anywhere you want, I'll take all the verbal abuse you got, but if you think you can put a hand on me I'll kick your fat little white butt. Is that understood? I'll use my black Cleopatra ass to take you places you never dreamed of, but if you mess with me big boy that little penis will be cut in half and I will pull your balls out of your scrotum sack. Is that clear?"

Auckland for the first time in his life had been one upped. Her sheer beauty and the deep black color of her skin high-lighted her physical stature. Her six foot one frame with large breasts that were capped off by silver dollar sized nipples had him in a state of total submission. He almost came in his hand with the anticipation of fucking her. She slowly walked across the room as he was holding his throbbing penis and she helped him take off the rest of his clothes. They entered a large sunken tub where they made love for more than two hours. Auckland was experiencing the first of three days of fucking before his imminent death.

Bill having total electronic eyes and ears on the sexual escapade said to Alvarez weeks later, "Man, if you have to go, what a fucking way to play out your final hand."

-----o-----

Auckland was sitting next to his black beauty, and realized he had never heard her name. He was too lazy, only interested in the sex and decided not to pursue it.

"I'm going to order from room service," he said, "do you want anything?"

Food came up to the room by 10:30pm. After eating she suggested a shower.

"Look my lovely," he said, "I've never had sex like this before. But that don't give you the power to tell me when to clean up or not. By the way I'm paying for your pussy not your opinion. I have always had multiple women and you were right when you said you would take me to places I couldn't imagine. But I can't take you out of this room, imagine that!" he said. "I have appearances to uphold and I can't be seen with a black bitch. Everything we do we do here in the room. Don't expect anything else from me except my money."

She held back her temper and said, "I've already been paid. I don't need any more money from you. As long as you don't put your hands on me or try to hit me I'm cool with just being in the room with you. So sure, I don't have to be seen with you in public. That's fine with me. And by the way I don't need no date. I've been paid to stay here for three days with you so just send up room service. That's all I need."

Auckland responded, "I usually sleep by myself but wrap those long black legs around me until I fall asleep. Then get to your own room. I'll come in tomorrow morning. Make sure you're washed up and that your pussy smells good."

She laid next to him knowing she was in total control. He was not as bad as Bill had said. He was tame compared to many of her past street clients. She was thankful she was no longer an Atlanta street walker. Now she only worked in the best hotels in Las Vegas.

-----o-----

His Caesar's card playing was not the animated sessions marking his usual participation. Auckland confided to Denton that he was more interested in the sex with a black bitch than the prospect of taking money from a bunch of rag heads or tobacco executives. He almost seemed indifferent after each five hour playing session. During breaks he would go up to his room and fuck his black beauty, as he called her, before the next round of play would start.

Denton was familiar with his braggadocio mannerisms when it came to women but going upstairs and having sex during the break was even over the top for

Auckland. The two days of uninterrupted play were monitored by Bill.

Kasogi held the game together as everyone felt the event's ineptitude. There was something missing. It could have been the Azizi's absence or the Auckland indifference, it made no matter because all participants were basically a wash when it came to their winnings. After two competition days, they were tired and wanted to call the game. The event's circumstances had cast a pall on the Las Vegas card playing.

Auckland informed his two tobacco associates of his plan to stay one more day with the finest piece of ass he had ever had. They were relieved to be homeward bound without the prospects of flying home with their narcissistic capitalist associate.

"What a reprieve," Denton mentioned, "Not having to be with that prick, Auckland, for one more moment."

"It must be karma for the two days of lousy cards," he thought to himself.

"I will just write this off as bad luck that extended past our friend Mohamed Azizi to us," said Player.

Auckland did not even say goodbye after the last hand.

He just said, "Well boys I'm going up to my room and getting into that black pussy until it kills me. Gentleman it's been a pleasure," as he cashed in chips.

Later those words, 'until it kills me', were reflected upon as being prophetic by his two former associates. Auckland opened the suite door with the anticipation of being greeted by his black Amazon.

"I'm here," he yelled. He started to undress as he talked as if she were waiting for him in the other room. "I can't believe that fucking game is finally over and I just about broke even. That usually never happens to me, I always make money playing against these losers. Just stay there on the bed he yelled. I'll be there in a second."

He took a quick shower and ventured into the master bedroom. As he opened the door he saw a still naked figure on the bed face up as if she were looking at the ceiling. Before he figured out the situation two men grabbed him. He was in a state of complete nakedness as he was thrown down to the floor.

Bill stood over him. He looked at the stupefied tobacco executive and said, "She's not dead but you will be."

He pointed to one of his men to bring in the medical kit so he could administer his handmade cocktail.

"Listen you miserable fuck," Bill said as Auckland shit himself. "No one gives a damn about you alive or dead. You are not going to make it out of this room but you can make it easier on yourself, a fast quick death versus me torturing you for hours. I don't care which one. I've got all day but you will tell me what I need to hear."

Auckland had no idea to what Bill was making reference or why he was in such a terrifying situation. He pleaded for his life, he begged, he offered to pay Bill any amount of money. He had no comprehension of why he had been assaulted and was now being drugged. There was a deep desperation in his voice. A terrifying thirst took over. His mind was racing to calculate what was happening to him. The fear and thirst paralyzed his every thought. He had no comprehension what these men wanted and had no means of meeting their information request.

Sobbing, trying to digest Bill's ever present proclamations, Auckland went into shock and passed out.

When he awoke tied to a chair in a state of semi-consciousness, everything was a visual blur. There was no physical pain but Auckland was in a state of mental paralysis. Bill was cautious not to leave any signs of physical foul play. The truth serum Bill had administered made Auckland's face flush and warm. He appeared to be in the middle of an out of body experience. Bill was standing over him and Jose was on the TV. monitor. He did not understand why he was being tortured and what Bill and Jose were talking about. He had no knowledge of the terrorist attack on New York or any other tobacco activities that threatened the world agreements on drugs and terrorist associations. Bill was at a blank wall and changed his line of questioning and pressed Auckland for information on the American Tobacco Institute.

"Yes, yes," he screamed. "I am on the committee. I'm the vice chairman of the finance committee. No, I'm not aware of the accounting for all of our marketing expenses."

Question after question on the internal workings of the Institute only generated oversimplifications. Auckland's approach to management decision-making was evidently that of delegation for he had no knowledge of the institute's specific inner workings. Auckland was not a micromanager. He was not privy to any organizational line decisions. He was a generalist acting as a symbolic figurehead approving all his immediate subordinate's decisions. He did not prepare or study any position papers leading to business activities. He was in effect a blank check for whoever was behind the terrorist plot. After three hours of interrogation Bill set up the room for Auckland's death. He prepared a new cocktail of barbiturates that would cause a massive heart attack. Once Auckland was dead he was cleaned up and placed on his companion. The cocktail she had been administered was a Rufalin category drug that would suspend her memory for at least three hours.

The john, Auckland, was dead lying naked on top of her when she awoke. She called the front desk in desperation.

Caesar's Palace like all major gaming corporations followed the letter of the law in the most discreet way. Internal security was at the scene in a matter of moments. The Las Vegas Police Department and paramedics were in the suite within twenty minutes. The coroner's office and medical examiners were on site within thirty minutes; all legal, all clean and all quiet. A guest died, a whore made money and Las Vegas was no worse for the incident. It was as if nothing out of the ordinary had happened.

The event was played out on a video for Guzman. It would later be sent to the other members of the American Tobacco Institute executive committee as a warning of Operation Leopard's resolve. One down Guzman told Gisele. He was clear on this point. They would die. All of the committee members, complicitors or non-complicitors would pay with their lives.

-----o-----

"Okay," Matt said to Frederic, "I see Auckland is dead," making reference to Bill's activities, "Now what?"

Frederic replied, "The good thing is BiBa was totally out of the picture and you were here in South Beach. As for Jose and Bill's interrogating Auckland, it didn't amount to very much information, but that's what we expected. Auckland's death only made the small print of the paper. Maybe a two line obituary. No one really cared about the SOB. He has a sister and she was notified but seemed really reticent to get involved in bringing his body back to Chicago. She finally acquiesced when the hotel said it would pay for the shipment of the corpse. Talking about the hotel, Caesar's Palace followed proper procedures and the police are satisfied that he died a natural death. The coroner's office expedited a death certificate that has the cause of death as cardiac arrest. As for the prostitute the cocktail of barbiturates Bill gave her produced temporary amnesia. She's a non-factor. She's just happy as hell to get out of there, she was compensated really well. Bill's electronics allowed us to videotape the interrogation.

We will use it later to intimidate the other members of the American Tobacco Institute's executive board. We're no closer to the responsible party of the planned terrorist attacks, but as José said, 'one down.' I'm making reference to his scorched earth policy of killing all of them if they're involved or not. He doesn't say it but this is what he did in Mexico and he feels it's necessary to make sure it never happens again. Denton and Players, the other tobacco CEO's who were there, are no longer targets. You can thank your relationship with BiBa for saving their lives. We didn't make the statement in Las Vegas we hoped but shit happens and we eliminated one target. Hey, that's more than ten percent, that's not a bad start if you look at things through Guzman's eyes. I think you said to me once, answers always surface if you have enough time and South Africa extended our time frame. José wants to pressure the other American Tobacco Institute committee members but we will hold off for at least thirty days. That way there's no tie in with Auckland."

"José, Gisele, and I will have a clearer operational plan for what must be done in a few days. Matt, I'll see you tomorrow at 11:00am. I'll get your ass on the court. It is just a matter of time fat boy. You were lucky as hell the other day," as he laughed knowing Matt was a much better player.

"See you tomorrow," ended the conversation.

-----o-----

PART V

MIAMI, FLORIDA

At 9:00am Matt answered the ringing phone. "Did I wake you?" asked Frederic. "Not really, I'm just being lazy before I go exercise."

"I have to cancel the game today. One of our investment partners called for a meeting at 11:30am. It's set-up at the Ritz-Carlton, the one near you on Collins Avenue. How about I meet you for lunch around 2:00pm?"

"Hmmm, Frederic, you know my schedule. I don't have plans."

"I'm really sorry but some of our investment partners, a group called Capital Solutions, out of New York a Morgan Stanley offshoot asked for a meeting. I've never talked to you about our partnerships or your holdings but I'm always in communication with your LA lawyers. They'll be representing us as well on the videoconference I put together this afternoon."

"I guess more attention from me would be in order."

"You have never asked any questions about any of your investments so I just figured you're okay with everything we've done so far. I can set up a feed in my office if you want to see what we're doing."

Matt said, "Why break tradition? Both José and I trust you. We figure it's your job, that's good enough for us. By the way, are you sure there's a meeting or is this just your way of getting out of racquetball? You still have to be pissed about how badly I beat you. I can't believe you'd make up this meeting crap just to get out of playing today."

"Just kidding, I'll go to the gym and work out and meet you. Where do you want to have lunch?"

Frederic responded, "How about the Lincoln Mall? There's an outdoor restaurant called DeLuca. It's right next to the Miami Beach Community Church. You can't miss it. I'll try to get there as close to 2:00pm as I can."

Matt said, "I'll see you there."

The e Lincoln Mall was in the old South Beach district. Its 1930's Art Deco architecture was reminiscent of Shanghai China. Many historians compared the two districts and held them as examples of better times in both countries.

The two men met at 2:00pm Frederic was dressed in an Armani suit, Prada shoes and wearing a Petite Philippe watch. His garb and professional look were new to Matt.

Coming directly from the gym, Matt was wearing a pair of jeans, T-shirt, and flip-flops. He was carrying an Adidas gym bag he put down as soon as he got to the table.

Frederic said, "How you doing?

"Not bad."

"We've got to do something about what you're wearing. There's a Bank of America at the corner of Lincoln and Washington. After lunch, its set up I got you an ATM card dedicated to a checking account with one hundred thousand dollars in it. The password is 4747 for Isis. She saved Osiris. I think that's what BiBa is going to do for you."

Matt actually turned red faced.

Frederic continued, "Anyway, your limit is fifteen hundred dollars a day. If you want to change it, let me know. After we eat we're going to get you some new clothes and for sure we're getting rid of that ratty old gym bag."

"That's my old buddy. Heh, heh."

"Wherever you got your clothes, South Africa or wherever, they have to go. We want you to dress more upscale. Appearances are important. I also got you a mall credit card. If the stuff around here isn't good enough we can go to the Aventura Mall. It's all upscale, you know, Hugo Boss, Burberry, Faconnable, that kind of stuff."

Matt reluctantly said, "Sure."

The day was too nice to argue with an old friend. During the three hours spent eating and shopping, not one word about Operation Leopard or tobacco crossed either man's lips.

Finally as they walked past the Soprano Café, Frederic said, "Let's stop here and have some coffee."

"It's pretty late in the afternoon."

"If you feel like a drink, that's fine by me."

Both men ordered the house Cuban Mojitos and for almost twenty minutes their discussion of the Miami Heat carried the moment.

Finally Frederic said, "We should talk about something important. I mentioned yesterday, we're at a standstill with regards to Las Vegas and tobacco. The other side must make another move sometime soon to keep up the momentum for a terrorist threat. For now they are probably just retrenching, figuring out what to do next. José thinks the connection with government operatives and the Christian right from Texas is definitely at the heart of all this.

Matt asked, "Is that where we need to focus? What do you think?"

"That's probably where we need to concentrate our efforts. That Texas Senator, James Richardson, and a guy named Ghram Winningham are links to the New York terrorist threat. I think, I should say I know Jose has an unconventional plan to get them both. I won't go into details, let's just put it this way. If he must, to get information, he will do stuff that doesn't happen in the United States. We will pressure the politicians and at the same time have totally backed off the American Tobacco Institute's executive committee. If they don't feel threatened, we think some point in the future they are so arrogant they'll try to proceed with their plan. Maybe just another machination but they're so greedy, if they think profits are in it for them they will cause some type of terrorist incident."

"How about the money trail?" Matt suggested.

"They're still throwing around money to every outside contractor they can and they are even trying to buy some European government information trying to find what happened to Al Bin and why things fell apart in South Africa. They are baffled."

"Is there any other area where they show their colors?"

"There is some grumbling about someone approaching the Las Vegas Police Department but they haven't pieced everything together yet about Auckland. Our sources say the committee doesn't know why things are coming unglued and the terrorist attack failed to get traction. It might be either Homeland or tobacco but someone is showing some interest in Auckland. Somebody thinks his death was too coincidental to the New York attack's falling apart. There have been some inquiries to the coroner's office about his heart attack. They have nothing but air. They're swinging at ghosts. We want to put pressure on the Texas Christian right and set off alarms. Jose wants to place a noose around the Christian's or Homeland Security's neck and every time either one feels pressure they will try to distance themselves from tobacco. He wants to break up their alliance. It's counterintuitive, the harder they try to distance themselves the easier it will be for us to follow their connections and relationships. It all starts with Senator James Richardson and Willingham."

"As usual there is one more thing," Frederic said, "If you are going to stay here in South Beach, you need a social life. I'm setting up a doubles match for us with some pretty outrageous women. One is nationally ranked and the other is a former tennis player from the University of Miami. They will be good competition for us. They might not be in your class, giving you a compliment is so stupid on my part, but they're really good for women."

Matt chimed in, "Really?"

"I guess I haven't lost my sexist attitude, have I? If it works out you have a companion to be seen with. Anyway if it's not one of these two then you should start dating soon. If you're not seen with female companionship here in South Beach, you'll be seen as gay. In itself that's not a bad thing but here, it's a complication we don't need. The gay community is too close-knit and gossipy. As long as you live in South Beach you are on gay community periphery and there will be scrutiny and that's not in the cards. If you don't have a woman, every social network, every work related reference; these guys will seek you out because they think you're gay. We just don't need it. So you're going to be seen with some female."

Matt interrupted, "That is the last thing I need. I have whored around the world for three years. I finally meet BiBa and feel I have a chance of being all right and you tell me I need to be seen in public with women. My marriage was wrong, the last three years have been wrong, and if I stay here long enough this will feel wrong. You want me to have a girlfriend, that's not for me old buddy."

Frederic said, "This is not what is good for you, this is about us. Look, you don't have to fall in love with anyone. You just have to be seen in public with a woman. Her name is Linda. If it doesn't work out with her, we'll find somebody else. But you have to at least have a social companion that's seen with you. We can make it a weekly outing at the sports Club, I don't care. You just have to be seen with somebody."

Matt said, "You're pretty sure about the setup aren't you."

Frederic replied, "This is the best I can come up with. She's cool, you got to trust me. It'll be just the four of us playing social racquetball if that's all you want. We just don't need any trouble. Oh yeah, you won't believe how outrageous they both are. I got to get going. I have to make money. I'm more than just a social orchestrator, I'm a financial wizard and you're my beneficiary. See you at the club tomorrow. You're rich now. We fixed you up at the B of A. Frederic handed Matt the card. You got money. All you need now is a woman. It won't be so bad."

-----o-----

Both Linda and Sophie were world-class athletes. Linda, a tennis player, and Sophie was an alternate on the US gymnastics team in floor exercise at the London games. They were in their late twenties and both had rock hard bodies. Matt was amazed at how attractive both women were for their size. They were both about five feet, ten inches tall and muscular, maybe in the hundred and forty pound range. They were both vigorous followers of the P90X training regimen for athletes. Matt felt a little embarrassed about his overweight body but this would be just another incentive to get back his body of three years ago. Both women felt their athletic performance could only be enhanced by training and it was something they did vigorously for an hour and a half every day. For Sophie it translated into a higher national rating on the racquetball circuit. They both felt being physically fit led to better emotional and mental health. It has made them more well-rounded as human beings.

As Linda said after the introduction, "Racquetball and working out isn't all I do, but I love it."

Frederic suggested he team up with Sophie and Matt and Linda would partner up. It was evident both women came to the club not for the social scene but to use the sport facilities. They had similar features; both were tall, athletic, brunette hair, and hazel green eyes. On many occasions they had been mistaken for sisters. Linda had softer features of the two, lower cheekbones and the base of her nose was more rounded. They were a pair to behold. It was evident to the two women this was not a date, it was an athletic competition. This made Matt feel more at ease.

Linda's immediate notice of Matt's somewhat out of shape condition set her a little askew about wanting to play doubles.

That changed in a matter of moments when she saw how athletic he was. It was evident how alive his right arm was as soon as he hit his first kill shot. He had lost twenty pounds and needed to lose twenty more. He had not lost the power of his golden right arm. Some athletes are considerably stronger or have more torque or a better swing plane than others and therefore have much more power. Matt was one of these extraordinary athletes.

Her first impression of him was no discipline, looking at his love handles and soft stomach through his T-shirt. The extra twenty pounds made him look meaty. This initially was a turnoff. Frederic was in better shape but he had very little muscle definition.

Both women asked themselves why they were here. Sophie's impression of Frederic ran similar to the point of Linda's impression of Matt. All this would change as the game proceeded. It was evident Frederic was the worst of the four players but Sophie and Linda were not in Matt's league.

His court knowledge and the drive of his forehand ferocity set him apart from the others. His pinch shots off the front wall, his ability to pull the ball off the floor on the backhand side, the easy way he drove the ball and more importantly his ceiling play. It was evident he had been a top player. His footwork was unusual for his size. He had both quickness and speed.

Frederic was a different story. He was at best an average club player but he extended himself to his best athletic abilities. They played three games, with the predictable results of Matt and Linda winning. It was competitive in a gentlemanly way. Linda noticed Matt tried to protect Frederic by lying off his backhand and only putting it on the ceiling to his forehand. She liked how he protected his friend.

Sophie was so bold to say, "I really enjoyed this. But to be truthful after seeing you guys when we came in I misjudged how good you'd be and how much fun this would be. I guess that says a lot about first impressions."

As they stood outside the court in the main lobby Matt put his hand on Linda's shoulder and said, "Thanks. I don't know how to say this without sounding like a real sexist but this is the first time I played with women and you two are really, really good. I can't play any better than I did today and I know both of you can."

"Man, this was really fun." Linda said, "Thanks, it was great."

"Frederic told me we were going to play doubles and in reality I hate doubles but I really had a good time. This is not what I expected, but it's been a real pleasure." Matt added.

Frederic smiled and said, "I don't want to say it but there's a tradition here at the club, losers buy lunch."

He looked at Sophie and Linda, "How would you guys feel about having lunch with us after we clean up."

"Sure." Sophie said looking at Linda. "We'll meet you downstairs and if you like we'll walk over to the Lincoln Plaza, it's near by. There are some real nice restaurants or we can sit outside and listen to some Salsa music."

She smiled and continued, "We'd love to have lunch. If you guys don't mind there's a place called Sosta's. I have a number on my cell. I can call and make reservations. We'll meet you guys in twenty minutes. I'll tell them we'll be there in half an hour.

The two men and two women went to their respective locker rooms to shower.

Sitting at the outdoor café they all agreed they would play again, maybe changing the teams up after two or three sets. It seemed out of place but Linda yawned and said in a real competitive way, "Maybe it's better if Matt and I don't play against you guys. It's not fair," and then she laughed.

When Matt's meal came to the table it looked disgusting. It amounted to what he called an all nonwhite diet.

"No carbs, no sugar," this is painful he said. "I guess I'm paying the price for letting myself go. I have already lost twenty pounds and there are only twenty more to go and then you're all in big trouble." He looked at Frederic and continued, "What will you do when you can't call me fat boy anymore? Today I was lucky but in six to eight weeks you'll see a new me."

Linda looked at Matt and said, "It's pretty evident you're very athletic. If you don't mind my asking why did you let yourself go? It's always harder to shed the weight the second time around than not gain it in the first place. I don't want to sound insensitive but I've never been heavy so going through the process of being on a diet doesn't make sense to me."

Frederic jumped in, "Matt's part of my financial team and we sent him to Spain and France and then on the way back New Orleans. I think he ate his way through his trip. Now I'm just kidding, he can speak for himself but he did gain weight out of country being away so long. I hate to give him a break because it's so much fun cracking up on him, but he was gone a long time. We have a closed end real estate hedge fund that focuses on foreign investment. Matt's our away guy. I'm not trying to make excuses for him but I think fatso," Frederic roared a belly laugh, "paid a price of making money for the firm."

Frederic apologized for interrupting and Matt chimed in without a break in the sentence.

"We are into buying distressed properties overseas and to tell the truth I just got caught up in a culture and was undisciplined."

He looked at Linda and said, "You're right I'm paying the price as he cut into a piece of grilled chicken. I'm a numbers guy; you know compulsive, work and food, not a great combination. The work wasn't glamorous but the economy is turning around and we want to be active in the market. The food was great though."

As if he caught himself he said, "This must be a boring conversation. It is set around my eating habits and my work. Linda, what do you do?"

She said, "I run an art gallery for probably the best photographer on the East Coast. His name is Paul Lester. In fact," she said, looking directly at Matt, "The gallery is right down the way. It's about two blocks from here on the Mall. If you have some time I can walk you over there after we're done eating. We do really well, when you see the place I think you'll know why. I think he's great. Besides running the gallery I'm always on the lookout for new talent. There's a kid from South Africa his name is Shawn Walkin. He is the next big thing. I'm negotiating to get some of his wildlife pictures in the gallery. There's a lot of money in photography and the new trend is black and white. Wait until you see the kid's stuff, it's just fabulous. I think what makes our owner, Lester's, photographs so striking is their size and all the new canvases and paper types he uses. Most of Lester's are on a crystallized photo paper. I'm just kind of running at the mouth, but you'll see."

Sophie started to laugh and said, "Your gallery and his food sound like the highlights of your lives."

The four of them realized it was a good day when new friends could compete as well as laugh at each other. As in all groups of more than one a selection process created the result of Sophie pairing with Frederic and Linda pairing with Matt.

-----o-----

Matt and Linda left the table saying goodbye before heading to the Lester Gallery.

Frederic asked Sophie when the four of them would play again. "You set it up. I'm sure Matt and I can make it any time convenient for the two of you. I didn't get a chance to say much at lunch other than picking on fatso," he laughed, "but I had a really nice time today. I'm looking forward to seeing you again. I have to get back to the office."

"It was a really nice afternoon," she said.

As Matt entered the gallery he knew exactly what Linda was talking about. He was looking at some of the most extraordinary photographs he had ever seen. The gallery's walls were bejeweled with the most beautiful still life photos. A 6 x 8 foot photo of the Grand Canyon, a 3 x 5 foot vertical photograph of a small atoll or outcropping in Tahiti, the most beautiful picture of a banyan tree emoting pure wisdom, these were but three of a collection of thirty spectacular photos. The one that struck his fancy most was an African elephant pressing its head against a tree in a sepia tone format. He looked at her and said, "I know why you love this place. This guy is amazing. I did not come here to buy art. I only came here to be with you and extend a wonderful day but, I want the elephant. No discounts, whatever the price is, I want it. I even want the frame."

He handed her the credit card Frederic had given him earlier and said, "Try this." He smiled.

"Matt," she said, "I didn't bring you here to buy anything, I am overwhelmed. If you are trying to impress me all I can say is this is over the top."

He smiled and replied, "I thought my game impressed you? I'm certainly not trying to buy your favors for a few bucks. I really like the elephant. It kind of makes a statement, doesn't it? Come to think of it, you can lighten up on the court until I lose some weight. Just kidding, I really do love the photograph. Someday I'll show you some of mine. I spent some time in South Africa. I just take pictures and certainly don't fancy myself as a photographer but I do have some good ones. Just wrap the guy up for me. I live a couple blocks from here if you don't mind I would like to take it home. I'm tall enough to put it under my arm so it's no inconvenience at all. And by the way, I would like to have a chance to play racquetball again. Are you up for it maybe later this week?"

"Sure," she said. "Thanks for a great day and I really didn't expect you to purchase any of our art. I think you are a person of many surprises."

He laughed again and said, "You have no idea. Really I didn't expect to have such a nice morning and I can't believe it turned into an afternoon. I never thought I would go on a binge and buy something for my place. I surprise myself sometimes too," as he smiled.

Matt slowly walked along Collins Avenue with the picture under his arm. He was conflicted. He had met another normal woman. He would develop a cover by seeing her but wanted to make sure he would not get close and complicate his life.

Just as Frederic had laid things out, he mumbled to himself, if he needed a woman as cover, she would fit the bill. He needed a destination to go to every day. He would venture to Frederic's office each morning and do research hour after hour trying to determine relationships within the American Tobacco Institute, the political right and Homeland Security. He would play racket ball twice a week. Being a person of habits and feeling comfortable following a daily pattern he crafted a mental picture of his new life in South Beach. He would work out every morning, including a jog along the strand behind the hotels off Collins Avenue. He would go to Frederic's office at nine o'clock each morning and he would play racquetball two days a week with Linda, Sophie, and Frederic.

His diet would have him down to 195 pounds in forty-five to fifty days. This would all bide time until Guzman needed his services. His office work would be dedicated to disentangling the tobacco relationships and following their money. He would leave Frederic to his financial dealings while combing all the information Gisele relayed to him. He believed in the adage, all answers to important questions surface, it's only a matter of time and effort. It appeared that Operation Leopard had time and he certainly didn't mind putting in the effort.

-----o-----

After a few weeks Matt fell comfortably into a platonic relationship with Linda. His daily exercise regimen, going to the office and delving into the inner workings of tobacco and Homeland and playing racquetball set well with his compulsive personality.

Linda called early on Thursday morning and asked, "Could you stay for lunch after the game today?"

"Sure," he said, "I'll make room. I'll clear out whatever I have to on my schedule, the afternoon is yours."

He didn't know if this was going to be a complication in his life but he felt he owed her. It was only a few short weeks but a friendship had been forged. The match that day was Matt's best competitive effort. He won three sets, even though he didn't put a goose egg on her score the extra weight loss and working out every morning was paying dividends. They decided after cleaning up they would walk over to Paul's Café.

Once seated, in a serious tone, Linda said, "You don't know me other than racquetball and that's fine. I don't need or want a relationship but I've got to ask you something."

He was puzzled. He had a premonition it might be something about his cover, Matt was attentive, all ears. His stomach was churning. He didn't know his feelings. Before she could get a word in he nervously said, "It's kind of different for me having a female partner. Especially when she's as good looking as you are. I'm sure you have some questions about me but let me just say something; I'm not gay if that's what this is about. I'm not married. It is nice having a non--

threatening relationship at this time in my life. So if that's what this is about I got it off my chest. Go on; ask me, what you need to know."

Then she hesitated. "I said you didn't know me. I call it my straight talk. Everybody else calls it my pain in the ass speak. Maybe it's a weakness but I'm really curious, so I have to ask."

He looked at her and said, "Go on, the floor is yours. I'll answer any question. Knowing me the way I do, I'm pretty close vested about personal things, but I will try. I usually don't offer up myself," smiling he continued, "but you are a special case," and grabbed her hand.

"Okay, okay," she said, "this isn't easy but. This is hard for me because I'm usually so much more straightforward. Here I go. Why the plastic surgery? It's a great job. I mean a really great job. I've been trying to figure it out, is it the work of Whitefield in Los Angeles? It's so good I can't complement you enough. It's really clear that you were good looking before, if you would like I will back off, but, why?"

Matt was stupefied and said so. "This is the last thing I ever expected, maybe the last thing I ever wanted to talk about. But I guess I owe you an explanation."

He was good at thinking on his feet. His mind was racing a million miles an hour trying to come up with a plausible reason that wouldn't endanger his cover. He said, "Let me think of the best way to tell you then he quickly developed another story to obfuscate the truth. He was talking as he was conjuring up yet another chapter of lies.

"Shit, I can't believe you noticed. No one, I mean no one has called me on it. Let me start at the beginning. I had a real bad accident and if you don't mind I don't want to get into the particulars. Let me just say it took a couple years off my life. My face got rearranged in a mugging. Three guys robbed me and beat the crap out of me. While I was on the ground they stomped on my head. I was passed out lying facedown and some guy kept kicking me in the head, that's what some witnesses said. I had a few surgeries and believe it or not I look pretty much like I did before. I was so disturbed by it emotionally that for comfort all I did was eat and I gained forty-five pounds. In the last six months I lost twenty and I need to lose maybe twenty to twenty-five more. But losing weight is the easiest part. It's the emotional stuff, well; it's taken me almost 2 years. It took a lot of time to get past the point asking 'why me' and all that shit. I finally came out here and met Frederic through common acquaintances; you know the investment community is really small. The circle of analysts is really, really small. We all know each other. Anyhow I'm here. Let's just say it's taken me a little over two years to get back to some semblance of what I call normalcy. I'm sorry I sound so serious but you asked," and he smiled. "Now my question. How in the hell did you ever notice my face? What did you see that no one else has seen?"

She said, "I'm really sorry for being so blunt, I don't have a real good filter when I'm curious. I could not help myself. It's such a good job. To be honest, I didn't expect the truth from you. Now for the first time in my life I think I'm at a loss for words. Ah, well, my dad was a face jockey. That's what we called him. So I've been around plastic surgery my whole life. I noticed your face's perfect symmetry, especially your eye orbits. It took me three times on the court to put it together. Your face is perfect. I kept saying to myself how gorgeous you would be if you were thinner. She backed off for a second and said that doesn't mean you're not really attractive. I feel like I'm putting both feet in my mouth. Then it hit me, he had to have had plastic surgery. I just knew. If my questions about your past cut too deep I'm really sorry. It's my filter."

She continued, "Matt, I don't need a relationship either emotional or physical so I didn't ask you as a come on. To tell the truth I really do like you more than just a two-day racquetball partner or some social acquaintance. I'm not trying to hit on you."

"It sounds like we both need distance in our lives. Oh hell, it's hard for me not to be truthful. He cut in. Linda there is more. I am still in love with someone even though it's been two years since I've seen her. I guess I sound like a sniveling wimp. She only knows I had to leave her and I cut her out of my life. When I got my face caved in it was on a business trip and she knows nothing about any of this. I just left her in the cold. I couldn't tell her, I couldn't even tell my family. It was better to have them hate me than see what I was going through. At least that's what I thought. I have this stupid notion that some day I will seek her out. She will give up what ever she has and what ever she is doing. She will give it up all for me and it will all come together. Does that sound f-ing stupid or what? Anyway very soon I plan on playing out my stupid dream and see what happens. Then I can start to live again. If she takes me or if she doesn't I'll be able to live my life again. For some stupid reason I feel that's how I have to play things out, perfect isn't it?"

He wasn't proud of himself but he felt Linda bought into everything he was saying by the way she was gripping his hand. He changed the subject as soon as he could once he felt that she was comfortable with his story. As she squeezed his hand he knew the lie was complete.

"I'm getting way too serious," as he decoupled his hand from her. "Actually I like you a lot but this just makes things a lot easier for me now that it's out in the open. I hope you understand why I can't get more involved. I have to confirm my past. Hey, we are way too serious or at least I am. Let's eat. Being truthful for a change is making me hungry as hell. Shit, I might even break my diet today."

-----o-----

Matt had been working in Frederic's office for more than a month before his research found how deeply involved one of the people of interest was. The person with such deep and far-reaching relationships in Texas politics was Ghram Winningham. Citations in blogs, magazine articles, political analysis on cable TV in the South, and conservative American Morals Movement internal papers were filled with apparent random news events. In one form or another all were related to Winningham. He was a leading advocate of the Christian Right. He was a stanch supporter of the Republican Party and its stances on immigration and abortion.

The young looking, Texan was more than he appeared. His actions were as titular head of his party's reactionary zealots but he also had at his disposal large sums of unaccounted for monies. He was

38 years old and could pass for early twenties. He had an out of touch Christian look on his face. Matt remembered the inappropriateness of Preacher Phil in Los Angeles and his aggressive assertive self righteous opinions. Phil lead his flock at the Sunshine Mission on skid row in downtown Los Angeles and it amazed Matt how anyone could follow such an idiotic Charlatan. He equated the two men. Winningham the Southern Baptist whose presence in any capacity was repugnant to Matt was a powerful insider in the Republican Party. What made him all the more dangerous was the fact he was United States President, Bill Mapplethorpe's, Godson. The president's ties ran deep in Texas. He was the former governor and US Senator from Texas. His relationship to ex-President Lyndon Baines Johnson and Lady Bird Johnson's communications empire was the basis of his political support. After the death of Lady Bird Johnson his affiliation with the far right was nurtured by money from the old John Birch Society and money from the conservative Moral Imperative Foundation.

Bill Mapplethorpe's family was the pen-ultimate in Texas politics. Its conservative tentacles reached almost as deeply into Texas politics as George Bush's family which produced the 41st and 43rd United States Presidents. The President's long time friend and Press Secretary, Silvia Blum, asked President Bill Mapplethorpe if he would be godfather to their only son Ghram and hence the Christian zealot's entitlement relationship began.

He used his godfather's name and developed Christian movement relationships. His pedigree in religious circles also came from his undergraduate education at BIOLA (Bible Institute of Los Angeles) undergraduate education, Masters Degree in theology from Auburn University and a stint as an adjunct professor at the Baptist Religious Institute in Clearwater Texas. On paper he looked good but just like Preacher Phil he was so reactionary in his beliefs he was dangerous. He spoke the Christian language, he sat at the feet of men in power, and because of his political DNA handed to him by President Bill Mapplethorpe he had a voice. His fanaticism directed against immigrants in general and Muslims in particular caught favor after 9/11.

His working relationship with the present Texas Senator James Richardson made both of them people of interest to Matt. Originally he was viewed as the mastermind of the religious right but his research showed Winningham was the principal in developing the Texas Republican Party platform. He had the connections and ambitions to move to the national level and with the tacit help of his godfather he moved up the ranks quickly. His money, position, hate and loathing for Muslims were the precipitant for the planned attack on New York. None of this was scripted out but the confluence of random events, the run-a-way fanaticism and political power mongering of President Mapplethorpe led to an eye turning situation away from the actual plot to detonate a dirty bomb in New York. What made it worse for Matt was once the plot surfaced it was rationalized as acceptable. There was a sickness of self righteousness and God's will that permeated the White House, the National Security Agency, and tobacco.

Matt walked into Frederic's adjoining office. "Frederic, shit, I think I have it."

He showed him Winningham's bio and threw out the theory. "I think he is our contact between tobacco and Homeland. He hates Muslims and his funneling money to political candidates in Texas is giving him carte blanche directing political appointments through Senator Richardson. Too many in the national security agencies particularly Homeland Security are his cronies for it to be a coincidence that no one noticed Al Bin and the plot to bomb New York."

Matt gave him a packet and said. "These are some of his early writings."

He also gave him an annotated file on the National Security Agency and its intercepts of e-mails and phone calls intentionally overlooked by Christians in Homeland Security. There had always been rumors of Christian involvement in military hierarchy; particularly the military academies and the Air Force but now he had proof of their involvement in Homeland. Matt had sifted through all the

Intel generated by Gisele and came up with conclusive relationships between Christian ideology and Homeland's activities. It was evident Winningham's reach permeated Homeland and National Security. Matt needed Frederic's financial expertise to follow the money from the Christian Right to Homeland to tobacco.

"I think these are the funding sources for the terrorist activities. These religious freaks get to extricate their enemies, you know they're like Christians on a crusade, they think it's the fourteenth century. The military gets more money and by definition more power. Homeland is seen as the protectorate of the democracy when it tries to stop the threat and has reasons for its existence and of course if narcotics become illegal again tobacco makes billions for a twenty-seven billion dollar investment. Here's where the shit falls into place. The New York attack was directed at an all African-American neighborhood."

"In the long run, the consequences of killing blacks in conservative political circles are none as far as I can see, just more frosting on the cake. These ass holes are no different from the fucking crazy

Arab extremists. I take that back there's one difference, they're a little bit more technologically advanced and have a hell of a lot more money. They're dangerous as hell!"

-----o-----

Matt had been reticent to tell Frederic about Linda's face comments. Maybe this was a good time. After his discussion about Winningham and Senator James Richardson he would describe his conversation with Linda.

"Frederic I probably should have mentioned this when it happened. It's all covered up now."

Frederic responded, "What the hell are you talking about. You just gave me a theory on how we should approach tobacco and Homeland, some real serious heavy duty stuff and now you tell me you forgot to mention something and it's all covered up."

He related her questioning of his plastic surgery and the ensuing cover-up story. "I'm one hundred percent sure she bought it. I just feel really uncomfortable and somehow I have to get out of here. I just think my time in Miami has run its course. I need your help on this. Two heads are better than one, even if one of them is yours. No kidding, Frederic what the hell am I going to do?"

"Well the first thing for sure is," Frederic responded, "we can't tell Jose. This is real heavy duty. We have to be careful. I almost feel like a traitor on this, but we can't tell Jose. Matt to tell the truth I am pretty uncomfortable about how brutal he has been in responding to the threats to our organization. I know we look to him for leadership and we are right in doing so but deep in my gut it's hard to understand how fucking, shit I don't know, different he is than us. I think he gave you a pass on BiBa. I don't know what the hell he would do about Linda. I don't even want to find out. So old buddy this is between you and me. Shit, this could mean our lives. So let's not fuck this up. My advice is to talk to her. Make up some story and get out of Miami and leave it at that. I have this feeling being with Jose is kind of like a mafia thing. Once you are in you never get out. Let me rephrase that, the only way you get out is feet first if you cross him. Here's my advice again. End it, and I mean, end it soon. You've developed some stuff on Winningham so we'll figure out another place you can continue to work on it. Leave that for me."

Matt called Linda and canceled their afternoon game.

He was surprised by the conversation when she said, "I was going to call and cancel myself. But it's important we meet for drinks if you are not busy later tonight. I'm in the middle of something so I can't talk. If you'd meet me tonight, that would be great. How about 8:30pm? Ohm," making it sound like she was playing it by ear, "meet me at the Loews Hotel. I will be in the Preston Lounge."

He entered the prestigious five-star South Beach Hotel lobby and was directed to the Preston Lounge next to the sports bar. He had figured out what he was going to tell her. As form would have it, the moment he saw her and how beautiful she was in regular clothing he was at a loss for words. He walked up to her and kissed her gently on the lips as she sat at a table overlooking the hotel pool area.

She greeted him by saying, "You dress up well. You look very handsome tonight. I have a lot to say so do you mind calling over the waiter. I need a drink."

He responded, "Sounds like I may need one too."

When the waiter came over she asked for a dirty martini and Matt asked for a double Vox on the rocks.

She began, "Matt, don't say a word. Hear me out. I am at a crossroads in my life because of you. I lied to you a little bit, and it's biting me on the ass." She held out her hand to stop him from interrupting. "I'm kind of a groupie. Paul Lester is more than just the job for me. We are casual sex partners. I am his assistant and he is my mentor as far as photography is concerned. We travel a lot together we enjoy each other's company and everything is easy. Then you came along. It isn't easy anymore. My whole adult life all I've wanted to do is be a photographer and he is the best. I can't jeopardize that. I am so close to going off on my own and I am frightened at what our relationship will do to my dreams. To make it worse I don't think this is a good time for you either."

"Slow down, slow down," he said. "I'll make it easier for you. I'm here to let you know I have to leave. I have to leave soon. Some of it is because of what I told you. I am not going to be good for anyone if I don't try to resolve yesterday. But there is more. I am not really working for Frederic; it's more of a partnership. He manages my assets and I have been here for a while working out of his office. Now it's my turn to be truthful. You have literally saved me. I did not expect to find someone I could have feelings for and that is really complicating everything. I can't subject you to my crazy life. That's why I wanted to talk to you. That's why I called you this morning. We can't see each other anymore."

She tried to calm him but to no avail.

He continued, "It's just better we stop seeing each other. There are some things," he became pensive as he measured his words, "you have to agree. This ends tonight. It's the right thing to do and we both know it. There's something else, and if our friendship means anything to you, you can't say no. Frederic will contact you tomorrow. You have no choice in this."

With a blank look on her face she said, "Matt I have no idea what you're talking about. And I always have the right to say no."

"Well just hear me out then. I am funding a gallery for you. You can open it anywhere in the world. I have the money so this is the least I can do. I will front expenses for two years. The only control I want is I want Frederic to help you oversee leases and help you control the business end of it. You will have final say on everything. He will be there just to help. He has your interest at heart. If it doesn't work out in two years than the two of you will revisit why and what you can do in the future. There's one last thing, I'm a little more selfish than you'd think," he smiled. "I'm going to ask you to place my photos, remember I mentioned I took some pictures when we were looking at the elephant in the gallery. I want you to put my photos in your gallery and see if you can sell them. I guess it's a way of seeing if I deserve any recognition. It certainly is not for the money. It's important to me that you put them on the right side of the gallery when people walk in. I want to see if I am as good as I think I am. My stuff from Africa, let me temper that, some of my stuff from Africa is at least as good as, what is that guys name?"

Again he smiled knowing full well that she knew he had Paul Lester's name etched in stone in his memory. He stood up and leaned toward her and kissed her on the lips gently as if he were kissing a cloud. "It's better. It's the hardest thing I've ever had to do in my entire adult life."

Knowing this little lie would make her feel better, Matt added, "It's just the hardest, but I have to go." He was amazed that his eyes started to moisten so he got up and started to walk off. He turned around after two steps, "Frederic will always be there for you."

She stood up and squarely looked him in the eye. "I don't need anything from you, you've given me more than I could ever have expected. All I want is to share the rest of the night with you. You're right, it won't work for us. Yesterday has a way of screwing everything up. There was a reason I picked this restaurant. I got us a room." as she handed him a key card. "Now shut up."

He smiled as he took her hand.

-----o-----

Matt and Frederic sat in the conference room of Frederic's office talking about his future. "Well old buddy, it's been great to have you here. I mean it. You know I really didn't expect to see you after the Porter incident three years ago. The last couple of months were totally unexpected. I think we both needed to see each other. How are you dealing with moving? It's going to be hard for me; it's been easy having you here in South Beach."

"To tell you the truth," Matt said, "I know I have to get out of here but you've been like an anchor to me. Shit, that's not nearly strong enough, you've always been like a brother to me and I can't thank you enough for giving me some stability."

He gave Frederic that look and continued, "The racquetball has been kind of marginal but it did pass the time of day. These have been the best few months of my new life. I owe a lot to you. After the Linda thing, and by the way it was over as of last night, I know I have to get out of here. You said once I made the decision and I could leave all the particulars up to you. Well, get cracking."

Frederic responded, "I've had things in the works for the last couple of weeks so let me sketch some things for you. We are making you a Canadian citizen. We had to prefabricate a new cover for you. This time it won't be as difficult as three years ago."

He started to get up from his chair and said, "I'll be back in a second I have a briefing book for you on Canada it's in the other room. I'm in the process of buying you a house in Toronto. It's on Embassy Row. If you want to look it up it's in the M4V2P5 zip. Some people call it the nicest area in the city."

"Do you really think that will work?"

"We are in the process of buying you a place virtually next to the British Consulate. You'll be in good company. Prince Charles uses it as his quarters when he visits the old Commonwealth. The neighborhood is quiet, obviously really expensive, it fits you perfectly. It's close enough to city center to walk there."

Matt questioned, "A great house on a short sale?"

"That says it all," Frederic continued, "Pretty much a strange transaction for this district because of its financial stability. An architect named Stephen Eskind refurbished the old French tutor mansion. He works on lots of these high-end houses and his office is nearby. He's considered to be the best restoration architect in Canada. He guts the houses and restores them to their authentic design. All the materials are original and he uses the best craftspeople in Canada. These are very prestigious houses but what you like about your new digs the most is, it's like all of the Eskind houses, it's really livable. It's on Russell Hill Road; I call it the top of the mountain. Nothing's too good for you, my friend."

"You are lucky to get in one of his projects. Like I said the previous owner had some difficulties and we purchased it on a short sale from Standard Bank. Eskind is in such demand he has a backlog of almost three years. When the house came up, it was perfect. Part of your cover will be a real estate investor who buys and holds properties. The real estate market in Toronto was minimally affected by the

2008 -- 2011 market collapse in United States. Their banks hold larger reserves and their real estate are very rarely leveraged to the same levels we are accustomed to here. The loan to equity ratio is about fifty percent. We don't see any downside to this purchase."

Frederic started to smile, "We haven't talked much about your portfolio but this is part of it now. You're paying lots of money per square foot, but I think it's a good deal. Eskind not only restored the structurally damaged part of the house he acts as the principal interior designer as well and replaced all the fixtures, the flooring, the wall fascia and he even made the furniture. Everything is to its original standards. He will be available to help you with anything in the house. You just call him, what makes it better is his wife Janet. She's a designer and she'll be there to help too, two great people. You even have friends built-in if you see fit. They are not part of our team just a lucky find for you in Toronto. We also purchased a horse farm."

Matt said, "Wait a minute."

"You don't have to do crap. It's part of your cover. It's a working farm with permanent employees. They live on the property. You have six ranch hands and two people to help you with the house. It's six hundred acres, there are twenty show horses, and an incredible twenty thousand square feet all weather stable. You won't believe the F-ing stable. It must've cost two million dollars Canadian. It's the size of an industrial building. It's all year-round weather proofed. It has thirty feet ceilings with incredible oak beams."

Matt, its temperature controlled and the temperature is always at sixty-seven degrees. It's got a one quarter mile walking track inside the stable. Contiguous to it are the worker's quarters. It is like a small hotel. There's a shed for all the farm machinery. It is utterly amazing."

Matt asked, "Frederic, how do you find all this stuff?"

"It just comes up," he grinned, "You don't have to get involved in the horses but you can if you want. They are for show and like I said you have permanent help with the breeding, their care, showing them, and subsequent sales. It is a moneymaking operation, don't screw it up. It's more than just cover," he laughed again, "its part of your portfolio. You can participate or not, it's up to you."

"Now for the tricky stuff," Frederic continued, "Your cover is you are a Canadian citizen. You graduated from Toronto University with a degree in finance. I have you tied into some of our investments in the United States. You've gone back to Canada because you think there are more opportunities and potentially higher rates of return in upscale residential properties not only in Toronto but in Montréal and Québec as well. All this is perfect for you. Your personality is a match for Canada. People there are honorable, soft-spoken and reserved. They cherish friendship and are really put off by arrogance or petulance. This is the old Matt, this is you."

"If you say so."

"We will set up your house with all of our best electronics. People will think you are a techie, but that is okay. I've been thinking of the war room we had in Las Vegas, something along those lines. On face we will set up everything to look like the electronics in my office just in case anybody gets nosy. I am sure when you have guests you will show off your great house.

-----o-----

"Since you'll be working directly with Gisele, Toronto will become our center for intel. Everything will flow through you and then be directed to me. It will give me a break to put more effort into the financial stuff. I hate to say it but you've done a hell of a job on this, certainly better than me."

"It's no big deal, Frederic," Matt added, "I just followed the money."

"You have some kind of knack. You'll be lead on the Intel project. Eskind does not know anything, like I said, he's not part of our team, but some of the subcontractors who come in will be. They'll place an electronic fence around the whole neighborhood, effectively making your activities black."

"Frederic, I've been thinking a lot about some of that information I shared with you on Winningham and the Christian Right. I'm trying to develop a new hypothesis. Let me just throw it by you for a second and see if it makes sense for me to put a lot more thought behind it."

"Hit me," Frederic said.

"It's very clear to me, he's crazy as hell. But everything is too clean, and no one is trying to hide any of his activities or the fact he has been dumping money around with impunity."

"Maybe, it's too warm?"

"Yeah, too hot, if you ask me. I just have this feeling deep down in my gut it's too easy."

Frederic added, "At the beginning when Gisele and I put our finger on Al Bin and all that came to light, he came off as a simplistic religious fanatic. We didn't think he could wrap his head around anything at all that was complex. We were sure he was kind of like a village idiot. Now we can't even find the son of a bitch. We totally underestimated him."

"I think Winningham's importance has been prefabricated to throw us off track." Matt continued, "I'll take the blame, I think I have overestimated the president's godson. President Mapplethorpe is a real asshole, but he is smart as hell. If he had any involvement in this he would have multiple trapdoors between him and the actual operatives who want to bring down all our relationships and criminalize narcotics again. He'd sacrifice his godson in a god damn second. And what makes it worse; he is such a fucking racist that he is not above destroying a whole black neighborhood and thousands of lives creating a national emergency to get his way."

"Wow, that's too similar to Al Bin. A second village idiot?" Frederic shakes his head, "It's just too coincidental."

"I'm not saying he was sitting around a table with his right wing buddies and came up with this idea and said, 'let's fuck some blacks and give our country a common enemy and I'll be king again' or anything like that."

"But, Frederic, he's a hate monger and all the negative chatter about Muslims can only bring him more political credibility with the fringe that put him in office. He showed how shortsighted by not wanting to decriminalize narcotics and trying to build a wall between the U.S. and Mexico. You know that Christian bull-shit. If something happened in New York or just public knowledge of a real threat came to light it would certainly solidify his re-nomination for president. I'm just throwing this out to you; I'm probably just grabbing at straws. There's just too much pointing at Winningham for him to be our guy. It's never this easy. This reminds me of the time when you and I were in Arenal, Costa Rica on that trip when we were younger."

Frederic jumped in, "That trust me, just trust me thing again."

"Yeah," Matt said, "I was so sure about the path down the volcano when it started to erupt. Remember how scared we were. We thought the pyroclastic belching was actually going to be a lava flow and ran like hell. I was so sure but so fucking wrong about our path down the volcano it could have cost us our lives. Everything is still so clear to me about running the wrong way because I misunderstood our surroundings. From that point on in my life if something is too easy I try to reassess it. And believe it or not I never use the phrase, 'just trust me', anymore."

Frederic cut in, "Let's not get going on this again. Let's just say we got out of there all right."

"Okay, okay, I guess this is my way of telling you I'm not really sure about Winningham. He might be a sacrificial lamb. I'll reflect on it when I get to Toronto. This gives me a little more time for looking into our data again, maybe come up with something making more sense."

Frederic nodded, "A little more time can't hurt."

"And by the way, thanks for understanding the Linda thing. Let her know what I said about helping her with a gallery is all true and I really do have the resources."

"Sure thing, Matt."

-----o-----

PART VI

TORONTO, CANADA

When Matt arrived at the Billy Bishop City Airport, a limo was waiting. Landing in Toronto was a pleasant experience compared to the overcrowded, haphazard and oppressive Miami International Airport he just left. The five-hour flight was easy. After deplaning, walking to the baggage claim carousel, he found his luggage in the hands of his limo driver, John Smith.

John introduced himself saying, "John Smith, I will be at your service until you purchase or lease a car."

"Thanks, John," Matt marveled at Frederic and Gisele's details.

"If you need a permanent driver, Mr. Shaw, and you feel my services are adequate, that can also be contracted. Arrangements have been made for my company to help you secure any services you need here in Canada." Frederic again had worked his magic. "The drive to your home will take approximately twenty-five minutes if you want to go there directly. I would like to make a suggestion. I can give you a city tour, acquainting you with Toronto."

He sounded like an enthusiastic tour guide. "Toronto has a population of more than a million, but it is quite provincial and small town, as we call it. Hopefully you will find it as charming as I do. It is ethnically diverse. We have large populations of Chinese, Italians and people of Jewish heritage. What makes Toronto so wonderful is its history. You will come to love the city. If you don't mind," as he pulled off the freeway, "I will take you into what we call metropolitan downtown."

Matt said, "Sure, that's nice of you."

They drove twenty minutes downtown where the Toronto Blue Jay baseball stadium or Roger's Center was the city's epicenter near the waterfront with all its tourist attractions. The financial district encircled the stadium. The University of Toronto was also mid-city with its bustling student population making the area seem younger and more robust.

"All this is accessible by tube or metro," John said, "you look fit though, it's close enough for a spring walk or outing. It's walkable although it might take forty-five minutes or so but it's lovely in the spring. I just wanted you to see our fair city."

As they continued driving towards Russell Hill Road, John continued, "This way you have a better feeling for Toronto and know there is more than just its wonderful houses. I say that because your neighborhood is the ultimate of living in Toronto. Forgive me for my opinions but as my mom once said, 'everyone has one but Jonathan why do I always have to hear yours'. I guess I'm excited for you. Toronto is a wonderful place. Take advantage of it. It's too easy for many people just to stay in their beautiful neighborhood and never venture out."

As they drove through the urban heart of Toronto Matt notice how un-congested and peaceful it was for a major city. He just sat back and watched as his new environment unfolded.

He said to himself, "I needed a break, this time I'm due. Toronto will certainly meet my needs."

After settling in he received a call from both Steven and Janet Eskind, kind of a welcome wagon. He was assured, if he needed anything from sugar to advice it was there for the asking. He was also made aware they were not seeking him out as a new friend. Their houses or projects were like children to them. They wanted to make sure he knew he would have the advantage of their knowledge and resources if he wanted.

"It's kind of a personal warrantee," Steven said.

It took about a week to get used to Toronto. The quick acclimation process was noted by Matt. He had been in many places over the last three years none felt like home until Toronto. Its more temperate climate with its sweet chill in the air, the dense maple tree foliage and the wonderful brick houses on huge plots were all deeply comforting to him. The foremost attribute of the city was the civility of its people. Matt liked his new home but he had things to do. He would follow an old Arab adage, rest before work. One week of leisure led him to his war room.

-----o-----

Sitting on the couch next to his desk, hands on his head in reflection, his cell began ringing. It was Gisele.

She started her conversation with her usual greeting, "Hello Matt, how are you this evening?"

Matt's reaction to her niceties was unusual. He was neither polite nor social, as was his custom, he was all work. "Well Gisele, I am ferreting out all the information you sent and it points to Robert Marleau, the Presidential Chief-of-Staff. He is part of the Texas good old boys club. I didn't realize how entrenched these guys were until I went over all the National Security Agency e-mails and office memos of the Texas Republican house caucus. It's amazing how arrogant they are. They don't care what they say. They don't care about a paper or electronic trail or anything. It's as if they think they're bulletproof. Well, I think we got them. Just hear me out. The Christian Right, the Republican State Committee of Texas, the lobbyists on K. Street, American and Continental Aviation, and tobacco are all involved to one degree or another."

"How did you find this," Gisele asked.

"It's all that American founders bull shit. They say 'we'll bring America back to the Constitution and the purity of its Christian beginnings.' The good old boys are playing the Republican Party Christian fringe through Winningham. He took money funneled through Marleau as a tacit agreement of the anti-immigration Christian agenda. Winningham's Arab bashing enthusiasm was ripe for manipulation. He and his operatives sent money to Al Bin."

"You've always said to follow the money."

"I can prove it. Although the dirty bomb materials acquisition didn't pan out, Winningham had his hands all over it. They're really stupid lazy people. They're arrogant as hell, because evidently he didn't try to hide this stuff. All of them felt they were above the law. Once I got into their accounts and followed the money it became evident what they were trying to do to anybody with forensic accounting skills. I uncovered it."

"There must have been others involved. A president doesn't have time to handle the details." Gisele prodded.

"Marleau used some position papers and polls taken by the Enterprise Foundation in Washington and came up with a new wrinkle for the neoconservative movement. Instead of God smiling down on white Christians and their singular superiority to all other races and religions by giving them the military power to inflict their will on the global community, he is casting Christianity as an underdog in the war on terrorism. The Arabs and their Muslim faith are being depicted as the religious adversary as they were in the Crusades. And to bring home their threat he was willing to bomb New York. To garner support of all Americans no matter what creed, color or religious preference he was willing to kill thousands of people. Just so happens they are poor and black and not his type of Christian. The bomb's detonation and its response would rekindle the nationalism fervor of 9/11 and entrench Christian ideals of preservation. Any relationships, treaties, 21st century political imperatives would be abandoned for seventeenth-century Christian ideas of our founding fathers.

The Enterprise Foundation's template for the future is pure and simple intolerance of anything not white or evangelical. They have perverted our founding fathers' historical paradigms. These Christian fanatics think we were a religious state. They have no clue about the separation of church and state, they have no clue about what Jefferson, Adams, Paine, Madison or any of the founders thought about the evils of religion. They have no understanding of the Constitution and how it gave people rights. All they want to do is take people's rights away. I'm sorry, I'm digressing, I am so pissed I can't see straight."

Gisele said, "I understand completely."

"Anyway this movement was hatched in Texas. I have all the players. I have a trail on all the money sent to Al Bin in Pakistan, in Afghanistan and in South Africa. Gisele, the frightening part is I can place blame all the way to the Commander-in-Chief himself. This isn't much different than when President Johnson faked the Maddox shelling in Vietnam's Tonkin Bay to increase our military presence in Southeast Asia stopping the domino theory and communism in its tracks. It's not much different than President Bush when he tried to convince the world Saddam Hussein and the Iraqis had weapons of mass destruction. These fucking Texas evangelists are so sanctimonious and self-righteous it sickens me."

Gisele questions, "Is there something about Texas I'm missing?"

"There must be something going on there that denigrates their thinking and perverts it so much they are willing to kill thousands of people and take away all our civil rights just to spread their Christian teachings. It makes me sick."

Gisele interrupted, "I agree with everything you say. They are religious zealots. They do have the resources to get their way. It sounds like you have ironclad proof. I will help you put this into the proper format so you can present it to our team. The big question is 'what do we do with it'?"

"It is a conspiracy theory."

"No one will believe it goes all the way up to the president. No one will believe the depth of the Christian right and the

Republican Party of Texas' involvement. Worse, no one will accept all our proof. What do we do? What do you do with the truth when it's unbelievable?"

"Give me a chance to work on it, maybe we can come up with a way." Gisele suggested.

"I don't want to sound like a defeatist but we are on dangerous ground. Up to this point by thwarting the attack in New York we have slowed up their pace to undo all America's progressive foreign policy that led to a more stable global atmosphere albeit one with legal narcotics and open relationships with terrorist groups. They are willing to cast out the 21st century new world order and implement 16th-century religious notions that never existed. They are no different, from their Muslim counterparts. They have a hell of a lot of similarities."

"I will come to Toronto and help you put this into a document. I know it's not necessary with all of our electronic abilities. I can just sit here and work with you like we're doing and be on the other side of the Atlantic from you and we have a virtual office."

"Hay, we are doing it right now." Matt added. "I guess I'm old-fashioned and think I should come over and have my feet on the ground. We will work together on this in Canada. I think it will be better for both of us.

Matt wavered for a second.

"Of course," he said. "Come over here and stay as long as you like. I certainly have enough room for a guest. I don't know if Frederic has mentioned anything about my new home? It is large and I want you to feel at home here. Set up a cover for yourself as my cousin from France. How's that for being original? The Canadian either love or hate the French. You won't be noticed much. Really, I think it's a good idea. You're right. I have all this information. I am going to need some help putting it in proper form so it is ironclad. I want to get all of us on board."

-----o-----

"Yeah, I'm pretty sure I nailed down everything and you're right, the question is 'what do we do with it'?"

Gisele said, "We have to get other people listening to us. No matter what resources we have, we can't take on the President of the United States if we don't have everything nailed down perfectly. I do not doubt you. I guess I just doubt our ability to go after him."

"Two heads are always better than one."

"I'll get to Toronto in the next two days. We better call Frederic and fill him in," she continued, "You better bring José into this as soon as possible. Initially it will be the four of us."

"After we sort all the intel," Matt continued, "we'll have a full meeting. At that point we'll bring in Alvarez, Bill, Pedro, and Malique."

-----o-----

Gisele called to give Matt her schedule. "I arrive Saturday morning."

Matt suggested, "I will be picking you up at the airport myself. You can accompany me to the city center art exhibition if you feel up to it after your seven hour flight. You could clean up at the house and rest until midday and then make up your mind." He said he would be waiting for her inside of the airport. No signs needed he said, "I have seen you so many times on our conference calls I think I know every curve of your face."

Matt she said, "I travel differently. I've literally let my hair down and wear makeup. Just to be safe, I'll be in jeans and my color is burgundy."

At 8:20am Matt was waiting behind the green immigration double doors opening onto the airport's arrival lobby for international travelers. He was standing behind a thin three-tier rail with thirty to fifty people who were family, or friends, or travel associates waiting for passengers.

When he first saw Gisele he was taken aback. She looked vaguely familiar but if she had not described her travel garb he might not have recognized her. True to her words she had on jeans and a burgundy top. What she did not tell him was how skintight her jeans would be and how revealing her Theory brand fitted long sleeve shirt in burgundy plaid would be. Her hair was down and straight. It almost looked Jerry Curled, but she was not black. Her face's features were elongated because of her hair length which was now a lighter shade of brunette. She looked like Halle Barry but white and French.

Matt was so taken aback he stammered, "Gisele is that you?"

She smiled and said, "It is I. I dressed up well, yes."

She was so striking that it was a total surprise to Matt. He had a skycap attend to her luggage and followed them to his Chevy Eldorado truck.

She looked at him and his silver gray pickup, "I wouldn't have expected this," she said. "You look thinner and much more fit than I imagined." she continued as her eyes gave him the once over.

Trying not to be too obvious and avoiding direct eye contact Matt said, "I can't begin to tell you how much I misjudged you. To say you're not as attractive on-screen is a vast understatement."

They looked at each other with a different level of appreciation. No longer conference call participants from across the Atlantic.

Matt said, "Gisele we'll go by my house it's about thirty minutes from here. There you can clean up and rest. Then we can go into the city if you are up to it. I have been looking forward to an art exhibition. I think you will find it interesting. To offset jetlag, I'll try to push you until you're really tired. If we keep you up long enough, tomorrow will be easy."

She said she was game for it.

Sitting next to her in the truck he could not take his eyes off her. He felt silly. Their conversation had degenerated into small talk. It was juxtaposition to all the intelligence meetings they had participated in for the last few months. Words being thrown about like life or death, or phrases like, we have the world's future in our hands, had been commonplace at these conferences.

His chatter was directed at her beauty and how he had misjudged her.

Finally she said, "Are you coming on to me?"

He looked stunned. "No, no, I guess I'm a little nervous. I don't know why. No, I am not coming on to you. I'm a little overwhelmed by your beauty. But no, I'm not coming on to you. I don't need any more complications in my life. A few months ago I finally found a woman who is levelheaded, smart, beautiful, and everything I had kept away from my whole life. Then I met someone in Florida when I was with Frederic that would have been just perfect for me under any other circumstances. Now you, I can't believe it. In my whole life I was never with women who were good for me. I've always struggled with women and now I have met three incredible females, and by the way one is you. Any man would give anything to be with you. Go figure."

She had a strange look in her eyes and was at a loss for words, which was out of the ordinary for her.

He continued, "I don't want you to think I'm coming on to you. In truth I'd be a fool not to, you are incredible, but believe me when I say, I'm not."

He ran out of air and verbalism. He was tripping over his words trying not to offend her.

"I'll let you off lightly," she said. "It's fine."

They both laughed.

"In France we call it timing. I know what you're going through because you have just described my life. Bad choices? I even dress down not to be noticed. You know the glasses I wear when you see me on the monitor; you don't see them now do you? I don't need glasses. I hide my face, I hide my body. Very few in our profession have ever seen me with my hair down. I do a lot of work in the gym and I feel I have to hide it. My looks are not right for my work. So yes I know. But I am not as fortunate as you. I have no good men in my life except the ones I choose to sleep with and that's just for sex then I dispose of them. Don't worry, I never jeopardize my work but I do have needs as you do. It flattered me to think you were interested in me as a woman. I take you at your word and believe me, I do understand. Now, when do we get to your house? I'll feel a lot better when I clean up, and yes I would like to go somewhere. It's a beautiful day. I think I would like to be outside if you don't mind. The art exhibits sound interesting but I have one request. We don't have very good Chinese food in Paris I would like to go to an authentic Chinese Canadian restaurant."

They left Matt's house around 11:30am and arrived at City Hall in the central district of town twenty minutes later. The art exhibition was being held at the Nathan Phillips Square. There were thousands of people milling around the annual Toronto Outdoor Art Exhibition. Matt was keen on walking over to the kiosks displaying photographs. He discussed his new passion for photography with Gisele.

Later he said, "When we get back to my place if it's not too much trouble I would like to show you some of my South African photographs. I need an analytical eye, your eye from work, not the glamorous side of Gisele Lapiner. I've not been at photography very long. Maybe it's the subjects, but my South Africa pictures are really good. I think I'd like to get your honest opinion. I would like to pursue photography when all of this is over. No kidding, I really think I can be good at it. But I need the truth, sometimes I overestimate my skills."

She said the truth was her strong suit.

-----o-----

Alright she said, "I'll just consider viewing your pictures as my payment for a nice day and Chinese food."

"Actually, it's my pleasure."

"You do surprise me. I guess we have a way of surprising each other."

"I will say it again, I am truthful. Some say, brutally truthful. So I will be more than happy to look at your photographs just as long as you know I'll be honest with you. Come to think of it," she had a nervous giggle in her voice, "my honesty is probably why I've never had a lasting relationship."

They continued walking through the numerous art displays and kiosks. Around 5:30pm Matt Shaw and Gisele Lapiner, two associates with much greater regard for each other, walked into the Sampan restaurant and had Chinese. A few hours later on the way back to Matt's home on Diplomatic Row Gisele fell fast asleep.

-----o-----

The morning came around slowly for Gisele. She awoke at 10am Toronto time. Matt was outside in the solarium reading some files that had been sent the previous day.

"You make me feel like a gracious host," he said, "its good you slept in late. It's a sign of comfort. You're the first guest I've had in my house and I like the fact you're comfortable enough to take advantage."

He had shown her the house the day before and she expressed how livable it was for a home its size.

"Gisele, after breakfast I am going for a walk, come with me. I want to show you off to my neighbors. I have this feeling they either think I'm celibate or gay. I hope you don't mind me saying it; all you can do is make me look good around here. You will be the best eye candy this neighbor has ever seen."

She looked bewildered not at the thought of being displayed but at the phrase, eye candy. Matt let her know it was a way of describing visual pleasure.

"It is beautiful around here," he said. "It will be a nice way for us to start our day. We have the rest of the afternoon to get serious, I mean really serious. So why don't we have a bite to eat and go for a nice walk through my perfect little Canadian world." After breakfast and an hour and a half walk they got back to his house on Russell Hill Road. They went directly into the communication war room. Matt walked over to the 3 x 4 feet touch screen monitor showing the matrix he developed to follow the money from tobacco and Homeland Security.

"It's the money, it's always the money," he said. "I can't believe they can't hide it or be less transparent but I guess that's the government's advantage in tracking electronic banking. There are no free zones or dead zones for money. Unless it's actual cash being transacted from one person or organization to another there is no way or place to hide money. I don't know why I'm surprised. This new information age is kind of mind-boggling. I just want you..." he stopped.

"I forget who I'm talking to. This is what you do for a living. Anyhow, let me continue. Once I got a good look at all the information it suddenly became very obvious someone had turned a blind eye to what was happening. It's virtually impossible not to be detected especially if you're arrogant and cavalier. It's good for us these people are."

He started discussing the flow chart with the President of the United States at its apex. He subscribed numbers to any agencies or persons having had a hand in the attempted terrorist plot on New York. He also annotated tangential political or operational associations as they applied to tobacco or Homeland relationships. Totally there were 36 individuals, three national security agencies, and the president himself who were responsible for these actions. The total money spent was one hundred-thirty-seven million dollars. The confluence of events was highlighted, some intentional, some incidental, some had unintended consequences, but in aggregate they all led to the misguided attempt to detonate a dirty bomb in New York City.

Matt's analysis showed no one individual's direct culpability but in aggregate they were all culpable. The perverted notion of a terrorist attack potentially killing thousands of people being good for America was the precipitant to the coordinated activities of tobacco, Homeland, the Christian right, and the amoral pragmatic administration in power. The assumption of the tail wagging the dog or vice versa was unclear.

What was clear was events spiraled out of control and America was at a tipping point. The perversity of people of faith abiding in God's will and politicians who started believing their own Crusader rhetoric could lead to such a potential catastrophic event was mind boggling to Matt.

"The nature of these Christians and far right politicians is not to question the ways of God." he said, shaking his head in utter disgust and embarrassment for humankind.

"Gisele this all sickens me. These dumb, mean spirited morons have so much power and unlimited resources it is beyond my comprehension. I can't believe people could be so self-righteous and uncompromising in their beliefs. They actually believe anybody with a different value set should be killed in an eye blink. It's all in front of you. Put holes in it. Do something to refute it. Please tell me it's not true."

Gisele said, "It's going to take me some time to digest your hypothesis. This will sound strange, but leave me alone in here for a while. I do my best work in private. I love your company but it puts pressure on me when I have to digest something so vast. Solitude is how I thrive. Give me some time. Then and only then will I give you my professional opinion."

-----o-----

Matt contacted Frederic, "Well, old buddy, we are pretty sure we have it all. The presidential tapes, I still don't know how you obtained them, confirmed our thinking. It goes all the way up to President Mapplethorpe. There is no clear plan. They didn't just sit around the table and plot this out, but it's evident, it's driven by the president in a default capacity. We sent you a file Gisele and I generated. You should have it by now, have you had a chance to look at it?"

Frederic said, "I have not."

"Well, after you view it you will know why we have to set up a conference call with José.

"Get it done as soon as possible. I don't want to sound pushy but if you can get it done tonight that's all the better."

Frederic said, "It's doable on my end. I will contact him as soon as we are finished. How bulletproof is your assessment."

"Frederic," Matt replied, "we have him on tape and have authenticated it. We also have a paper trail of all the money spent in the Middle East and South Africa on Al Bin. We have it all. Just look at the file, its extensive. Call me after you have reached Jose and set everything up. This cell phone is dedicated to you and we'll make sure it's open, so assume when you've reached him you can instantly get back to me. And if you need some time to prepare for our discussion with José that's fine."

"I don't want him to go off."

"I'm frightened what he might do. We need a measured response to all this and I don't have a clue how or what he's going to do. Sometimes with him it's how you present stuff that determines his response."

"Okay," said Frederic, "because it's so important and our lives are at stake, I don't know if that's the case, but I need some time to think about it and be measured in how I approach him."

Frederic got off his cell by saying, be available. "I'll give you an hour before I call."

Matt looked at Gisele, "This is what we have been waiting for. Why am I so tense and nervous? Why do I feel so isolated? We have ceded all our control on how we would deal with this stuff to Guzman and I'm all right with that. He's the man. There's no question about who has to make the final decisions and I'm still in knots over it."

"Why do we feel so powerless?"

"When we give all this to Jose it's frightening, but we have no other choice. This is a lot to digest."

She said she had similar feelings. "Matt, I don't know if you know much about my background, but at one point in time I worked for the French National Security Agency as an alternatives analyst. What I learned was simple, when I passed the information on to someone in power I had to wipe my hands of it. Once it passes from your palm put it out of your mind. From here he is the best, yes? Then we have done our job, yes?"

The hour between communications with Frederic seemed like an eternity to both Matt and Gisele. The cell rang. He was told to get on Gmail and opened up an e-mail with instructions for a video conference call. Within three minutes Jose Guzman was monitoring the call between the four of them.

"Matt," he said, "I have just looked at your work and it is good my friend. It's really good. This is what we needed."

Both Matt and Gisele drew a breath of relief.

"We had our ways with Mexico government officials, this will be no different. Your president is no more than a corrupt businessman trying to bleed people not for money but for some political or religious gain. It makes no difference. He is a miserable weak fuck and we will take advantage of his weakness. He is no different than the Mexican Presidents who bled people for money and power. We have had the past two Presidents of Mexico in our pockets. They have stolen billions and billions of dollars from Pemex, by skimming money from the taxes, and most importantly by doing business with the drug cartels. But do you know who runs Mexico? It is us my friend. It is me and my cartel brothers. Every president, every governor, every mayor, every police chief, and the Army, are all in the cartel's pocket. Your president will be no different. It's because we have information on every one of them that makes us the most powerful people in all Mexico. Because of the threat we might expose them and their corruption, they are ours. They are frightened of us but they are terrified of the people. Because we have knowledge of their dealings, they can't touch us. They partnered up with the wrong people because of their greed. They are arrogant my friend, and that leads them to believe they had the upper hand. We ripped out their guts in Mexico by showing them what we had and how we would use it. Your president is no different. I can get to him. Leave it to me. That peacock is too full of his own shit to smell it, but very soon he will know whose pocket he is in. We don't have to kill him."

Matt and Gisele could not believe Guzman would ever entertain the idea of killing the President of the United States.

"His involvement in this will limit how many people we have to eliminate. When we kill a few, the right ones, it will make a statement and Bill Mapplethorpe will be mine. Like I said, leave it to me."

The tapes in the oval office with the president himself discussing national security matters with his Chief-of-Staff, Robert Marceau was all Guzman needed.

He became much more articulate and said, "The president was not directly involved in his godson's anti-immigrant coalitions but his tacit approval and his parallel political leaning pushed the security agencies to back off any threats the Christian Right posed to national security. It was implied the vitriolic rhetoric of the right was not only acceptable but it was the stance of the president himself. Homeland even seeded money into the Al Bin operation and recruited him as a double agent. They would let him run with the project until at the very end, when they would step in and stop the attack on New York to reestablish their importance with the President of the United States. They would turn a blind eye to anything that red flagged the attack until it came near to fruition and then intercede in a hero's manner. On NSA briefing tapes the President's response to his godson and Al Bin was all Guzman had to hear. Even if the Arab radical pulled this off, the president said, all it will do is kill some good for nothing blacks in New York. Who gives a fuck? It will give us the ability to impose martial law like we should have after 9/11. Can you imagine, no matter the end result of Al Bin actions we are winners and we'll be able to push our agenda in Congress. There is no downside. Even if the fucking bomb goes off and kills thirty or forty thousand people, in this political climate who cares? The other side of it is if we stop them from detonating a bomb it would be a dramatic victory against terrorism and that's a win-win. You see, we can't lose. Let my godson and all of those crazies have a long leash. We can't lose either way. I don't need to say this but, you distance us from all of this. I don't give a fuck who you have to bring down when this happens but you keep us out of it. Set up whoever you want as a fall guy. You better have a position that protects us no matter what. Put it on tobacco, put it on some crazy rogue in homeland, or put it on my godson, if there are any problems but make us clean. I don't care if something goes wrong keep us the fuck away from it. You understand me? One more thing, the eventuality is that it will give us reason to break all our treaties. We can suspend all of our quasi-treaties with those Arab radical states. I don't care what the past administrations have done I don't trust those bastards and I think the only reason we haven't had any terrorist episodes up to this point is vigilance not those tacit narcotics agreements for safety. We'll even have a legitimate reason to break our official treaties the liberal Senate passed with all the socialists' countries they did business with. This is a win-win situation all the way around."

-----o-----

"Gisele, Frederic, do you mind if I talk to my friend Matt in private?"

They both went off-line.

"Matt, I will talk directly to the President."

Matt thought he must be joking.

Guzman continued, "I'd like a copy of the tapes and a transcript with his conversation in red. I also want an electronic one on just one disc. I need a jacket for all of this saying 'for your eyes only.' Tell Frederic to get it to me as soon as possible. You will hear about this tomorrow on the news, I have been nominated for the Nobel Peace Prize just like Arias, the former President of Costa Rica, had been years ago. You know our work with the Organization of American States and the CIA trying to smooth out relationships between Venezuela, Colombia, and Ecuador. We have just formed a regional trade agreement with them and to get it accomplished I have been pumping in a lot of American money. All this has been done with the backing of the U.S. National Security Council to bring about more stability and slowdown the Venezuelans. This is some of the staff you helped set up. It has stabilized and protected our investments. So my involvement in all this shouldn't be a surprise. Being nominated for a Nobel Prize though, that's kind of crazy. My hands-on leadership in this alliance has lead to some regional political recognition and this Nobel nomination. I don't think I will win, and you know my history well enough that this is just crazy considering who I was, but it will give me some credibility in getting to Bill Mapplethorpe. I'm going to invite him to San Jose. He wrote me a letter of congratulations on my nomination and said he would be coming to Latin America; actually he has a trip to Antigua, Guatemala. I am going to persuade him to come to San Jose. The invitation will be about three to four weeks from now so by then I will have everything in place. It is amazing how our lives have changed and how far removed we both are from our pasts. Now things are different. Sometimes I can't believe it but I am President of Costa Rica. Everything has changed my friend. My new powers give me greater range as to who I can affect. I know I can get him; he will be mine when I get him alone. Leave it to me. You have to stabilize everything on your side for the next three or four weeks. Tell Frederic I have my way of getting to the president. Tell him it has something to do with Mexico. He has no reason to doubt it. I just don't want him to question how I have access to Washington. My friend, once I talk to Bill Mapplethorpe he will do what I ask. He'll have no alternatives. I'm going to give him your files. That's all he needs to see. That fuck will quiver with fear and I will take his fucking soul. His God will not help him with me. I will pressure him to end this terrorist attack craziness and stop pressing our Arab allies. He is not one half the man Calldenaris of Mexico is and I own him. This is over when he gets to San Jose my friend. You did well. This is better than anything we could have expected."

Within twenty minutes Gisele was back in the communication room sitting across from Matt. He filled her in on what he could of his conversation with Guzman.

Matt once more placed a call to Frederic and the same progression of electronics as earlier that day lead to a three-person video-conference call. Matt proceeded to fill in Frederic and placed responsibility for keeping the Homeland and National Intelligence busy squarely on the shoulders of Frederic in the United States and Gisele in Europe. A concerted effort would be launched to heightened security worldwide from terrorist plots as a subterfuge until Guzman could have a one-on-one meeting with the president of the United States.

All Matt could tell his counterparts was Guzman needed thirty days free of any Al Bin activity or any other group sponsored by tobacco or Homeland. The thirty day window would be sufficient to get to the president. Matt felt funny having to hide the truth from his cohorts but knew it was imperative to protect Guzman's cover. It was agreed monies would be appropriated to third parties who tried to secure information on airports, the national grid or major infrastructures such as dams, bridges, the national highway system, or any important national targets pointing heightened terrorist probes into the American security net. The object was to set off multiple red flags and bring the

United States security apparatus into higher alert. The same pressures would be applied in Europe by Gisele's designees.

Frederic said he would enlist Pedro to have third parties inquire about US embassies, consulates, and military bases in South America for the same purposes of red flagging potential terrorist activities. Frederic was strident in his attitude that US security must be brought to the accelerated state of red alert. He said he would alert Pedro to set into motion a kidnapping plot of US diplomatic assets in Central America as well.

Everything would lead to international terrorist groups with Arab or Muslim ties. Anything and everything setting off national security alarms and bringing the Western world to a greater state of readiness would be used. In further consideration Matt said, "We can only push this so far. We can't overload national security with so much it causes a paralysis and incapacitates government. We can't cause a panic. We just need to put enough pressure on Winningham's people through National Security pressures that any rogue elements associated with the far right or tobacco will pull back for at least the next thirty days. Once the word gets out there are other players threatening the United States, anybody involved in Homeland will back off as fast as they can because of the scope of the investigation. If we can set off creditable alarms at arms length, we can get our thirty days. That is all Jose asks."

Frederic and Gisele both said they grasped what had to be done. They would act with clarity and caution in setting off concerns in the national security agencies. They said they could collectively guarantee Guzman more than thirty days if necessary.

-----o-----

President Bill Mapplethorpe arrived at the Guatemala City International Airport and took the thirty minute helicopter flight to Antigua where he was a seated member of the Inter-American Regional Council. He would play his last card in forming Central American Trade Association.

The thrust of the association was to quell the rising tide of communism spread by Venezuela. He was there to sign the final treaty agreement. His two-day stay at the Hotel Santo Domingo was punctuated with tours of the old colonial city and photo opportunities with South America's common people not the perfunctory slate of political and business dignitaries. Bill Mapplethorpe's image as a Christian, every day man, would be bolstered by his trek up the Volcano Palaya's viewing trail. He and his entourage hiked up the active volcano located three miles west of the fourteenth-century Tzutujil Maya Nation capital, Cakchiquelian. Antigua, the site of the council, became a Spanish colonial city in 1717 when it was made the colony's primary military outpost and regional capital. It became the center for acquiring precious metals, gold and silver in particular. From its beginning as a military outpost it became a self-sustaining agricultural center producing bananas, sweet potatoes, corn, and other vegetables. Today Guatemala's second city's primary agricultural production is coffee but its greatest economic activity is tourism. The Inter-American Council chose Antigua because of its continuity and stability. As with all presidential activities, every detail was managed. The presidential trip was choreographed and scripted for maximum political exposure. The outwardly spontaneous walk from the hotel to the central plaza, Parque Central, viewing the production of Cakchiquelian fifteenth century sacrificial masks produced in jade in one of the city's many jewelry factories and the climb up the western face of the volcano were all political activities directed toward winning support from the Latino community in the next general election. Everything went as anticipated but for one fly in the ointment. The Costa Rican diplomatic contingency led by Consulate General Juan Estrada had a "for your eyes only" document for President Bill Mapplethorpe from President Jose Guzman that was delivered just as the conference ended and Bill Mapplethorpe was walking up the steps of the helicopter that would transport him to the airport. He accepted the diplomatic pouch and put it under his arm as he entered the chopper for his trip to Guatemala City and a short flight to San Jose.

Estrada's parting words were, "Mr. President this is an urgent matter of life and death. It must be attended to as soon as possible. President Guzman feels it is so potentially explosive and far-reaching that he doesn't trust Costa Rican security to handle it and feels he must speak to you in person in the presidential palace on the matter during your official visit."

He opened the folder and looked at its contents. It was a false accounting of terrorist activities in Latin America that needed an analyst eye to prove. Made up intelligence pointing to US involvement from ex-CIA operatives creating instability in Costa Rica with negative American political overtones because of its Christian evangelical leanings in a Catholic country was the crux of the analysis.

Guzman said he needed personal assurances from the president to thwart the perceived threat and give security resources to his country if necessary. Costa Rica was the only country in Latin America without a military and Guzman said he felt vulnerable. He wanted a heads up from Bill Mapplethorpe because of their perceived personal friendship.

Bill Mapplethorpe arrogantly felt he had relations and respect from all Latin

America's Presidents. Guzman was not special but needed his reluctant attention. The United States was the steward of Costa Rica's defense and Guzman wanted to play on that. The politics bait and switch would pull the President of the United States into this meeting with a false sense of power. His first intuition would be his ability to save an ally but Guzman's ploy would pull the rug out from under him.

The power of the unforeseen was immense and Guzman was the master of it. As Air Force One came to a stop on the tarmac in San Jose, Guzman and his entourage were flanked by a marching band playing the stars and stripes. Bill Mapplethorpe's arrogance and self-importance of coming to the aid of an inferior was written all over his face.

Guzman warmly embraced him as if he were a savior and said softly as not to be overheard, "Mr. President, I need to speak to you personally, one on one, no others around. I am embarrassed but I need your guidance and counsel. I have some other documents for your viewing that are dangerous for the both of us. I need your help."

He said, "I'm in San Jose for five hours, there has to be a couple minutes where we can get away by ourselves. You set it up at the end of the day, wanting to put pressure on Guzman for his tactical advantage. Do you have this other document with you he asked?"

"No, Mr. President because of its importance it is in my office. After lunch we can walk alone in the Rose Garden and I will share it with you. Then you can have your people look at it if you think they will be helpful, but I have not had the courage to pass this along to anyone else. The files are personal, I can vouch for their authenticity. We will talk later, thank you Mr. President, thank you very much for your indulgence."

Bill Mapplethorpe was an ideologue as a politician and not terribly bright. He was inert when it came to new ideas or thinking on his feet. But he did delegate all important matters to his Chief-of-Staff. The thought of not having instant input because of his one-on-one conversation with Guzman was foreign to him but he would deal with it as he always dealt with anything new. He would dismiss the importance of the issue until after lunch. This was his mode of operation. He called it self-discipline. Don't overwork an issue until you've delved into it with other people of knowledge. He would act on all of this after lunch. "Let Guzman panic," he said to himself.

"He would attend to the overly dramatic Hispanic leader later. He would look at the documents in private with Guzman and then pass them on to his Chief-of-Staff," he said to himself.

-----o-----

PART VII

SAN JOSE, COSTA RICA

Guzman played his role as a sniveling overmatched president to perfection. His posture was softened as was his speech. To the United States President Stephan Mapplethorpe, the inappropriate needy pressing for attention and help was simply weakness.

Finally the President of the United States in what he thought was complete control of his inferior counterpart said in front of all of the other guests at the luncheon, "Mr. President," looking directly at Guzman, "if you may, I would like to chat with you privately for a few minutes. He made it seem as if it were his idea."

Guzman responded sheepishly, "It would be my pleasure, Mr. President. It would give me an opportunity to show you the Matt Shaw garden, named after the American Matt Shaw, who died last year. He was my Chief-of-Staff and for all of the services he gave to our country we have set aside a memorial garden in his honor."

Guzman had prepared for this meeting. He walked Bill Mapplethorpe over to a solitary bench in the middle of the three acre garden. It was electronically shielded from surveillance. Effectively blocking the US Secret Service form listening.

As soon as President Mapplethorpe sat down Guzman's demeanor changed instantly. He pushed a new set of files into the president's face and said, "You fuck, read this, you are mine."

The startled president responded, "Do you know who you are talking to?" He began to stand up.

Guzman said, "Al Bin, that's right Mr. President, Al Bin. Now do you know who the fuck you are talking to? I know all about your fucking involvement or lack of response to the threat in New York. It's undeniable, you fuck. It's all here. Set your ass down. You are mine!"

He turned on the little handheld tape recorder and played the tape of the president in the Oval Office with his Chief-of-Staff.

"That you fuck, is your death sentence," Guzman said. "I think it is called treason in your country. You have no options. I am the safest person in the world; I've got you by the balls. It's simple! There is a list of thirty-six people including your godson, your Chief-of-Staff, some top administrators in Homeland, a couple Army generals and of course there is tobacco. I want all thirty-six of them killed and proof of deaths within two weeks or all of this will come out. I want Al Bin personally. Make it happen or you'll be in jail the rest of your life. Smile you fuck."

Looking over at the Secret Service he continued, "Your men are nervous because I blocked out this conversation, this part of the garden is electronically black. They are nervous. Let's not disappoint them, so get up and we will walk to an area where they can listen to our conversation."

Bill Mapplethorpe clutched the documents. He was dead in the water.

Guzman put his hand on his shoulder and whispered in his ear, "You are my bitch, now! You self righteous fuck. See how your God smiles upon you now, you Christian hypocrite. You got two weeks. If there are any threats on me or anyone around me this will be given to every major news source in the world. There is nothing you can do to protect yourself. You've got two weeks. If I ever call, and I will, don't ever fucking disappoint me."

On the way back to Guzman's office, both men's posture had changed and so had the posture of the Western world. Guzman walked as if his body was inflated; he had the physical stature of tempered steel. Mapplethorpe's shoulders were slumped and his eyes looked down.

Political events played out over the next two weeks. Winningham and the gathering of Christian leaders in Austin, Texas were attacked and killed by a mentally ill man with an assault weapon carrying an apocalyptic message. Robert Marleau the Chief-of-Staff and three Homeland Security Administrators were in a military aircraft when it crashed. The cause was deemed to be pilot error. A meeting of the American Tobacco Institute executive committee came to a tragic end when the yacht taking them to a golf outing in Bermuda hit a reef and sank. The president delivered all but one of the 36 men within his two-week deadline. Al Bin was still at large.

Guzman sat at his desk in San Jose, picked up the phone and called President Mapplethorpe's personal blackberry. "Your time is short there are no excuses. I want Al Bin."

-----o-----

Matt called Las Vegas. BiBa answered her cell after seeing the name Matt Shaw on the iphone screen.

"I didn't expect to see your name or hear from you. I can't tell you how much I've missed you," she said.

"I have missed you too. It's over. I've got a lot of explaining to do," as he once more wondered how he would make up another story. He continued. "Can you come to Toronto? Let me rephrase that, I need you to come to Toronto. Please, can you clean up your schedule and get here as fast as possible? I have a wonderful surprise for you and I don't think I can stand to be without you another day."

She said, "I don't need a surprise, I just need and want you. I'll be where ever you want me to be, just give me three days to clear my work here in Las Vegas."

For the next three days all he could do was talk the ears off the Eskinds about the love of his life. He made future arrangements. He would later ask BiBa to accompany him to Costa Rica. The new slimmed down unrecognizable Matt Shaw would take BiBa to meet a friend.

Frederic and Gisele went back to their respective jobs in Miami and Paris.

Alvarez, Bill, and Malique went back to Mexico to be with Pedro and finish their work in the narco-business.

Jose Guzman a nominee, but not winner of the Nobel Peace Prize, was in Costa Rica waiting to see his friend and brother in arms.

-----o-----

Those People

BY RUSSELL C. ARSLAN

David Russell arrived in Africa to share experiences with his grown sons. After clearing customs, the boys waited for David outside the airport terminal. By the time their father arrived with an old Land Rover the boys were wondering why he had brought them to this horrid *other world* place. The people seemed different. The place stank to high heaven.

When dad rolled up in the Rover saying how beautiful Africa was, they looked at each other thinking he must be delusional.

As they drove to the hotel both boys realized not only was this place different than anything they had ever known, but so was their father. They are introduced to David Russell a Kenyan revolutionary. They saw *those people,* a strange non-emotional brutal, other kind of person. But this was just the beginning. They had encounters with *those people* found the loves of their lives, establish a new business, and realize their lives could expand beyond even their expectations.

-----o-----

HIGHEST STAKES, "ALL IN"

BY RUSSELL C. ARSLAN

After being charged with Homeland Security crimes he knows nothing about, Matt Papaz goes *All In* to prove his innocence.

This Russell C. Arslan mystery grabs you and makes you a part of Papaz' quest for survival.

Matt Papaz's life depends on the intelligence and strategies needed to win Texas Hold'em or any card game of skill. Going full throttle, *All In,* means take a commanding position, based on odds and reading your opponent's hand. Papaz plays from the power position in the game rather than from weakness. Taking an aggressive stance gave him the edge in life and death situations.

Acting from strength, *All In,* is what the best players do and is the template for Papaz's dealing with forces more powerful than himself who are bent on his elimination. *All In* uses gambling tactics and strategies as a guide for Matt Papaz' dealing with adversaries. His ability to read danger, adapt and overcome all odds was a successful trademark in the world of national security, gamesmanship and professional poker.

-----o-----

ABOUT THE AUTHOR

Russell C. Arslan is the author of the bestselling Matt Papaz novels and "Those People". He lives in Bel Air California with his wife and travels throughout the world. Readers may learn more about him and his work, report mistakes in this book and correspond with him on his Website at www.russellcarslan.com

www.ingramcontent.com/pod-product-compliance
Lightning Source LLC
LaVergne TN
LVHW020647110826
845149LV00012B/1936

* 9 7 8 0 9 8 5 7 6 9 5 2 9 *